REVOLUTION

An Apocalyptic Thriller

M.L. Banner

Toes in the Water Publishing, LLC

ISBN (Paperback): 978-1-947510-28-9

ISBN (eBook): 978-1-947510-27-2

ISBN (Audio): 978-1-947510-29-6

V1.9

REVOLUTION: Highway Book #4 is an original work of fiction.

The characters and dialogs are the products of this author's vivid imagination.

Much of the science and the historical incidents described in this novel are based on reality, as are its warnings.

Author's Notes

Thank you for picking up *REVOLUTION,* the conclusion to the *HIGHWAY Series*.

Don't forget to get your freebies, which includes an eBook copy of my USA Today Bestseller, *TRUE ENEMY*. Details at the end of this book.

Enjoy!

Michael

Revolution

"When dictatorship is a fact;
Revolution becomes a right." - Victor Hugo

~

"If Tyranny and Oppression come to this land, it will be in the guise of fighting a foreign enemy."
- James Madison

~

"Power is not a means; it is an end. One does not establish a dictatorship in order to safeguard a revolution;
one makes a revolution in order to establish a dictatorship."
- George Orwell

July 14th

49:00:01

49:00:00

48:59:59

Prelude

Upon hearing the old dispatch transceiver emit a pulsating beep-tone, Sinclair bounded from his desk on the opposite side of the station and dashed toward the sound. He'd been waiting much of the day to hear something from federal authorities.

Earlier that morning, his police radio crackled and then transmitted a pre-recorded broadcast announcing, "This is an announcement from the Office of the President. All public service authorities are required to monitor their radios for further instructions."

Since there had been nothing from anyone in the government after the surprise morning television broadcast from the new female President, he was eager to get information. More so, based on that TV broadcast, he was expecting a potential windfall to him and his team members. He had even radioed each of his team to be ready, as he suspected their department might be federalized to carry out the new President's Executive Orders. This was what he was waiting to hear.

It was not that Sinclair was restless to get back to work: the terrorist attack meant that he and his team members were officially retired, as everyone needed to take care of themselves and stay close to home to protect their own families. Since the attacks, Sinclair hadn't returned to the station, other than to take whatever he and his team could use, including the station's cache of weapons and ammunition.

Once he heard the Presidential call to authorities, he had rushed to the empty police station, fired up its generator and plugged in their old dispatch system—Their high-tech, Computer Aided Dispatch or CAD system was fried from the enemy's EMP.

As instructed, he waited. And waited. There wasn't much else to do at the station.

Hours passed by without a peep. He was even about to call it a day, when the pulsating beep-tone sounded.

Approaching the radio, he slowed when he considered that this might just be another jamming signal from the terrorists. Though, to him, this one sounded different.

When he halted in front of the radio, the rapid beep-tone stopped.

He sucked in a breath and held.

Then the speakers thundered, with a voice reminiscent of James Earl Jones.

"Attention, all law enforcement and other governmental agencies with enforcement capabilities. This is a message from the President of the United States..."

There was a pause, followed by the now familiar shrill, female voice of the President.

"To ensure our fragile peace is maintained and to help your government root out any terrorists at large, you are ordered to begin the enforcement of the new Emergency Weapons Ban in your area.

"To facilitate this process, we have set up an analog fax service with further instructions to each local authority receiving this broadcast. To access your instructions, simply use your analog fax machines to call the phone number given at the end of this announcement. When you are prompted with a tone, type in your area code and we will fax you detailed instructions of your orders, along with a list of every person in your area who is suspected of having militia ties. Each name will include a complete listing of their current firearm holdings, culled from ATF databases.

"Here is the phone number..."

Sinclair jotted down the phone number on a pad. Then he went to work.

From a storage room, he pulled out one of their retired fax machines, plugged it into the analog phone line, which had been connected to the dead CAD system.

He strained his memory on how to make this relic work.

It only took a few minutes until he was dialing the phone number. Almost instantly, a tone sounded through the fax machine's tiny speaker. He entered his area code, as instructed, and it began spitting out page after page of instructions, followed by lists of names, addresses, and current weapons holdings.

Sinclair licked his lips.

Sinclair

One Hour Later

"Police! Weapons search. Open up," demanded Swat Team Commander Sinclair. "You-have-five-seconds." He hollered his count so that his team along with the house's occupants could hear him.

Only yesterday, he was breaking down doors without any authority but his own, and solely to plunder for his and his men's benefit. Now he had the Presidential power to steal at will.

"Four."

If the houses he targeted didn't turn over their weapons or didn't comply with his team's search, he was given Presidential authorization to use whatever means that *he* deemed necessary to gain their target's compliance, as long as he followed their rules, which were minimal. The cherry on this cake was that the list they provided him contained every household in his area code that possessed purchased firearms from a licensed gun dealer. This was much easier than having to stumble from house to house, not knowing what those occupants—if they were still alive—possessed. More often, they came up empty. It would be different now.

"Three."

Sinclair nodded to his masked team-member who was clutching the handles of the Enforcer, their euphemistically named battering ram. It was his signal to get ready to break down the door. At the same time, Sinclair switched off his rifle's safety and took a full step back.

"Two."

This residence was only the first name on the list. It would be one of many they would raid this evening. He hoped this house would bear a lot more fruit than his previous targets. His assumption was that the homes with multiple weapons were more likely be occupied by prepared-minded individuals, and therefore those with a large storage of food, ammo and even gold coins. All of these were valuable now a days. And if the occupants resisted, which he expected with preppers, his men could shoot everyone with immunity and confiscate everything.

"One."

His man pulled back the thirty-five pounds of steel, getting ready to release three tons of force on the weak point of the owner's front door. But before he could let loose, the door clicked and swung wide open.

Standing inside the doorway was a rotund man, who appeared to have just rolled out of bed before answering the door. He was clad in olive green boxers, a T-shirt, and a giant cowboy hat.

The man's arms were thrust into the air in submission, but each hand clutched a can of beer in an obvious mockery of Sinclair's demands. "You coming in or are you going to stand out there until nightfall?"

Sinclair and his men hesitated, momentarily unsure how to react to this unexpected behavior.

"Any of you gentlemen want a beer?" The man held out one of his beers while slurping down two abundant gulps from the other. His belly poked out from the bottom of his T, as if it were begging for more beer.

"Engage," Sinclair commanded, ignoring the homeowner's offer and sending his men inside to secure the area around the doorway and engage with anyone inside who might pose a threat or obstruct their search. Despite the homeowner's nonplussed attitude, Sinclair was leery of those who possessed weapons: they might be more prone to react to his team's demands with violence. Especially once they found out his team was here to take possession of their weapons away from them.

While his men were taking positions inside, Sinclair addressed the pot-bellied man, purposely telegraphing his voice for all the home's occupants to hear. "Robert P. Jones, you are commanded to turn over any and all firearms in your possession or face severe consequences."

Jones let his offertory beer hand drop and used it to point inside. "It's on the coffee table," Jones said, punctuating his response with a belch.

When Purdy, Sinclair's team leader called out "Secure" from inside, Sinclair pushed past Jones and then directed his team to begin their search of the house. He felt certain that based on his list and Jones' attitude, the man was hiding weapons somewhere.

His men would find them. They could sniff out the proverbial needle out from a football-stadium-sized haystack. Especially Purdy.

After his men's flurry of movement out of the living area, their flashlight beams disappeared into predesignated points around the home, leaving Sinclair and Jones in semi-darkness. Sinclair focused his attention on the room's only source of light, since the shades were drawn—which was odd when the sun wouldn't set for several more minutes. He was also startled to find that he had an audience.

At a dining room table, just off the living room in which he stood, was a woman in a nightgown and two young kids. All sat, with their hands visible, while nonchalantly consuming cereal and watching Sinclair as if he was providing them their entertainment. Other than their being dressed in their sleep clothes during late afternoon and the glowing Coleman lantern on the table's center, it looked like they were having a typical family meal, albeit cereal.

"Sure you don't want one?" Jones asked, again motioning with one of the two cans. Without waiting for an answer, Jones crumpled his empty and began drinking the second beer he had just offered.

Sinclair overtly crinkled his nose, closed his eyes and gave his head a shake. Then he marched over to the coffee table Jones had pointed at, so he could better examine the rifle resting on its glass top. He turned on his own rifle light to see it better.

At first glance, Sinclair thought it was a vintage Mosin Nagant, which would make a nice addition to his collection. But upon further inspection, he could see it was a rusted piece of metal that only loosely resembled a rifle in its former lifetime. It was certainly not functional now.

Two of Sinclair's team members returned to the living room, each one calling out, "Clear."

"What the hell is this?" Sinclair glared incredulously at Jones, while pointing at the junk rifle with his light.

"What's what—*burp*—Mr. Swat Man?" Jones asked.

Two more of his team returned, both announcing, "Clear." In other words, their searches in and through their preassigned rooms were clear of guns or any other interesting contraband that they could confiscate.

"What is this piece of shit?" Sinclair asked, no longer hiding his frustration with Jones, even though he swore to himself and his men to not let their searches get personal.

"It's a firearm. You told me to turn over all my firearms, by someone's command..."

"The President's—"

"What?"

"It's by the President's command that you are required to turn over your weapons or we have..." Sinclair waited for the last two of his men to return to the living room with their reports. Each simply shook their heads, rather than announcing what the others had and interrupting their commander. "Nothing?" Sinclair almost begged them.

Purdy, his team leader and most senior man, continued his head shaking. "Not a damned thing, sir," Purdy said. "Even the gun safe was open and there was nothing valuable in there, except some useless sterling silver jewelry and Poke Man Cards."

Jones scuffed. "Those things are worth a fortune, so n—"

"Shut up!" Sinclair demanded. He returned his glare to his clipboard, with its assigned list of targets, thinking maybe he had somehow read it wrong. Seeing the first line, he pointed at it. "This says you have fourteen weapons total, that you bought over the last ten years, including... one, two, three," he looked up at Jones, who was ignoring him, now holding the second beer can vertical, just above his lips to get its last few drops. "Where are your *three* AR 15s, and all the rest of your guns?"

"Let-me-see," Jones said, who craned his head so as to get a better look at where Sinclair was tapping with an agitated finger. It was Jones' full name at the top of the list of names, along with a list and description of all of the man's firearms.

After a minute of feigning any interest in Sinclair's question, Jones simply shrugged his shoulders and crumpled his second can of beer. "I'm guessing... a boating accident?"

Sinclair responded immediately, "You mean to tell me that you lost all fourteen guns and rifles in a boating accident? Not that you would even have a boat, as there's not a lake for miles"

"That list of yours tell you who legally owns a boat too?" Jones eyed Sinclair, finally giving him his full attention, adding, "Besides, I thought the federal government was not supposed to keep records of gun purchases. That's why gun stores must keep their paper Firearms Transaction Records, Form 4473 in a physical book rather than in a comput—"

"Shutup-shutup-shutup!" Sinclair screamed. "Where are your other damned weapons?"

"Oh, weapons; not just guns? I have a couple of pocketknives and a boomerang from Australia somewhere in the house." he turned to address his wife, who had long ago stopped eating her cereal to watch the show. "Hey, Sheila,"—Jones said this in a mocking Aussie voice—"where did we put the boomerang we got from our trip? You know—"

"Stop!" Sinclair gruffed. He wanted to shoot these people just for their insolence. But he really couldn't. Per his instructions, which he accepted by turning on his fax machine and receiving his orders, the US Military was supposedly looking over his shoulders now. This family had technically done everything he had asked. His men had conducted a proper search of the house, without finding anything that would give them cause to take any further action. Jones gave up the only visible firearm immediately upon request, satisfying their mandate. It was time to move onto the next home on the list. Surely they would have better luck there.

"We're done here," Sinclair huffed.

He and his men exited the house.

As soon as the last set of boots was out the door, Jones slammed it shut and engaged the lock.

Jones

"Great job, Team Jones," Rob announced, while squinting through the door's peephole. Once he was sure that all the police were back in their truck, he trotted over to a desk in the living room.

Picking up a box, which covered up a CB transceiver, he snatched the microphone up with one hand and clicked on the radio with the other. It was powered by a spare truck battery, also hidden out of sight. He turned up the volume and pressed the mic to his mouth.

"Hey Boomer. This is the City Cowboy. You got your ears on?"

The response was almost instantaneous, as he knew Boomer McKenzie was monitoring his CB for Rob's call. "I'm here, City. Feds leave?"

"They just left my place and you're next on their list. Thanks for the intel."

"No prob. Thank you for the update, City. Stand firm. Soon we'll be part of the revolution."

"We're ready. Out."

Jones switched on channel 9 and caught the excited voice of someone he'd heard before; their local version of Lieutenant Grimes. Jones turned up the volume louder, so his family could hear too.

"... My sources are telling me that authorities have already started door-to-door searches and seizures of firearms. We urge you Patriots to continue to follow our arrested brother's suggestions...

"Hide your weapons. Because we will need them soon, when it's time for our revolution."

Chapter 1

Former Basecamp of American Eagle Patriots

Faisal

Sacrificing five of his warriors to kill most of his enemy's fighters was an acceptable loss to Faisal. But he wasn't about to call it "retribution" for the enemy's initial attack on their convoy. He would not do this until every one of the militia members was hunted down and killed like the dogs they were. Only then would he allow his men to celebrate the victory, and then he would find a way to tell all of this to his Mahdi. For now, there was much more work to do.

Their secondary goal was to find the rifles and ammunition which were stolen from them after the militia's ambush of their convoy.

The primary goal was to find the remaining militia members. Two of his men were sent to different positions to watch out for any militia who might return. This was their best chance to find them.

That left fifteen remaining men who were tasked with locating, "anything which might prove valuable to hunting down these dogs." After this, they would prepare for whatever their Mahdi demanded of them next."

While Faisal sat in what the infidels called a director's

chair, he waited for each of his men to present to him what they had found after a thorough search of the militia's campsite.

By the second presentation, one truth was evident, proving wrong one more assumption from their dead commander: these Americans had many of the finest weapons, as evidenced by those they had found in the camp. None were automatic fire, like the AK 103s they had received for this war. But several of these guns were worth keeping.

His fourth man presented him with a large bore pistol that he was immediately enamored with. It was called a Desert Eagle, and it was heavy even for him. It used a sizable caliber of ammunition, which seemed excessive for a pistol. Though he couldn't help but smile when he imagined targeting his enemy with it. So, it ended up in his waistband.

The Americans were not short on ammunition either. This militia certainly had much more than their own units carried. Unfortunately, most of it was for their popular military-style rifles. He wasn't about to complain though as they were able to also salvage a fair amount of their own 7.62 variety.

Still no sign of their own cases of ammunition—at least twenty-thousand rounds—and the AK rifles stolen from their convoy. Based on what he and his men witnessed, they weren't in possession of the wood crates during their escape. So they must have hidden them somewhere. Faisal's men were soon going to extend their search perimeter outside of the immediate camp until they found them.

Meanwhile, there were other items worthy of keeping,

besides the two pornographic magazines called Sports Illustrated—he told his men he would hold them for educational purposes. The greatest find so far was the military transceiver.

In hindsight, they probably should have been more selective in their killing and saved the operator, because its keypad was complicated and not like the transmitters they had used. Praise Allah, one of his men, was former Hamas, and his unit had used a similar radio taken from an IDF soldier during a border war. Soon his man would figure out the radio's secrets, so that Faisal could call Mahdi Abdul directly at Mt. Weather and tell him what they had done to win glory for their Mahdi and then await further orders. They had been headed there when they were ambushed by this militia. He could not wait to tell his Mahdi of how he alone had secured a victory against these American *najis*.

Faisal eyed the man working hard to decipher the radio's keyboard, before averting his attention to the next of his approaching men, seemingly excited about a box of electronics clutched in his arms.

"Sir?" Samir begged for permission to approach, giving a quick bow. Faisal beckoned him forward. "At first inspection, we missed these." Samir—the only albino he had ever known—held out the box so that its contents were visible. Faisal was interested at first, as Samir had already proven himself to be fearless as a warrior. But then Faisal glanced at the box's materials.

"Portable radios?" Faisal asked, noticing the five or so handhelds. They would not do him or his men much good as they would only work for short distances. They already had handhelds such as these.

"Even better, commander," Samir said, his white eyebrows raised as he laid the box down. He snatched out one of radios with an unpronounceable name etched on its face and turned it on.

Faisal felt sure this exercise was a waste of his time, but Samir had a reason for this demonstration. So he waited for his trusted warrior to finish before having him move onto his next assignment. The man earned the right to waste a little of his time.

"All of these radios were taken from dead infidels. Each are pre-programed to the same channels. We also found more than five empty chargers plugged into their solar batteries. This means that there are as many as five other radios we didn't find, and they are likely still being used by the infidels who only temporarily escaped our assault. We cannot hear their conversations on them now, because they are likely too far away. However, if you had your two sentries listening to the pre-programmed channels, in addition to what you have them doing, maybe we can catch the infidels through their radios if any of them try to return."

Faisal sat up.

One of Allah's warriors had just demonstrated his intellect to be equal to his fighting skills. This was excellent. Faisal had assigned Hamza and Ali to keep an eye out for the surviving militia members' possible return. Faisal felt certain two or more would come back to reclaim his stolen weapons or more stupidly, to attempt to bury their dead. The radios were a perfect complement to his sentries' assignments: they could listen to their channels while they also watched for the infidels.

"Excellent job, Samir. Give one to Hamza in the north

and one to Ali in the south, each of whom is on watch for returning infidels. Have them listen on all pre-programmed channels. If they see or hear any sign of the infidel's return, have them report back to you on one of the middle channels."

"Yes, sir," Samir replied. He grabbed all five of the radios, turning each on and methodically doing a quick examination of every radio, though Faisal didn't know why he was conducting this exercise in front of him.

While Samir was playing with the buttons on one of the radios, another of his men approached, but waited until Samir was either finished or dismissed by Faisal. Despite his different look, Samir had earned the respect of the other men too. When it was time, he would give Samir an elevation of rank befitting his abilities.

After making several *beep*-sounds with one of the radios, Samir handed it to Faisal. "Here, sir. This one is all set. Any reports from our men or me will come in on this channel. Just push the button and talk."

Faisal accepted the radio and Samir dashed out of sight to the north with the other four.

Faisal leaned back in the folding chair beside the table where his radio expert was still trying to figure out the infidel's military transceiver. He placed Samir's gift on the table, hoping he would hear of something from it soon.

He ushered the other man forward and sighed when he saw the man was carrying multiple bed rolls, which they did not need. He cut off this man's excited words about his find and dismissed him as another man approached right behind him. In truth, Faisal was already disinterested in whatever was about to be presented to him. Instead, he let his eyes fall back upon his new radio.

He couldn't wait for it to report some good news to him.

He didn't have to wait long.

Hamza

Hamza was not happy. What warrior would be joyful, waiting like a coward, under the protective cover of bushes, all for the remote possibility that one or more of the infidel dogs would stray back into the camp again, to pick through the garbage his warriors had discarded. To further add to his anguish, if this did happen, he was now being ordered to call it in on the new radio he was listening to and ask for permission before he could shoot any of these infidels. Not that any of these cowards would even return. So he sat under a bush, wasting his time.

But what angered him the most was that he was stuck with this duty while his brothers were given first choice at the spoils of their decisive victory over the infidel soldiers. Some of those spoils could have been their women. During the battle, he saw at least one young woman he would have liked to have found first. Alive was preferred, but dead would have been fine, too. Not that he was given that choice...

His new radio beeped at him.

Hamza snatched it from where it was hooked on his front pocket and examined the foreign object. Samir had told him how to work the thing, but it was still a mystery to him. He was good with a knife or other weapons; he was not good with electronics.

He switched to another channel, as the albino had shown him, and hooked it back to the front of his shirt. He would listen to this channel for one minute before repeating the process of switching to the next. When he checked to see where he was, and confirming it was channel number 6 on the display, he caught sight of something in the distance.

That something was coming *his* way.

Hamza switched the channel to 4 and pushed the button to talk. “Samir, this is Hamza. A truck is approaching from the west. Do I have permission to engage on behalf of our commander?” He let go of the button, unsure the thing was working or that anyone heard him.

“Hamza,” the radio boomed. It was Faisal, his commander. “Do not engage. Just watch and report.”

“So you want me to continue hiding, sir?”

“Allah’s warriors do not hide. However, we must know where the other infidels are hiding so we can find them and then kill them all.”

That made sense to Hamza, who thought Faisal was a better commander than the one previously assigned to their unit. If Faisal had been in charge to begin with, they would have killed all of these infidels before they were given the chance to slaughter so many of their own warriors.

Even though he didn’t like the waiting, he would follow his commander’s orders.

Hamza watched the truck approach to within ten meters of him before pulling off the road. This was only fifty meters before the road turned into the camp. The action was obvious and proved that the driver was familiar with the road and the camp.

A man exited the truck without a visible weapon and stepped carefully into the thick of bushes and trees.

Hamza followed.

Jimmy The Axe

Jimmy The Axe—so named because he carried it everywhere to fetch and cut up firewood for the camp—left his axe and rifle in the truck. He didn't think he'd need either. He slunk down low and trudged through the weeds as quietly as possible so as to not alert the enemy. Not that there'd be any still in their camp.

He firmly believed the terrorists would be long gone by now, having stolen all of their belongings, leaving only their dead patriots behind—that was one thing he did not want to see. Besides checking on the camp's status, Slim wanted him to retrieve the hidden cache of weapons and ammo, if the jihadis hadn't found them yet.

Since there was a chance the jihadis might still be here—no matter how slight—he'd do as Slim asked and approach carefully. The kid might not have been military, but he was a pretty smart understudy to Cappy.

Before he could see anything, Jimmy heard the busy sounds of activity coming from their abandoned camp... and voices.

Twenty feet from where the roadway's bramble and brush began, it opened up, providing a partial view of the camp. When he saw them, he sucked in a breath and let himself drop to the ground.

They were like a plague of locusts after having feasted on the summer corn: they buzzed all around what used to be their camp, having already picked through and spat out what they didn't want. There was debris everywhere, where their tents and belongings used to be... Then he saw their dead.

Jimmy had to turn away, as he was instantly repulsed by what he saw. The image he just took in would surely occupy his nightmares from now on.

How could fellow humans act so barbaric with the dead? he wondered and then quickly concluded; *they aren't human*.

Bile worked its way up from his stomach and threatened to erupt. He held it back, but he had to get away. Quick.

There was nothing he could do here. These disgusting pigs would have certainly found their stash of rifles and ammo by now, and if they hadn't, there were too many of them still there for him to attempt to retrieve them. He'd leave and report back exactly as Slim had asked.

Jimmy backed up, remaining prone so he could keep scanning the camp... and the carnage. He averted his gaze away from the bloody pile of maliciously desecrated bodies.

The thistles and thorns bit at his palms and arms, but this didn't slow Jimmy. When he had made it out of the overgrowth, he did a quick double-check to make sure no one had seen him and then dashed for his truck and left as quietly as he could. As far as he was concerned, someone else would have to come back here to check further. He couldn't bear to see it again.

When he was back on the highway, returning to the Senator's home, where his people were waiting for his return, he tried his radio. "Hello Eagle Base, this is Axe. Eagle Base, this is Axe, you read me?"

A flash in his rearview drew his attention from the road ahead. He studied the blacktop behind him through the shaky mirror and then studied it even further through his more wobbly side mirror. For just a moment, his heart skipped when he thought it was the reflection of another vehicle. In the end, he decided it was nothing more than his imagination.

Every minute that passed, he tried his radio again, desperately needing to connect with his friends.

It wasn't until he turned down the Senator's long private road, that he finally reached the remnants of his militia.

That's when the tears came.

Chapter 2

The Bookeater

With no answers on how to save their country, much less her brother, Travis, Lexi, and a few of the remaining members of American Eagle Patriots drove to the most rural part of North Carolina. Their hopes now hung on a mystery that appeared to be protected by concertina topped chain-link fencing and an equally fortified gate with posted death threats.

Until this moment, quiet reflection had been each member's companion. The enormity of what had happened in the last couple of hours seemed too overwhelming: Frank and the Senator had been captured by the enemy—which appears to have included some of the US military who were acting as terrorist allies; they had buried Randall White, who had helped them succeed in Endurance; they lost most of their supplies, including their newly acquired weapons and ammo; and finally, they received Jimmy's frantic report about their camp.

They had nowhere else to go and didn't know their next step. Their failures felt too vast to ponder any longer. Their only hope was that Frank's note and GPS coordinates might lead them to an answer.

Fearing another trap, Samuel had the other American Eagle Patriot survivors remain at the entrance to the dead-end road they had headed down. Their people would remain there, hidden but ready to intervene, if any threat attempted to box them in or if they radioed for help.

Samuel was driving their beaten up Hummer, with Gladys at shotgun, Lexi navigating from the back and beside her, Jonah, who was always ready.

Upon seeing the warnings at the gate, Lexi couldn't help but wonder if all of this was a waste of their time.

The gate signs were sure to telegraph to strangers like them that this mystery person did not welcome company: "Private", "Keep Out" and Lexi's favorite, "Trespassers Will Be Eaten".

"I don't even want to know what the last one really means," Samuel half joked.

During every slow mile preceding this, Gladys' head had been on a swivel. "Looking for any threats," she told Lexi. So was Jonah, who seemed more concerned with who might come from behind them.

Now idling at the gate, their heads remained fixed to their left side: a keypad just outside of Samuel's open window. Gladys startled them when she stated, "Better press the button so Lexi can tell 'em not to eat us."

Lexi sighed. She was in no mood to laugh.

Samuel reached out of his window and poked a round red button on the pad, probably not expecting it to work like most electronic devices these days.

Almost instantly, a speaker above the keypad announced, "Go away!"

It was as if its owner had been hovering over a microphone, waiting to immediately respond to all requests coming from the gate. More likely, this was a pre-recorded, albeit automatic reply to anyone foolish enough to press the button.

"Do it again," Lexi said mono-toned to Samuel, out her own passenger side window. As soon as he punched the button, she craned her head out further and yelled, "Frank Cartwright says I should ask for the Bookeater. I'm his goddaughter."

This time, there was no verbal demand from the key-pad's speaker. Only a solid *click*-sound, followed by the gate cracking open. The hum of a motor kicked in, and the gate slid sideways.

It halted abruptly once it offered them a space just wide enough for the Hummer to enter.

As they pulled through, Lexi remained in place, hanging out her window, her head fixed upward so she could continue to stare at the camera focused at them. She wondered who was behind it and why, of all places, Frank sent them here?

They continued down a long white gravel road, which appeared to be leading them up toward the highest hill. A small structure glinted in the distance.

Lexi reconsidered Frank's note to her. She had read it out loud to Jonah, Samuel and Gladys, because they were mentioned by name in the note. Lexi felt many parts of the note were too private for the others.

Frank's words felt so absolute to her: his cancer, her need to seek help from others "because he wouldn't be there for her," not to mention his writing this just before his and Senator Chase's arrest. But this mystery person seemed so...

A brown blur raced past her window. Upon realizing what it was, she was more shocked of this than she was by her thoughts. "Did you see that?" she huffed.

"See what, Lexi?" Samuel replied to his rearview, eyes flipping from her to the road and back.

She turned to glance at the same location before answering. "Never mind. It was nothing."

It *was* something. And that something resembled a cougar or even a female lion. But no one else saw it. She'd have to check it off as her own paranoia. Instead of stoking her jitters further, she peered ahead and considered their destination, now fully in view.

Admittedly, it was a disappointment.

She expected this person's house to be more palatial, perhaps akin to the Senator's mansion. They were, after all, hanging all their hopes on whomever came out of what was a very tiny ranch-style home, that was unremarkable in every detail, except for a roof carpeted in solar panels.

Samuel parked them steps away from the dwelling's insignificant front door.

"At least the paint looks somewhat new." Gladys' comment made Lexi wonder if she had been sighing out loud or what else she had done to reveal her frustration.

The front door popped open. An overt welcome sign. Or was it a trap being set?

"Someone wants us to come in?" Lexi stated, immediately regretting her comment because it sounded as if she was volunteering to go first.

Gladys turned her head and flashed a look that hollered, "No, really?"

Jonah, who had been mostly quiet the entire way up, spoke up. "I don't think Frank would send you into a trap. However, you should probably lead us in, Lexi. He would seem to be aware of you."

"We're assuming he's a he," Lexi mumbled. This time, she purposely exhaled loudly before jumping out of the Hummer. She had to stiff clutch her AK, while readjusting her pack.

"Hold up," hollered Samuel. "It's a... lion?"

Lexi caught it out of her periphery. It *was* a female lion, after all. Now it was silently sashaying toward them, having already crossed the drive they'd just come in on. Lexi pointed her AK toward the sleek, but older looking animal. Not that she could even consider hurting such a majestic animal.

"Bathsheba won't bother you," said a loudspeaker. The voice reminded Lexi of her father's, like that of a radio personality. At once, it put her at ease. With barely a moment's hesitation, Lexi marched right up to the open door, giving the animal an apathetic glance.

The lioness seemed equally disinterested by their presence, now ignoring the visitors. She sat down on her haunches and gave a wide yawn as if she were about to take a nap.

Lexi halted her progression in, just past the home's threshold. The others must not have been bothered by the large predator either, as she could hear their rushed movements to catch up while she scrutinized the inside of the small home.

The entry foyer was utilitarian, lit by a single wall sconce—further indicating the occupant had working electric—and a shotgun hallway with multiple doors on each side. All shut.

A reassuring hand squeezed her shoulder, telling her it was Samuel. "That was exciting. Now what?" he asked from just inside the doorway.

"Welcome, Lexi," announced a warm but authoritative voice from a hidden speaker just inside. Again, it was remarkably like her father's. "You and your friends are welcome to come in. I'm looking forward to meeting you."

It is my father's voice, her mind told her, even though that was impossible.

Near the end of the hallway, in front of her, a door on her right *clicked* open as if were released by an electronic switch. She doubted the mystery man or woman would be waiting directly behind it.

Lexi exchanged a quick glance with Samuel, Gladys and then Jonah. *Here goes nothing*, she thought, and she stepped tentatively toward the open door.

When she placed her foot into the darkened doorway, a flicker of fluorescents bathed a stairwell with light. It led down to a basement concrete floor that appeared to do a right jog out of sight. On the left side of the stairwell, attached to the wall was a small metal rail, hanging a foot above each step's edge, spanning the entire distance of the stairs down.

The three of them gazed at her, no doubt eagerly anticipating some sign from her. She gave them a nod before decisively advancing down the steps. Her need for a solution to their predicament, and Frank's, far outweighed her apprehension of what awaited her below.

About midway down, the noise of her new friends' footfalls gave her further assurance from above. Gladys must have been the next one down, as she whispered a correct summery of their situation from close behind, "Well, we're either walking into the lion's den or to someone with answers we desperately need."

Lexi was starting to doubt they'd find any answers because before them were even more questions.

A few feet from the base of the stairs, directly in front of her, was an open bunker-like door, at least a foot thick leading to a very small room.

Without fear, she continued through, just wanting to get to the end of this puzzle. She stopped in the room's center.

Her parent's Tucson home had a walk-in closet much larger than this room. Midway along each wall, including the entrance wall, was a single side chair—three total—as if this were a waiting room. The wall opposite the stairs had no chair, only a sealed metal door with a keypad to one side, similar to the one at the gate. This pad didn't have the red button.

"Looks like he or she had prepared this for us," Samuel stated.

"Or he only ever had three chairs for his waiting room," Gladys quipped. No one made any motion to sit or go much further than just inside the doorway.

Lexi was done with the games. She marched up to the keypad and stared upward at what looked like a domed camera mounted on the ceiling. "When do we get to actually *meet* the Wizard?" she asked, not holding back on her sarcasm. A pleasant memory flashed of the many times her mom and she watched The Wizard of Oz. She couldn't help but think this man was all pomp and no substance, just like the movie's Wizard.

The door buzzed open and silently swung inward. It continued swinging, perhaps from its own inertia, on precisely machined hinges, until it disappeared out of sight on the other side of the wall.

"Guess it's time we all meet this Wizard," Jonah said.

Lexi proceeded into what appeared to be a vast room, shrouded in semi-darkness. It's only illumination coming from successive rows of blinking-colored lights on both sides of the room. She had seen a server room at the University of Arizona, which looked somewhat similar to this, except for the darkness.

At the other end of the expansive room was a J-shaped arena of giant flat screens, stacked three-high, surrounding what she expected would be a luxurious gaming chair holding their host. The computer screen backs immediately in front of her, blocked her view of this wizard. The visible screens at the back of the area flickered multiple images of maps, videos of battles, satellite pictures, and one containing an image that made her swallow her breath.

It was an older picture of three men. The man on the left was her father, in the middle was her godfather Frank—both were considerably younger—and another, smaller man she didn't recognize. All were dressed in Army uniforms.

"So you're Lexi Broadmoor," an unfamiliar voice startled her, coming from her right side. It was completely different from the one projected over the speakers.

Of course he would know my full name, she thought as he continued, "Did your godfather tell you that I knew your father too?" Another thought hit her: *this man was somehow using a copy of her father's voice when he spoke over the speakers.*

She had immediately turned to address the unfamiliar voice. He was coming from the room's murk into a patch of light which illuminated the area in which she stood. He was the skinny man in the photo, only now older, wearing wire-rimmed glasses, disheveled hair and a just pressed white button-down shirt, gliding toward her in a modern-looking, motorized wheelchair.

"Honestly, until just recently, my godfather never mentioned a word about you." She didn't know whether to address him as Mr. Bookeater or by some other name.

"Holy crap, get a look at all of these computers," said Samuel.

"Come on in," said the Bookeater to the others and then turned back to Lexi. "Your godfather, and your father and I go way back. Let's talk about that and then we'll talk about what we're going to do about Major Cartwright's arrest."

Chapter 3

Frank

An Undisclosed Number of Years Earlier

"Comm check," crackled a voice from their command center.

"Cartwright here," Frank whispered, while eyeing their target across the street.

"Broadmoor, check," Stanley stated. His eyes were also on the target, but he was also fussing with his tie. He'd already grumbled about not being used to wearing one.

"Smith here," said the new member of their team, whose attention was fixed on Frank, their team leader.

"So why the hell do they call you Bookeater?" Stanley asked, his eyes still glued to their target. This was his way of dealing with the pre-op jitters... Talking.

"Ahh," Smith glanced at Stanley and then back to Frank.

He wanted to ask Smith this same question, but his mind was on the operation, and they barely had spoken five words together. Once their meeting was confirmed, the op came together very quick.

"Well, I learned at a young age that I could speed read

books. Lots of books. I was practically eating them up."

"No kidding? So why was the Company interested?"

"Well, as I read each book, I'd see patterns and connections with other books I had read in the past. Before AI, they had me read twenty to thirty books a day and find connections between them and the terrorist communications that we had intercepted—"

"Cut the chatter," a loud voice hollered in their earpieces.

At the same time, Frank gave them a nod and the three men, all dressed in civilian clothes, crossed the street, in the busy Karrada neighborhood of Baghdad. He led them toward the ornate entrance of an otherwise nondescript Iraqi office building. On each side stood two thick-necked security guards, who became instantly animated upon seeing Frank and his men walking their way.

Mentally preparing for what he had to say, Frank mouthed the lines of the Russian nursery rhyme, "May There Always Be Sunshine." A few feet from the two guards, he stopped and stated in English, but with a thick Georgian accent, "We have appointment with Khalid."

The older looking of the two security guards whispered Arabic into his lapel, telling the ears on the other side that, "Three civilians are here for your appointment."

After a pause, the same guard appeared to be receiving a reply in his earpiece, which was nearly invisible.

Definitely better tech than theirs, Frank thought.

After a few seconds, the guard nodded twice to the unheard voice, looked up and asked Frank in very bad Russian, what he translated as, "If looking at rain today?" His voice inflection at the end was overly exaggerated.

Despite the poorly worded question, Frank's answer

was immediate, again in English with his practiced accent, "It looks like sunshine."

This silly repartee was their pre-agreed upon code for entry to meet with the representative of a secretive and yet unknown imam, to whom they were supposedly going to sell nuclear weapons. Frank was posing as the lead representative of a cartel of Russian arms dealers, and they were meeting someone named Khalid, who was the lead representative of the mystery Imam. After all, it wasn't every day that someone had the balls to try and buy nuclear arms from the black market.

"Wait here," the guard barked, while the other stepped forward and told Frank in Arabic, "I'm searching you for weapons."

Frank lifted his arms as the man systematically patted him down and then moved on to Stanley. He would find nothing on them either, as they were unarmed. This was simply a meeting for introductions to feel each side out about their seriousness in transacting suitcase nukes. They didn't expect resistance, but if needed, their back-up team was waiting near the back of the same building, to be dispatched by their superiors if the op began to go off the rails.

Frank was leading this special op primarily because he had done so well in his first operation along with his knowledge of languages, including Russian. Stanley Broadmoor, with whom he'd already become close friends, had a basic knowledge of Arabic, but no Russian other than what Frank had taught him in the last couple of days. Hopefully, Khalid wouldn't either.

More important, Stanley was the only one Frank trusted to have his back. Smith was another matter altogether.

The young man was on loan from the CIA and allegedly had previously been Army. Though he seemed too nervous to have seen any combat, and the man was nothing but skin and bones. Frank guessed the guy would barely top out at an even hundred pounds, and only after a big meal. The man was certainly not there for his combat skills. But for what they didn't know.

Stanley and he were told in their briefing that Smith was supposedly a master of several languages, but mostly written, not spoken. And he was brilliant, with a brain like a computer. Oddly enough, his superiors referred to the skinny man as the Bookeater.

Regardless, Frank had wondered how any of this would help them on this op. But it was an order. His CO explained, "the guy had skills which would be uniquely necessary for this operation." Whatever that meant.

After the younger of the guards had finished pat-downs of each of them, and they had been standing exposed far too long for Frank's comfort, the older, no-neck, security guard nodded their approval to proceed inside.

The man's big frame belied his agility: in one ballet-like move, he spun in place, swiftly swiping a card from his palm at a black plate on the front door to generate a click, while smoothly opening the door for them. The other guard stated in Arabic, "You can go in now."

The three men marched inside, arriving at the entrance of East-West Consulting Ltd. The door to the office was already open, beckoning them inside its opulent waiting area.

As they approached, an attractive young woman stood up from behind a large wooden desk adorned in brass and gold embellishments. Her head was covered with a red and gold silk scarf, her black hair teasing its way out. But the rest of her clothing was traditional, albeit expensive looking.

When they entered, Frank caught a whiff of Jasmine, which was either her fragrance or a recently brewed tea.

A smile accentuated her perfect ruby lips. "Before I escort you gentlemen in to see Mr. Khalid"—her accent was an aristocratically smooth British English—"could I bring you some tea?"

"We're fine, thank you," Frank answered, still in character, though uncomfortably, not even returning the smile.

"Very well, gentlemen. Follow me." She bowed, turned and walked gracefully to a set of golden double doors. Both opened before she could touch them, as if they were mentally willed open.

The doors folded open into a giant office, offering them a wide view inside. And what an office it was.

To Frank, it was obviously all for show: the pretty female receptionist, the opulent entries, the reversal of roles... all for their benefit.

He didn't doubt that this office was that of the mystery imam: its excesses screamed this. But Khalid was more likely the one who worked at the front reception desk and the attractive woman was either the imam's daughter or his mistress.

A man, wearing the traditional dress of an imam, entered the mammoth office at the same time they did, coming from the left side of an automobile-sized desk in the middle of the office. Frank entered on the right, processing toward the man, who, with his hand extended and a beaming smile on his face, said in Russian, "I am Khalid. Welcome, gentlemen, to my humble office."

"Thank you, Khalid," Frank said in his practiced Russian. "I am Vladamir Prochenko. Your accent is very good." He lifted his hand to receive a handshake.

"Thank you," Khalid said in an educated Queen's English, just like the woman. "If you don't mind, that is the extent of my Oxford-taught Russian. So let's carry on in English." Khalid shook Frank's hand firmly and then with the same hand, welcomed them to four plush leather seats in a sitting area, away from the desk.

Frank's orders were to have Smith get a look at any documents on the desk and tables. There was nothing on the sitting area's table, but the desk was carpeted with stacks of papers and a large map. He hadn't been sure how he was going to arrange for Smith to get enough of a look there. Until now.

"If you don't mind, my two associates will remain standing over there," Frank pointed toward the right side of the desk. Smith and Stanley proceeded there and immediately hovered beside it. "You and I can sit and more privately discuss our business."

Khalid remained in place, halfway between the desk and the lounge. He snapped a concerned glance at Stanley and Smith, then to the back exit he had just emerged from, and finally back at Frank.

"Excuse me for just a moment," Khalid said, before he curiously dashed to and out the door at the back of the office.

Smith didn't hesitate, going right to work. He maneuvered around the ten-foot-long desk, eyeing every document there. Frank watched him and Khalid's door, as did Stanley.

Near the center of the desk, Smith halted, his eyes

scouring the contents of one pile of documents. He quickly shot a glance at Frank—his face visibly moved—and then back down to the first document in the pile. He removed a page and glanced at the one below it. Almost instantly, he did this with the next page, and then the next and then another, when the door popped back open, and Khalid emerged.

Everyone but Frank shuddered in place and then froze.

Smith flopped the pages back down where he found them, but otherwise remained unmoving, hanging over the desk.

Stanley took a half-step forward toward Smith.

Khalid remained two steps in front of the open doorway and then scowled at Smith.

What was behind Khalid caused Frank to spring into action.

Just inside the door, behind Khalid, were two men, dressed like Al Quida, with AKs, attempting to hide in the shadows and behind Khalid. "Attack!" Frank yelled, as he dashed right at Khalid.

"Behind me," Stanley hollered to Smith, while also rushing toward the door. At the same time, he launched, like a pitcher throwing a baseball, a paperweight he had picked up from the desk, connecting with one of the two gunmen, who were also now in motion.

Frank reached the door first, moving past Khalid, who was diving for the floor. Frank drove himself forward, shoulder first into the second gunman, who had just raised his rifle and fired a round.

Before the man could recover, Frank let loose with a combination of an elbow and then fist to the man's larynx, causing the soldier to buckle and gasp. Frank ripped the

AK from the man and drove its butt into the other soldier who Stanley had hit with the paperweight. Both were out of commission.

Frank turned the gun to where Khalid had thrown himself to the floor, but he was already gone. What he saw instead shocked him.

Stanley was doing the fireman's carry of Smith, and both were covered in blood.

"Smith took one in the side and can't walk," Stanley grunted.

"Come on," Frank said. He scooped up the other AK from the unconscious soldier while slinging the first rifle around his back.

Doing a quick check that it was loaded, he led them through the back doorway and toward the rear of the building, to where he hoped was their exit.

A rush of movement followed. The lead of a group of Rangers demanded, "Report."

"Cartwright, plus two," Frank immediately answered. "Two tangos down. Two tangos up front. One civilian female and male. Location unknown."

"Copy. Your evac vehicle is outside, sir," the Ranger said. His team rushed past them as Frank led his two men to their exit.

Before they crawled into the opened doors of the waiting van, there were explosions and gunfire coming from inside the building they had just exited.

Stanley hoisted Smith inside the van and someone who identified himself as a doctor attended to his wound.

"They're planning an attack on the US," Smith said. His voice shaky. "I read their plans. Some new terrorist group called the Islamic Caliphate of America. It's happening soon..." Smith lost consciousness as they sped off.

It was the last time Frank saw Smith, but by far not the last time he spoke to him.

The Bookeater

Present Day

"That day changed everything for each of us... Certainly, it did for me," Smith shot a glance down at his wheelchair. It was the only reference he had made to his paralysis.

"Unfortunately for America, our superiors never believed our report. All of the "Intelligence Services"—he made air quotes with two fingers on each hand—said they had never heard of the Islamic Caliphate of America; also told us that they never really had any intention of buying weapons of mass destruction; and said that it was too insignificant of a group to spend any resources on them..." Smith bit back at the anger, which he felt well up in him again.

"Bet they wished they could take back that decision," Jonah said from behind the others.

"They're all dead now, Mr. Price," Smith continued.

"Anyway, long after this, there was an incident where some Iraqi kids were killed, prompting Frank Cartwright and Stanley Broadmoor to leave military service.

"Frank... Well, Frank just went on being Frank.

"As you probably know," he looked directly at Lexi, "Stanley was recruited into the FBI to ironically join in the hunt in the US for Farook, the mystery imam we stumbled across, and leader of the not too insignificant, ICA."

Lexi nodded, her eyes becoming instantly watery.

"I owed them both my life. So I did my best to look after them ever since. I only wish we could have stopped Farook before..." He looked down at the tips of his Italian slip-ons and then back up at them. He too had to work at holding back his own waterworks.

"We all lost so many loved ones, all the while Farook's troops spread across our country like a biblical plague..." He was allowing himself to get lost in his thoughts again.

Time to take action and change things, he thought.

He snapped his gaze forward, took a breath and exhaled.

"Anyway, I have a plan to release Cartwright and Senator Chase out of captivity, and it involves all of you.

"Please follow me."

Chapter 4

Travis

Travis was miserable.

He huddled under the sharp edge of a Steelcase to escape the frigid air blasting down around him from the vent above. Every time he shifted, the desk's unsteady legs wobbled on top of a dusty clog of other desks and tables, causing shots of pain to his fatigued body. In the darkness of what he guessed was an unused storage room, he waited as uncontrollable shudders wracked his body.

At least for now, he was somewhat protected from the vent's direct airflow... his pants were almost dry... and the bleeding from his hand had stopped. Most importantly, he was still alive. Though he wasn't sure how.

When Abdul's psycho-hunter turned on the giant suction fan, he was almost done for. Somehow, he held on. In the process, he pissed his pants, lost all his supplies and his hand sutures reopened causing him to bleed like a stuck pig.

Yet, they didn't get him.

When the sucker fan was turned off and the psycho hunter stuck his head inside, he could hear the man's slow respirations, so Travis sucked down on his own breath.

For the longest time, he didn't dare move a muscle, waiting for some sign that he could get away. Minutes turned into an hour, as he listened carefully to the continued wash of Arabic spoken near the vent opening.

It was only after hearing Abdul-Aziz, his newly given name, along with the word "dead" or "killed" enough times that he came to understand what had happened…

They think I'm dead.

Maybe another half hour lapsed after they had sealed up the vent opening and any remaining voices were too distant to matter, that he dared to move. By then though, every part of his body horribly ached, especially his maimed hand.

When Abdul's henchmen had severed his pinkie, they also injected something around it to anesthetize it, causing most of that hand to go numb for days. So whatever phantom limb pain he experienced had been manageable. Now, that the numbness had worn off, and the pain was awful. It was even worse than when one of his madrasa teachers had struck him so hard his shoulder was dislocated.

At least the bleeding from the mottled mess that was his hand had stopped. So he gave up tortuously tapping on the bandaged area to check it. He knew he should investigate further, but there was not enough light.

He remembered thinking, p*erhaps this is a good thing*: he had no interest in examining it or all of the other places which stung from the multiple cuts along his legs, feet and arms.

Everything hurt at the same time.

That's when he felt a good cry coming.

It's not what Godfather would do, he chided himself and bit his lip.

One of his godfather's Frank-isms—that's what Lexi called them—came to mind... "Pain is a friend, there to remind you that you're alive."

Stop reminding me, he wanted to yell, but again he bit down, not wanting to make a sound.

No, like Frank, he would act, instead of wallowing in his own misery. That was when he slowly shimmied a distance away from his torture chamber, even though every movement was noisy and pure agony. He had planned to take it slow and maybe find some place more comfortable... Until they turned on the A/C. Full blast.

Going from chilled to downright freezing, he had scurried as fast as he could make his legs move, gunning for the first vent he could find and getting out of the duct work. At the time, he really didn't care where it went. Turns out, it was a dusty storage area which had been unused for years.

He woke to the sounds of new voices, *Speaking English?*

The cooling fan had stopped and somehow, he had dozed off. Though still feeling uncomfortable, he was not as miserable as before. Even his aching hand no longer throbbed like when they hurt him.

The words "prisoners" and "execution" were all he could make out. He wanted out of this dark and unstable area, and he was downright curious what these people were speaking about.

So back into the vent ducting he went. It was his new home.

If only I had knee pads, he thought. Maybe he'd make

himself a pair, if he could find the supplies.

When the ducting crinkled under his weight, he stopped dead.

Slow lizard walk, he instructed himself, starting back up and moving himself toward the voices. Just like a lizard, his movements were nearly sound free.

Somewhere in the distance, a heavy metal door slammed.

At the ducting's dead end, he had to either turn back, go up, go down, or double back and take a different set of ducting, going further into the complex.

He wasn't sure exactly where he was, other than he was not at the main vertical intake vent; this was a little smaller and when he looked up, there was only darkness and not the light of the outside world coming in through a vent.

Was it night, he wondered? He didn't have any idea of the time of day or even what day it was.

More whispered conversations. This time they were easier to hear… "So how do we escape?" a younger man's voice asked, fairly near.

They were coming from above him; maybe one floor.

You're on the C level, he reminded himself. *Only two more levels before the ground level, my way out.* If he went up one more level now, he'd be that much closer to his exit.

His discomfort didn't feel so insurmountable now. Hunger and thirst became his new friends. Perhaps there would be food on the next floor, and he could see what the whisperer meant by asking about escape.

He shimmied up one floor. Each grip-hold was as agonizing as it was difficult; much harder than when he mounted the first two floors. Twice he slipped and almost fell.

Flat Travis, his brain joked. A snicker tried to burst out, but he easily repressed it. He wasn't feeling very humorous now.

After making it up, and scooting away from the vertical vent, he laid flat on his back and panted. *Like Mr. Smithy.* He pictured the old man who walked a two-mile circuit around his Tucson neighborhood, often stopping near their home, breathing so hard, face tomato red. Travis always thought the man was having a coronary. Old people were having those all the time.

Waiting to catch his breath, Travis seized on a whiff of something magical... *food!*

The noise he made, and his physical discomfort were no longer a concern. Travis lizard-walked through his suffering until he came to a large patch of light. There, on the other side of a vent, below him were two adults, one man and one older woman, eating what looked like protein bars.

He licked his lips.

The man stopped and looked over at the woman and said, "Here, you can have the rest of mine?"

Travis wanted to yell out, "I'll take it."

Instead, the woman snapped angrily at the man, "You know where you can put your protein bar, you male chauvinist pig." She moved away from the man, out of sight.

Travis had no idea what was going on, and he didn't care. He just wanted one of those bars. Wherever they got them, there would be others.

There were other lights ahead from other vent openings. So he moved forward.

The next vent also revealed a similar room with a different man in it. This one had his back to Travis, kneeling on a prayer rug, in the middle of the floor.

These are jail cells, Travis' brain yelled. If he was right, they couldn't help him. He needed to keep searching.

He moved on to the next light, which went out as he approached the vent. There was a sound of a door closing and locking. Whomever was in that room had just left. So maybe it was not a jail cell.

Travis pressed his forehead to the backside of the vent register to get a better look. He couldn't see much, but he smelled something. Several somethings even. There was definitely food in there.

He listened for several long moments to pass. When he felt certain, he did what was becoming second nature and easy for him: he kicked in the vent register, sending it into the room with a clatter.

Remaining in place for another long minute to make sure no one else heard it, Travis then let himself into the room.

Even with the overheads out, the room was partially illuminated from the bright light squeezing in under the door, from the other side. With it, he could make out that this was another storage room. However, instead of old unused desks, there were supplies. Even better, this room had food in it, and something else...

Water!

A shelf was stacked full of bottled waters. He weaseled one out of its shrink wrapping and sucked it empty in a microsecond. After snatching another, he found boxes—one already opened—on shelves opposite to him. Inside the open box were bars like those he saw the man and woman eating. With no effort, the wrapper was off, and the bar was shoved into his mouth.

This is the best.

While he chewed and sipped some more water, he marveled at all the things stored in this large room. It was not unlike the storage area in their father's house in Florida. He would have to check it out in full. But later.

At that moment, fatigue hit him like a brick wall. He could fall asleep where he stood.

He shambled to the back of the room, around the end of a tall shelving unit, to find a place to curl up and nap.

Blankets?

There were stacks of folded, dark blankets, and... Until he put his hands upon them, he wasn't sure. It was a hanging rack of jumpsuits, like those that Abdul's workers wore.

There must have been a hundred, ranging from very tall to very small...

Like me.

He shed his soiled, ripped and bloody clothes.

Like a snake, slithering out of its skin.

He slid his legs into the smallest of the jumpsuits. It didn't quite fit. Standing on the cuffs, he reached over to the blanket stack and grabbed three.

Below the blanket shelf was an empty area, like someone else had cleared it out. He ducked in and worked his way to the wall, behind some other items which he already couldn't remember. He could sleep here and wouldn't be seen if anyone came in.

So tired.

Laying his head upon two of the blankets and slipping into the other like a sleeping bag, he noticed the silhouetted shapes of his discarded clothes on the floor. He needed to pick those up, so as to not alert anyone who entered. But before he could move. Sleep consumed him.

Abdul

"Where is Ali Baig?" Abdul hollered into the phone. Without listening to the response, he yelled even louder. "Send me Ali Baig, now." He slammed the phone's receiver down so hard it cracked. He was near cracking himself.

There had been no word from Ali, or anyone else to him about what had happened: no details about Hassan and the capture and killing of his son, Abdul-Aziz; not one update about Suhaimah, who long ago should have been captured; nothing about Imran, who should be accompanying her, and soon should take over for Ali; not one single report about how their Peacekeepers were doing with the US Military; or even how the new Emergency Weapons Ban was being enacted... Nothing from anybody for several hours.

There was a knock on the door.

"Come in," Abdul bellowed, and at the same time, launching himself out of his chair.

Ali Baig slunk through the door, yellowpad held in an armpit. He closed the door meticulously, as if it were the most important action of his day, all with his back to Abdul.

"Where have you been? Why have you not given me a report? What is going on..." He was yelling now.

Ali turned to face the wrath of Abdul, and his eyes went wide.

Abdul had an AK rifle pointed at his second in command, forefinger hovering below the trigger guard to make it obvious he was ready to squeeze it. "You have ten seconds to start answering my questions, or you will be replaced." He wasn't kidding.

Out of Ali's lips poured a word salad, unaided by his yellow pad, which he didn't even check once.

"Sir, I am happy to report that the American Senator, Thomas Chase and retired soldier and agitator, Frank Cartwright have both been captured and are being held for transport to here. In the process of capture, four of our Peacekeepers were killed by Mr. Cartwright, but the US Army—"

"What of Suhaimah?" Abdul cut him off. "What of Imran? Were they not traveling with them?"

Ali looked at Abdul's rifle, which had been lowered just slightly, at Ali's feet. Then Ali's eyes met Abdul's. "Ahh, well, I don't think—"

"You don't think?" Abdul's rifle was directed back up.

"No, I mean, we *know*... That Imran was also killed by one of the Americans. But Suhaimah is unhurt."

"Where is she?" He lowered his rifle and fell back into his seat. *Imran dead? Suhaimah not captured?* He couldn't believe it.

"The reports are sketchy because we had no other Peackeepers there, so we are dependent upon the report from the American troops. But it was stated to us that an American militia abducted her and fled before they could be stopped by the United States National Guard unit patrolling the Virginia-North Carolina border. We have Peacekeepers searching for her now."

Abdul didn't say anything. Everything had been going right for him, until late today. And it all started with the death of his son, Abdul-Aziz, at the hands of his assassin, Hassan Sabbah. He still hadn't heard from Hassan first-hand. All of his information had come from overhearing conversations from others and a cryptic report from Ali hours ago.

Now this.

"Why did it take you so long to give me this report? Weren't they at the border hours ago?"

"I have been trying to confirm the information from people on the ground. At first, I was getting reports that Suhaimah was shot too. But I have at least two separate confirmations that she was not hurt. And the Americans are not being as cooperative as we had hoped. Anyway, I only received a confirmation about the Senator and Mr. Cartwright a few minutes ago. So, naturally I came when I had something confirmed to tell you."

"Naturally," Abdul said, with more than a hint of sarcasm. "Fine. Where is Hassan? I have been waiting to hear from him since you told me what happened to my newly adopted son, Abdul-Aziz. Again, that was over an hour ago."

"Hassan Sabbah is at the mosque, praying."

Abdul sat back up in his chair. "Go and tell him to come to me. Now! And if he is not here within an hour, I will come to him and shoot him dead. Then I will find you. Have I made myself clear?"

"Yes, my Mahdi," Ali said, nodding once and dashing

toward for the door so fast he crashed into it.

Abdul had already turned around in his chair and now stared at the blank TV. "What am I supposed to do?" he asked it, as if he expected it to answer. In fact, he waited for a reply.

Chapter 5

Longhorn Munitions Storage Base

Grimes

"How the hell did we get here?" Aimes huffed after pacing around their cement confines. With a heavy sigh, he plopped himself down onto a foldout chair. Grimes, who sat opposite, watched his friend, but he had little desire to answer.

Waiting long enough to make the open question sound rhetorical, Aimes continued, "I recognize this place." Aimes' eyes once again traced the surfaces of the cement floor, walls and then ceiling, before drilling back onto Grimes, who still didn't say anything. Instead, he massaged his own neck, which with his back, ached like crazy.

Aimes kept talking. "You know, these were old munitions storage bunkers for the Army. Some years back, they were being marketed as prepper condos. My wife wanted me to buy one of these, so we could live off grid."

Grimes hadn't heard this story before. So he bit. "What happened—"It just occurred to him at that moment "—is that when she got sick?"

"No." Aimes offered his friend a warm smile. "This was a couple of years before that. Anyway, it turns out that the whole thing was a scam. The developer went bankrupt, and the federal government pulled its lease and so this place just sat here, unused... I guess until now.

There was a rumble of voices outside the only window of their cement prison. If you could call it a window. At best it was an afterthought, where a rough opening was drilled out of the twenty-four-inch concrete wall and a thick pane of glass was then installed later. Perhaps as part of the prepper-condo offering just mentioned.

Because Grimes didn't budge—*it hurt too damned much*—Aimes hobbled over to the window to check it out. Onto his tippy toes, Aimes propped himself up to see and listen.

He hung there for a solid minute, before letting himself fall back onto his heels. Standing in place for a moment, strained creases burrowed into the forehead of his bald melon, his tongue worked around his mouth as if he were probing for something caught in his teeth. Suddenly, he turned back and shambled over to his seat. He sat hard, glaring at Grimes' feet without saying a word.

"Well, what did you see or hear?" Grimes bellowed, surprised he was now the one getting the silent treatment from his normally talkative friend.

Aimes looked up. "Four National Guards and what looked like two local police had stopped just outside our prison window...

"The policewoman said there was talk about the military shooting prisoners. The policeman asked what was happening with *their* prisoners.

"One of the Guardsman said that he heard talk of a military tribunal for quote, "Those two," and he motioned toward us. Then he said, quote, they were to be executed."

Corporal Porter Grimes

"I'm guessing it's fifteen feet," Porter said, while tilting his head down to not appear to be interested. "Of course, the razor wire on top is a bit of a—"

"Shhhh," Wallace hissed from a few feet away in front of him. She was kneeling, pretending to tie one of her boots. On the other side of the chain-link fence, two guards were conversing quietly, with their backs to their makeshift holding cell.

Porter bit his tongue and waited for her to report.

One of the two guards—Wallace called him Tweedledum—appeared to take notice of her there. He yanked at the arm of the other guard. They both nodded an acknowledgment and stepped further away from their temporary jail to privately continue their conversation. Tweedledum excited the Fighting Warrior's gymnasium, leaving the other guard behind.

Wallace ignored them while straightening the laces of her regulation boots. She rose, marched forward and purposefully sat in one of the chairs behind Porter. It was an obvious attempt to make it look like she did not have anything to share. She dipped her head and appeared to be working on a deep cheek itch.

"Thanks," Wallace said in a low whisper, "for interrupting Tweedledee and Tweedledum from spilling the beans."

"What did you get?" Porter said to his watch.

"Neither of them like this duty. Tweedledee said he was going to quit. Tweedledum said he needed the food, and he wanted to at least wait around until, "the prisoners were executed." But then he noticed me standing there and stopped talking."

"Great. Now we have an even a bigger reason to find a way out of here."

"I have an idea on that. I think Private Tweedledee will be more open to our persuasion than the other guy. Meet me over at the same place by the fence and then follow my lead." Wallace rose quickly and stepped back over to the fence. Porter was facing her seconds later.

"This is horseshit," Wallace yelled in Porter's direction. "Don't you agree?"

Porter didn't know where she was going with this, but he was already used to her "on the fly" planning.

"I completely agree," he said, projecting his voice, though nowhere near as blaring as her. He peeked through the open chain-link to catch Tweedledee looking their way. "You have a bite," Porter said under his breath.

"Yeah," Wallace continued her act. "I'm thinking when cooler heads prevail, our superiors will come down hard on those who followed like sheep to break the law."

Porter did his best to add his two cents' worth. "All of this is clearly against constitutional law, and they know it."

Wallace smiled her acceptance that Porter caught on so quickly. She added, "I wouldn't be surprised if everyone who so blindly followed their bogus orders, even though they knew they were wrong, didn't end up getting shipped to San Quintin."

"I've heard of dishonerables going away for a lot less."

"And we will stand witness to the injustices done here today—"

Tweedledum startled both by banging on the fencing with the butt-end of his rifle. "Pipe down in there. No one gives a pile of poop what you two think."

"You will," Porter continued playing along, "when you're staring at a firing squad."

"Oh, I'll be in a firing squad alright, but not on the receiving end like you two," Tweedledum said, grinning wildly. He chuckled and walked away.

"Well, that didn't work," Porter said.

Wallace remained quiet, watching Tweedledum practically get accosted by Tweedledee, who stopped him from leaving and then began arguing with him, while pointing their way.

"In fact, I think it worked just fine. We'll let that germinate in both of their wee brains for a bit."

Frank

There was nothing unusual about the nondescript brick building discreetly appointed with a Greenville County Sheriff sign. What should have been remarkable to Frank was the unit of National Guard troops stationed in front of and surrounding the station's grounds. He barely looked, but Chase took notice.

They were driven past a lone entrance guard directly to the side of the building, no doubt to be out of the public eye. Not that anyone was around to witness the lawlessness occurring there and perhaps everywhere around the country.

Authoritarianism, like a fungus, needed darkness to germinate, often in closed rooms and protected fortresses, away from their subjects' prying eyes. By the time an authoritarian regime revealed itself, it was often too late to easily destroy. Frank feared they had passed this bulwark, and he suspected Chase felt the same.

The two Army privates and colonel handed over their prisoners to a National Guardsman with colored hair and dangly earrings. A younger twin, without the trans make-up, joined their processional and fell behind Chase, as Frank was led toward an open door into the station.

Chase cleared his throat. "Gentlemen, I'm Senator and President Pro Tempore, Thomas Chase. I demand you take me to see—"

"Keep moving," commanded the younger guardsman from the rear.

Frank didn't slow, because it hurt too much to stop and start again. After the jarring ride in the Army transport, he was anxious to just sit in some place quiet and be left alone.

"I wouldn't waste your breath, Senator," Frank said with a slight turn of his head. "These guys"—The trans-guard turned back to give Frank an angry glare—"are just following orders. I'm sure we'll be seeing someone in authority soon enough."

Chase didn't give a reply, and one wasn't expected. But Chase's footsteps continued from behind.

Upon entering the murky building, they were assaulted by a din of activity, noise and the all too familiar jail odors. He'd visited enough unclean prisons overseas, being on both sides of the bars, to recognize their acrid smells.

After walking nearly the entire length of the building, they were led to a small room, whose only light came from the other side of an observation window. Usually set aside for questioning witnesses, it looked to be their destination. There also didn't appear to be any shadows on the other side of one-way window separating them from the dimly lit room.

Frank took the seat facing the still partially open door and observation window. Chase took the other chair on the opposite side of a table in between them.

"Are those the two prisoners we were told to hold on to?" asked a gruff voice on the other side of the door.

"Yeah," answered the trans guardsman. "I understand they're going to be tried for treason."

"You're relieved," said the gruff voice. "They're under my authority now."

As two sets of footsteps marched away, an older man, who looked as if he might be the sheriff, poked his head inside the door and eyeballed both Frank and Chase. "I'll be with you two in a few minutes." He then shut the door and clicked a latch, telling them it was now locked.

Finally quiet, Frank's mind pounded away at his psyche.

He closed his eyes and let his head to fall forward.

At that moment, a wellspring of anger broke free. He had missed so many red flags and ignored those he did see. Jasper's were obvious and plentiful and yet he took no notice of them, putting his goddaughter in jeopardy more than once. Then he disregarded the overt red flags surrounding Chase's hand-off to the Army...

Frank had learned long ago to put failures behind him so that he could focus on how to tackle the problems which lay ahead. It was a waste of his energy to lament on actions that couldn't be changed. Instead, all thought should be directed on the mission and only the mission. But this time, he felt different.

Lost battles were part of being a soldier. It was surviving those losses and learning from them that helped him to become a better soldier. This time, he allowed his self-directed anger to persist. With the buildup of anger, he felt less in control. Without control, he was losing something which he had not felt before... A sense of hope.

He'd been in much worse situations, even recently. This time though, he felt too damned old, too physically damaged and too bloody tired to be able to do anything further. To even want to do anything further.

Maybe this was the end of the line for them. As much as he would have liked to have solved the many problems for Lexi, Travis, Chase, or his country, he wasn't sure that there was anything left in him to give.

What could one used up warrior and one elder statesman do against the overwhelming forces directed against them?

Right then, he could have just laid down on the floor and sleep until he was taken to whatever fake tribunal and subsequent execution awaited them. There was little he could do to prevent all of this from happening. He just—

Frank was startled when Chase had reached across the

table and grabbed his hand. "Frank, would you join me in a prayer?"

He examined the Senator, who didn't look as beat up as he remembered. The expression gleaming back at him was genuine.

"Yeah, sure," Frank responded with admittedly little enthusiasm.

A dim, pin-sized light of hope poked through his gloom.

Chase dropped his head and began addressing God on their behalf. The words poured out of him effortlessly and as polished as any preacher's Sunday delivery. Yet, every syllable had impact and meaning to Frank, as if they were crafted on his behalf.

After less than a minute of asking God for forgiveness, and giving thanks for their many blessings, including that fact that He had yoked Frank and Chase together in this seemingly hopeless situation, Chase asked that He guide them out of this. However, if it was not their time to do His will, they would accept whatever punishment awaited them...

When Chase was done, Frank repeated an "Amen."

He looked directly at Chase. "Thank you, Thomas. That's exactly what I needed. Now, let's find a way out of this place."

Chapter 6

The Bookeater

They were the first visitors Matt Smith had ever had down in what he called his Bat Cave. Next, he would lead them to his second most cherished room. It was his intent to wow them. He needed to.

"This place is a lot bigger than it looks from the outside," Lexi said.

"About ten thousand square feet underground, as opposed to less than two thousand above ground."

"No shit?" Gladys quipped. "Oh... now the tiny house thing makes sense."

Smith halted his chair before a wall of floor-to-ceiling brushed metal panels, where he waited until his rubber-necking guests caught up.

"Miss..." Smith flashed a grin at Gladys from his wheelchair.

"It's just Gladys. My new adoptive family, at least what's left of them, simply call me Grandma."

"Okay, Miss Gladys. You're perceptive. Because of my previous employer, I've learned that the best thing for me was to stay off everyone's radar."

"Or satellite," Jonah added.

"Correct, Mr. Price."

"Meant to ask, how did you know my name?"

"As I mentioned, I've been watching after Frank, Lexi and Travis for a while now. Yes, I knew of you and your reputation in Endurance. So I made sure Stanley and you met; knew you two would be of help to each other…

"Mr. Slim and Miss Gladys are new to me.

"Anyway, now that I have your attention, let me present my second favorite room in my home… my armory." He made a show of pressing one of several recessed buttons on the side of his wheelchair arm rest. The hidden Bluetooth device transmitted an encrypted code to the secret door's locking mechanism, which silently opened up the middle ten-by-ten, one-ton panel. The concealed door swung left to right, its arc just barely missing the edge of Smith's chair. Though he was quite sure none of them noticed this. They would be certain to notice what was inside.

For this reason, he savored each of their non-verbal reactions like a chocolate lover's entrance into a truffle shop.

Slim was the first to speak. "Is that what I think it is?"

"Looks like a gun-nut's best wet dream," Gladys said.

"Looks like all of our wet dreams," Jonah said, his mouth equally a gap as the others.

The lights inside the twelve-hundred square foot space flashed on, revealing a room filled with every conceivable variety of weapon Smith thought he might need for every contingency. It had taken him ten years of quiet purchasing through many entities to hide his identity and their ultimate delivery location.

"Geez, are you planning on taking over a small country?"

Slim asked as he walked in behind the others.

Smith snickered a little. "In a manner of speaking, yes, we are."

Lexi didn't seem at all impressed. Her hands were planted on her hips, her eyes drilled into Smith, as if she were the one gaging *his* reaction. "Yeah-yeah, I've got one of these back home too. That doesn't explain how you think you're going to break my godfather and Senator Chase out of custody, if we can even find them now."

Smith couldn't help but laugh. Neither Frank nor Stanley ever provided any details about Lexi. He had basic data, but nothing about her personality. So he had no idea what to expect. But after a few minutes with her, he knew he liked this young woman.

A lot.

"No worries, Lexi. I know *exactly* where they are and how we're going to break them out. But first, let me show you something and then we'll talk about how you and your friends are going to help."

Jonah found himself standing in front of and gawking at a wall of select-fire Uzzis, HKs, and Glocks.

He whistled, "Seriously, how did you happen to purchase all these fully automatic weapons as a civilian, when I wasn't even able to get tax stamp approval to buy a pre-1986 antique? Didn't think that was even possible, unless you were military, police or licensed private security.

"It helps having friends in the CIA."

"I'm pretty sure my father didn't have one of these in his gun room." Lexi was standing in front of a rack of shoulder-fire rocket launchers. This time, she looked a little impressed.

"No, it's not likely that any civilian possesses one of these. They came from a surplus purchase during the Russian-Ukrainian war." Smith glided past Lexi and stopped at a designated area of what were certainly high-tech looking weapons and turned his chair to face them. "This is what I wanted to show you."

The group ambled over to him and examined the display.

"You're not suggesting we toss bean bags at Frank and the Senator's captures?" Jonah asked.

"No, Mr. Price. That's just one form of non-lethal weapon. Let me explain what I have in mind."

Hamza

"I found them... Can... you... hear... me?" Hamza barked into his walkie talkie. Tossing it to the seat, he grabbed a hold of the wheel with both hands and navigated around a dead car blocking both lanes of the two-line highway. Snatching it back, he stabbed the button. "Repeat, this is Hamza. I have found the American dogs. Do you hear me?"

"Hamza. This is Faisal. Where are you, brother?"

Hamza straightened the steering wheel and jammed his foot onto the accelerator, before again picking up the hand-held... "I'm about five kilometers from you and fifteen from the militia camp. I have found the remaining members of that militia. I recognized their trucks on the side of a road. They are guarding a private entrance to some capitalist's property. We need to attack now, sir."

There was a long pause of static. Hamza thought maybe that his message was not received, so he lifted the radio back to his lips, intending to repeat the message, when it beeped back at him.

"Return to the camp, Hamza. We found the rifles and ammunition they stole from us. When you are here, we will plan our attack. Then, before tomorrow's first light, we will finally get our justice."

Lexi

They were all upstairs now, admiring Smith's front library. He seemed most pleased with their reactions.

Lexi guessed the room, with its vaulted ceilings and floor to ceiling bookshelves, must have taken up half of Smith's above ground floor plan. Like the complex below, it served a purpose but was also built to impress. As he said to them multiple times, "It's my favorite room." To Lexi, if the gun room wasn't proof enough, bringing them to this room was an obvious attempt to show off. Though she didn't know why.

He had already taken Lexi aside and revealed to her some secrets about his residence and his life before the collapse: he inherited a lot of money from his family, so building all of this was easier than it looked; his former employer, the CIA, left him alone because he had faked his death and everyone believed it, or just didn't care enough to investigate; and he was the one who helped Stanley find the home in Florida, because he knew Stanley would need a bug out house for him and his kids.

He was funny because he'd show off something and then do a reveal. Such as, "Did you see I have Al Capone's Tommy gun" or "Hey, did I tell you I'm responsible for Osama Bin Laden's capture?"

Then, to all of his new friends, just before showing off the library, he stated that Frank and Chase were being held as traitors, even though they had not been formally charged. Smith's source even said there was talk of an execution in the future. He told her that his source, feeding him the intel, was very high up in the current government.

Everything Smith told her appeared to be for the purpose of making a good impression on her. Lexi stared at the man, who looked a little like a skinny adult Macaulay Calkin.

"Impressive collection," Gladys said. "Are most of these first editions?

"You have a good eye as well." Smith beamed. "Everything here is first edition, even the newer books."

"I've read this one," Slim pointed to a book titled, *Stone Age*.

"Yep, helped that author with his research..." A red light blinked on Smith's arm rest. "Oh good, I see the rest of your militia are at the gate. After they park in back, we'll break some bread together and then we'll call it a night."

"Do you need to do something with Bethsheba?" Lexi asked. She didn't want the beautiful lioness to get hurt by a nervous militia member.

"No worries, Lexi. She's out hunting now, away from the house."

"There's a lot to hunt out there?"

"You never know what she'll find.

Chapter 7

Abdul

Hours after not hearing anything from Hassan and Ali interrupting him multiple times with "nothing to report," Abdul was finding himself desperate for some good news. Any good news.

This time he lifted the broken receiver without anger, pushing the Zero button and waiting for someone to pick it up.

"Yes, my Mahdi," answered a voice he recognized, Salman Asad. Sometime during the night, he had almost beheaded the phone receiver when he slammed it down again. Ali had duct-taped the two pieces together so at least it was functional.

"Salman, call Colonel Meer's phone," Abdul said. "Ring me back when you have him."

There was a knock on his door.

"And send someone to replace my phone receiver." Abdul hung up when there was another knock. He was starting to feel better.

"Come in," Abdul said. Maybe it was Hassan. He was hours late, but he would still welcome anything his trusted assassin had to report.

The door cracked open, and unfortunately, it was Ali Baig. He bowed, closed the door and marched toward Abdul's desk, this time without his yellow pad.

"Stop," Abdul barked. "If you don't have any news, I don't want you any closer." Like an annoying little fly, it was obvious that Ali was going to buzz around his office and then leave. This was the last thing he needed.

"Apologies, my Mahdi. We still cannot find Hassan Sabbah. I have notified everyone to locate him and escort him to your office. I just wanted you to know since it has been almost an hour since my last update."

Abdul didn't respond. He just held his hand up and shooed him away like he might have done with a fly swatter. He glanced at his AK rifle, lying on his desk and then up at Ali, thinking that this might be a more enjoyable fly swatter. Instead, he just continued waving his hand until Ali simply bowed and walked back out of his office.

The phone rang and Abdul snapped up the receiver, feeling the two pieces move independently of each other. "Yes."

The receiver answered. "This is Secretary Meer. You called me."

This man's attitude needs to be corrected, he thought.

"Mr. Meer, give me some good news," Abdul said.

"Sir? What good news, sir?"

"Tell me how it's going out there with our Peacekeepers and with your military arresting citizens for weapons violations."

"You mean the President's new gun ban?"

"Yes," Abdul huffed.

"It's going well, Mr. Farook."

"Excellent. So we've made lots of arrests?"

"Not a lot, but some."

"How many?"

"Excuse me?"

"How many arrests have you made across the country?"

"Did you mean how many people have been arrested or how many total arrests?"

This man was annoying to the point of madness.

"I will make it simple, even for you. How many US citizens have you arrested so far for breaking the weapons ban?"

"Well, let me see... It looks like... twelve."

"Twelve?"

"Yes, twelve."

"Only twelve people out of over one hundred million gun owners were arrested?"

"Yes."

"What is wrong? Why are not more people getting arrested? Surely there are more citizens than this violating the law?"

"Yes, there are."

Abdul squeezed the receiver, causing the two pieces underneath its temporary bandages to separate and wobble.

"So why don't you get them... all of the violators?"

Meer paused a long period before answering. "Because we are having difficulty finding US Military men and women to go along with the new rule."

Abdul pounded his desk with his other fist.

"What do you mean? How can you have a problem? They are in the military. Just order them to follow their new orders."

"Sir, many have gone AWOL. That means, absent without leave, sir. They—"

Abdul threw the receiver at the phone. Both pieces now free of their duct tape bonds flew apart, its few meager wires held.

"Ahhhhhh," Abdul screamed his disgust, picking up his AK rifle, with no intended target.

Mohammad Number One

The first of Abdul's two door guards named Mohammad, was nodding off again. He'd been at his post for ten hours, barely alert from Ali's coming in briefly and then leaving. The noise caused him to spring to attention. When no one was about, he guessed the noise must have been his Mahdi, perhaps summoning him. He dutifully darted inside.

Just inside the doorway, he asked, "Can I get you something, my Mah—"

He was cut off by the booming thunder from ten rounds of Abdul's AK.

Travis

Pop-pop-pop-pop-pop-pop-pop-pop-pop-pop-pop.

Travis' eyes snapped open and his heart beat rapidly in reaction.

He knew what automatic gunfire sounded like, even one distorted by distance and carried to him through the HVAC's ductwork. He'd been around enough of them lately to also know what kind of gun it was.

When his heart settled, he considered what this meant to him...

Nothing, he thought.

He closed his eyes and went back to sleep.

Chapter 8

Lexi

All eleven remaining members of the American Eagle Patriots sat in Smith's living room, around the fireplace and its giant screen TV. They all anxiously awaited their mystery host to go over his plan to free Frank and the Senator. Lexi was so tense, she couldn't control herself from visibly shaking.

Only an hour earlier, she, Gladys, Samuel and Jonah heard the simple version of the plan. But that's not why she trembled. It was the enormity of what had to be done and the fact that she was central to its success.

When someone sat down beside Lexi, her nerves fired a startling jolt. Turning in that direction, she saw it was Samuel, who had grabbed her hand and gave her a reassuring smile.

Just like that, she felt better.

"You're going to be great," he said. "We've got this, together."

She nodded, squeeze his hand back and returned his smile. It was genuine.

"May I have your attention," Smith said from his wheelchair, just below the big screen. He waited for everyone to be quiet, the last of whom—no surprise—was Moondog.

"Thank you. As I had mentioned before, my name is Matt Smith. Besides serving in the Army and working for the CIA, I have also watched over the man you know as Major Frank Cartright, along with his goddaughter, Lexi Broadmoor..."—all eyes momentarily fell on Lexi and then returned back to Smith—"and I am a personal friend of Senator Thomas Chase."

That was the first time Smith had shared that fact.

"In other words, this operation has significant personal meaning to me. However, it has even a greater significance to our country.

"Tomorrow, before sunrise, your militia is going to conduct one operation, at the same time as other operations, all focused on freeing American political prisoners from our government's jails."

There were a couple of murmurs in the audience, all asking the same thing: "There are others?"

"Yes, there will be other militia groups, breaking other Americans out of captivity, all wrongly held by local and federal government authorities. But you, my new friends, will be tasked with the most important of all of these breakouts. That is because you'll be breaking out the rightful President of the United States, along with one of the finest warriors and heroes you have ever met."

The room erupted in cheers. Lexi sucked in a breath.

Faisal

"Thank you, Hamza, our brother, for bringing us this information. " Faisal said, slapping Hamza's shoulder. Faisal stepped away, turned to face his men, with his back to a newly created campfire. "We will use this intelligence to finally bring retribution to our brother martyrs."

Every single one of the fifteen men cheered, each clutching a new AK-74 in hand.

"Now that we know the location of the remaining militia members, we must prepare for our attack tomorrow, at first light."

"Why wait," Samir asked. "Should we not attack them now, using the surprise to our advantage?" His blue eyes glared at him like a white wolf calculating how it might devour its next meal.

"Samir, my brother, you have proven yourself to be one of Allah's greatest warriors, as well as possessing a keen intellect. But planning is needed here for several reasons.

"First, it is already dark, making it difficult to approach their position without first alerting them to our approach. We must not take our enemy for granted. The previous commander did this at great cost to our many brothers, who are now martyrs. It is better that we approach slowly, like a mighty predator does when it spots multiple prey and doesn't want to lose even one. We will be careful to ensure that we capture everyone before they have a chance of escape.

"Second, we have a few more tasks we must complete at this camp before we can move on. Let's finish packing up the remaining supplies we have taken from these infidels and get them into our truck. We are also close to figuring out the infidel's radio, which we hope to use to contact our Mahdi. Once we do all of this, we will take our truck, with Hamza driving the infidel's truck in the lead, in tomorrow's early hours.

"Finally when we are done here, we will set fire to everything we have not taken, except for the bodies. We will leave them as they are. This will be our sign, to all who come upon them, of what lies ahead for any of those who do not submit to the will of Allah." Faisal withdrew his newly acquired Desert Eagle pistol. While pumping it in the air, he yelled out, "Are we ready, my brothers, to get retribution on the infidels?"

His men responded, first cheering and then chanting, "Allahu akbar. Allahu akbar. Allahu akbar."

Lexi

"But what about the military?" Moondog asked in his usual backwoods drawl. "The US Military, even with it being woke and all, is still bad ass. I don't think we want to fight against any of our boys."

"And girls," Gladys stated, shooting laser beams at Moondog.

"Moon..." Smith started to say.

"—Dog. Moondog is my name."

"Yes, of course. An ode to Gidget. You must have been a surfer. I get it," Smith continued with a nod.

Moondog shook his head and mouthed, "I don't understand."

"None of you have to worry about fighting against our US Military, nor our men"—Smith flashed a look toward Gladys—"or women in blue.

"First, we will be using non-lethal weapons. They're still highly effective, but we won't be drawing blood.

"Second, as I mentioned, there will be minimal personnel guarding the station."

"Excuse me, but how could you know this?" Jonah asked from the back of the room. "How do you have this kind of intel from... here?"

"Besides being tapped into their security systems, which are only mildly operational, I've been flying drones above there for the past few hours. I even know exactly where Major Cartwright and Senator Chase are located in the jail."

A picture appeared on the big screen, which showed the black silhouettes of two men sitting at a table.

At first, Lexi assumed it was an example of a still thermal representation of a jail cell. But then one of the figures rose from a table separating them and proceeded to walk around it, with a limp.

"That's Frank!" Lexi stated.

"Yes, Lexi. And with a little luck, this time tomorrow, he and the Senator will both be free."

Faisal

"Allahu akbar," the men continued their chanting. Some firing their weapons into the air to punctuate their excitement at the prospect of getting revenge on the infidels.

"Commander," hollered Aadam, his radio operator.

"Yes," Faisal yelled back, hurrying around the campfire and darting into the tent, where the radio operator waived an arm rapidly.

Before Faisal could get to him, Aadam bellowed, "I did it, sir! Their radio. We can now contact Abdul Mahdi."

"Excellent," Faisal said inches from the operator's ear. "We will do this in the morning."

Fiasal slapped Aadam on this back and then turned his attention toward the cheering men and once again took up their chant...

"Allahu akbar. Allahu akbar. Allahu akbar."

Chapter 9

Abdul

"My Mahdi," the jail keeper mumbled, while bowing. Abdul marched past him, commanding, "Open." He halted before Saleem Hafeez's cell door.

The jailer seemed startled more by his Mahdi's unexpected presence, than the AK rifle slung over his shoulder. But he should have been. Abdul rarely carried a rifle: that was for his little mice and his warriors. Though lately he found he had to do his warriors' work and execute a few to make an example.

"This cell; open it now," he barked even louder.

"Yes, my Mahdi," the jailer said, while sprinting over to the jail cell. The jailer, who had a simple job, fumbled with his keys, as if he had forgotten which it was. When he finally found the correct one, he slammed it in the hole, and with a loud clang and rattle, swung open Sal's jail cell door. The jailer backed away in supplication.

There, on one of the prayer rugs that Abdul had given him, Sal was kneeling, going through his nighttime ritual prayer of the *Salah*.

It occurred to Abdul that he had forgotten to do this. So he grabbed another *sajjadat* or prayer rug and laid it out beside Sal's. He would pray with his brother now as if they were equals.

After this, he would do what he came to do.

Travis

Crash-bang, were the sounds echoing from the distance, followed by two voices... One yelling.

Uncle Abdul, Travis thought.

His eyes popped open. Wide.

Uncle Abdul is here and... it's almost completely dark wherever here is.

Where am I?

Then it occurred to him: he's in the big storage room. He'd been sleeping. Now he really had to pee.

There was more yelling.

That is Abdul, he reasoned. His building panic was real. Was it possible that his Uncle Abdul found him?

"He... can't hear you," Travis slowly whispered to himself.

There was another voice, but Travis didn't pay any attention to it either. His Uncle Abdul was *not* in the room. So he could focus on what was most important... He *really* had to go.

Travis pushed himself through the bottom shelf, knocking over a pile of towels which had been neatly stacked in front of where he'd been sleeping. He didn't care.

He scanned the shelves and then the floor for what he could use. He saw it: the discarded bottle that he tossed on the floor. While shuffling over, he slid out of his newfound jump suit—*like a lizard molting*—snatched the bottle and relieved himself inside it.

Now what?

The discarded bottle top was found nearby, and a plan came together.

Still holding his partially filled bottle, he shuffled over to the light switch and flipped it on. Light was needed and wasn't likely to be seen from the other side.

He had to get rid of this and his abandoned clothes.

In the process of scooping those up, he stopped. Dead.

What the hell?

His clothes were all brown and black, and it wasn't just dirt.

Blood.

He remembered it was from where his hand wound had opened up. Not only had his blood spilled all over his clothes, but it was also caked up his legs, on his belly, up his arm… He dared a glance at his hand, afraid he might get sick at the sight of it.

Weird, he thought, after giving it a cursory glance.

"Not too bad," he reassured himself.

It wasn't bleeding anymore; just crusted over dried blood. But it still hurt. A lot.

For a long moment, he just stood there, bloody clothes and bottle of piss in one hand, misshaped hand held outstretched, unsure what to do next.

Your mission is to leave and see if those people can help you get out, he commanded himself.

Now it clicked.

After jumping back into his newfound jumper, he snatched one of the overturned towels, wrapped his soiled clothes and the bottle of urine in it, and slid the bundle in the back of the shelf where he'd slept.

Because his cuffs were getting in his way, he upturned them until his bare feet were exposed. They too were brown and black from blood and dirt. He couldn't imagine what his face must have looked like.

Supplies.

The storage room had many things he thought would help: a set of keys, a penknife, gloves—albeit over-sized—to protect his hands, several more protein bars, and a couple more bottles of water.

He turned out the light and after listening at the door for voices and not hearing anything, he opened it and peaked out.

Abdul

When they were done with their prayers, Sal waited for Abdul to arise before he did. "Are you going to execute me now?" he asked, as Abdul picked up the rifle he'd left on the floor during their prayers.

"No, my brother. I have come to ask you for advice. As to whom I am executing with this rifle, and when, that is not yet decided. Let me explain..."

Sal, to his credit, didn't question him at all. Instead,

he listened, as Abdul described to him the most recent events, from the loss of his son to the capture of the US Senator who was the rightful heir to the US Presidency and the trouble-maker Cartwright, as well as the loss of Imran and Suhaimah. Finally, he explained the reason for his concern: it was the state of the Americans' compliance with his demands. He gave Sal additional recent data from the reports of non-compliance by its citizens, to the many members of the US military who were simply ignoring their orders or even walking away from their duties.

He explained that until yesterday; he felt he was very close to achieving the promised caliphate in America. But now he was receiving too much push-back, and he understood that if this blatant disregard of his leadership continued, it might ultimately result in their defeat.

"I even warned them about the doomsday device; that I would not turn it off if they didn't follow my commands. Yet, they still resist."

Sal had taken a seat beside Abdul and fixed his eyes forward. It was obvious he was listening intently—as he always did.

Abdul continued, with only a slight pause. "I understand you have disagreed with my methods, especially in my not revealing everything to you. But I'm asking you, what you would do now to change the behavior of the Americans and force them to accept the inevitable?"

The inside of Sal's cell and even outside were abnormally quiet. The only sound Abdul heard was the heavy breathing of the jailer, who was right outside their door, eavesdropping on their conversation. The jailer might be the next one he executed today.

For a moment, Abdul was not entirely sure Sal was going to answer his question, as he remained pensive and silent.

Abdul glanced over at his long-trusted adviser, now thinking this whole exercise was foolish: why would the man who attempted a coup and scheduled for execution be willing to help him now?

But then Sal answered.

"Yes, it is true, my Mahdi. I had a disagreement with some of your methods, but I have always trusted in your faith in Allah and his profit, Mohammad—praise be upon him. Additionally, I certainly do not want to see the Americans succeed and for you to fail."

Sal turned toward Abdul, blinked his black eyes once, and continued.

"Your problems are not only just as you explained. Many of your people, here in this compound, are having doubts in your abilities to achieve your stated goals for ICA. I have even heard this from my cell."

Sal paused, perhaps to see how Abdul would react to his words or maybe to see what he would be offered in trade for his assistance. But Abdul did his best not to react or show any emotions. Instead he held onto Sal's attention.

"So I will tell you what I would do right now to solve all of this, if I were in your position..." He paused again. His reasons for this were obvious.

"Fine," Abdul huffed, snapping to his feet. "I will forgive your treachery and reinstate you as my Chief Deputy. I will do anything you ask to succeed."

Sal's eyes were glued on Abdul, stoic and unemotional as usual, but always calculating. Again, Abdul started to wonder if he would answer.

"What you decide is up to you, my Mahdi. I only serve you and Allah—praised be his name."

Sal gave a slow nod and drilled his eyes back into Abdul. He was about to say something when Sal gave his response.

"You need to make an example of those who resist your will, and you need to make sure that everyone sees this. Start with Mr. Chase and Mr. Cartwright. They need to be brought here, and in front of a national television and radio audience, you must pronounce their sentence of death by hanging and immediately carrying it out in front of everyone.

"At the same time, have the US Military leaders take some of their soldiers, along with additional citizens, and in multiple locations around this country, the same exercise must be carried out: that is, publicly pronounce their sentence because of their resistance against the rules that *you* had set out, and hang them.

"Leave all the bodies hanging, so that all can see and remember what has happened.

"Finally, stop wasting your time with the American government. Meet with them directly and demand compliance, or else they will meet the same fate."

"Is all this necessary?" Abdul interrupted, causing Sal's expression to change for the briefest of moments. "Because I also have the threat of the doomsday device."

"Immaterial since that is just an empty threat. This device does not exist, and you surely do not have it set up to go off at some pre-designated time... Am I correct?"

Abdul fixed his eyes on Sal, not sure why he would disbelieve his words. Abdul moved closer to him and held out his wrist so that Sal could see his watch face. It showed numbers counting down. 39:39:15... 14... 13.

Sal's face twisted, his scars forming odd indiscernible shapes, as if his features were becoming fluid, while his brain attempted to decide on which expression it should show. Then his face snapped back to its inscrutable norm.

"It is not some sort of nuclear weapon, is it?"

"No, it's biological. We have one here and several spread out throughout the United States. If I don't turn off the device, it will release a cloud of bacteria—something with over a fifty percent mortality rate—into the air here and be carried to where the winds blow. Additionally, this device will communicate with the other devices, telling them to do the same."

Abdul could see that Sal was scrutinizing his every word, probably to confirm his truthfulness.

"Very well," Sal said. "Once the executions are completed, and the American government has offered their supplication to you, you would turn off the device—Is that not correct?"

"Of course." Abdul offered a knowing grin. "I would only allow the device to countdown to zero, if they didn't comply."

Abdul put a hand on Sal's shoulder. "Thank you for your advice. You have always been the wisest of all men I have known."

Abdul turned on a heel and walked out the door, offering nothing more to Sal.

The Jailer slammed the metal door of Sal's cell, locked it and attempted to catch up to Mahdi Abdul, who had already left the premises.

Travis

Only ten feet away from him was another one of Uncle Abdul's men. His back was to Travis, and it looked as if he was eavesdropping on the conversation, which Travis could only make out small bits and pieces taking place inside the jail cell. Regardless, he could not go that way, unless—

To Travis' surprise, Uncle Abdul burst out of the cell, turned away from him and walked toward what he assumed was the exit.

Before risking being seen any longer, Travis silently backed away and closed the storage room door. At the same time, he heard the cell door slam shut, followed by one of Abdul's followers shuffling after Abdul.

He could have waited until the coast was clear, but he reasoned that even after everyone had gone, he couldn't leave that way. At some point, he'd be seen and as far as everyone was concerned, he was dead. It was better that he remained dead in everyone's' minds.

All he had to do was stick to his plan by returning to the main vent stack, going up one more story and then exiting out of the bunker complex and making his escape. Or...

He could stay and find new ways to hurt Uncle Abdul. He could move about the bunker, unknown to Abdul's men, like a ghost in their ventilation system.

He liked that idea best.

Change of plans; I'm now a ghost.

Travis eyed the register on the other end of the storage room and flipped off the light switch. As a ghost, he didn't need light to find his way to his exit, or rather, his entrance.

July 15th

39:37:51
39:37:50
39:37:49

Chapter 10

Dayton, Texas

Sinclair

Swat Commander Sinclair clawed at his angry rash. The tentacles of its itchy reach were spreading faster under his shirt than the betrayal that was infecting his whole team.

It was understandable that they had expressed anxiety about continuing after yesterday's debacle: one day's work yielded the arrest of just one person and confiscation of a single-working illegal weapon under the new Emergency Weapons Ban. He had assumed that the root of his team's ire was the the yield of only a few usable supplies from the one household. He had no idea, that their treachery was grounded elsewhere.

Sinclair announced to all of them last night, "It would be different from now on." He told them he alone would choose their next target, which would be randomly selected from the middle of the list, so that their movements couldn't be followed. He suspected one of their targets had a copy of the list and were communicating with each other. And because they had been following the list in order, their movements were more easily tracked.

So by selecting names randomly, even if their targets

knew they were on the list, they wouldn't be able to guess Sinclair's arrival. Finally, he assured his team, that he would cherry pick from the list, making sure only those with many verified weapons would be their targets.

His men were less than enthusiastic, but they agreed to start fresh early, the next morning.

This morning.

But at zero-five hundred, when they all had agreed to start the next round of seizures, only Purdy showed.

After ten minutes of scratching his skin raw, Sinclair had had it. He demanded Purdy call out to each team member on their portables.

Meanwhile, Sinclair pulled off his hot tactical equipment and scratchy undershirt—perhaps the source of his rash. He opted for a simple and well-worn SWAT t-shirt and slipped over it a short tactical vest. Since it only had one small plate on the chest, it wasn't as safe. It was the only way he'd be able to continue. Assuming any of their team showed.

Every one of Purdy's calls where unanswered, despite each team member assuring Sinclair that they would monitor their radios in the morning.

Only after Sinclair murmured an "I don't get it" did Purdy finally reveal the real reason why his men abandoned him... "They're uncomfortable enforcing laws which are plainly unconstitutional."

"How could you possibly know this?" Sinclair asked, while adding three loaded magazines to his vest and slinging his rifle over his head.

"Larry confided with me, after you left..."—Purdy looked down at Sinclair's feet and then he lifted his gaze upward to meet his superior's eyes—"He said the others felt the same."

"Damned pansies." Sinclair punched a dent into the van's back door, right beside where Purdy was sitting.

Sinclair took a breath and then glared at Purdy. "So they had no problem breaking into everybody's' homes, before we had the official pretense, but now they're worried about the constitution?"

Purdy screwed his eyes at his commander and shot back, "We were only breaking in when there was no answer at the door. Now, we're breaking down the door and confiscating the only thing people have to protect themselves."

Sinclair felt his blood boil.

He had to take a long breath as he wanted to ask the one person, who was his closest confident, why he didn't share any of this with him until now and whether he agreed with their thinking. In the end, he ate his words, ignoring their bitter taste. At least Purdy was here, with him now.

"Fine. We don't need them. Let's do this ourselves." Sinclair glared at Purdy, almost daring him to say "no." Instead, his most trusted team member—now, the only member—nodded in the affirmative.

They slammed shut the van's rear doors, climbed in the cab and zoomed off to their first stop. Sinclair hadn't said anything more to Purdy and to his credit Purdy didn't ask.

As they raced toward this morning's first target, the humid morning air blew through their open side windows, crawling up Sinclair's shirt and prickling more irritation at his rash. Still, Sinclair smiled.

He felt better about this. There were fewer mouths now to split their spoils amongst. And he was certain their haul today would be huge. He could feel it in his bones.

Their first target was going to be a gold mine: number 138 on the list, but probably number one in potential weapons… Over fifty rifles and pistols bought over the past ten years. That's what the ATF tracked, and didn't include any private sales.

Pulling into the residential street, that was five or so blocks from their target, he decided they would start shooting as soon as the target answered the door. They would set it up to look like they were being shot at. Further, they would take all but a couple of the weapons and all of their supplies. He wasn't going to tell Purdy this was the plan, knowing his partner would have to go with the flow.

"Get ready," Sinclair hollered through the muggy wind swirling around the van's cab. "It's only two blocks away."

Purdy eyeballed him, no doubt he was considering repeating Sinclair's own warnings about not wearing full tactical gear.

Purdy remained silent.

Sinclair would have told him the reason why if he'd asked. But he didn't.

Sinclair brought them to a screeching halt on the short driveway's concrete apron, the truck's headlights trained on the target's front door. Both men burst out of the truck at the same time, hoofing it to the front door. This time, Purdy clutched the Enforcer. Sinclair's hands were on his rifle, already clicking off the safety. The page from the list was folded up and in one of his front pockets, but he wasn't going to show it to their target this time. The moment Sinclair saw the man, he would blast him.

Purdy arrived first, standing to one side, battering ram

already lifted. Sinclair hollered, "Police! Weapons search. Open up,"

Sinclair slid to a stop in front of the door when he heard the crashing sound of a shotgun blast. The immediate sledgehammer punch of a twelve-gage's double-ought buckshot pounded his chest so hard it knocked him backwards onto the ground.

Not being able to breathe, his initial thought, *did that bastard just shoot me?*

At least I wore... Then he realized he wasn't wearing his full tact gear, only the shorty and the buckshot got him in his neck. He coughed up something, but he could hardly move. Everything felt wet.

A muffled voice yelled out, "I got more of that if you wan' it?"

"Don't worry, sir," hollered back Purdy. "You got us good. I'll be leaving now."

It made no sense to Sinclair. *What does he mean, he's leaving?* "What about me?" he croaked, his own voice sounding unintelligible.

He coughed again, this time sending a large amount of something into the air, most of it landing on his face and covering one eye.

I'm dying, he thought.

Purdy stood over him, staring down for just a moment, before he shook his head and left.

"Don't you dare go," Sinclair gasped. He attempted one last breath, "We have a job to d..."

Chapter 11

Hamza

Hamza felt proud to be leading their soldiers toward the militia's new camp. It was Faisal's reward to him for his finding the remnants of their enemy.

Driving the militia's truck, of which he already had familiarity, Hamza sat high in his seat. With Samir beside him and eight more of their finest warriors in the truck bed, they were ready to strike a final blow.

Hamza first needed to get them to the meeting point that he had suggested to Commander Faisal, near the entrance to the enemy's private road. From there, Samir's team would start on foot to gather information and secure one side of the enemy's compound.

Like Samir, he just wished they had left earlier: they would have already secured a victorious battle. Instead, they were forced to start after sunrise, and risk being seen in the daylight. All because Commander Faisal wanted to wait for orders from Mahdi Abdul, before they began their attack.

Less than a kilometer away from their turnoff, Hamza caught a glint on the road and two faint headlights in the distance. It was about where the militia's road was located.

He hard turned off the visible blacktop.

"What are you doing, brother?" Samir asked from the passenger seat.

As he navigated to a stop, behind the cover of a short stand of trees, Hamza answered, "Apologies, brother. I see one of their vehicles coming our way."

Hamza lifted his AK and pointed it down the road, flipping off the truck's ignition.

"Do not shoot, you fool," Samir stated.

"Only if they see us first." Hamza glanced in the rear-view mirror to make sure their men did not do anything to call attention to themselves. Everyone remained where they were, sitting low and watching the approaching vehicle. A few of them had their weapons readied too.

"Do you think they are leaving?" Hamza asked in a whisper.

"No," Samir said. "This is only a small van, which I do not recognize. They escaped their camp in three vehicles like this one."

The white van sped by them, appearing to have taken no notice.

Hamza reached for the radio.

"Do not bother to try to call Commander Faisal. The radio's range is too short. We should go to the agreed upon meeting point and wait for the commander's orders. Perhaps the van will have returned by then."

Hamza, like any good warrior, hated the idea of waiting any longer. That was all they had been doing. Yet, he felt sure Samir was correct.

When he could no longer see the van, he babied the truck back onto the road and checked both ways to make sure no one else was coming in either direction.

As he got them back up to speed, he kept his eyes on the road in front and behind him. He would get their team to the meeting point without being seen. Once there, after Samir's team had left, he would wait for their commander's orders of attack. Hamza would make sure it happened, whether the white van returned or not.

Former American Eagle Base Camp

Faisal

While they were still waiting to reach Mahdi Abdul, Faisal had sent his best ten men to take up positions around the infidels' new camp. Now, after multiple attempts, over several hours to make contact, Faisal was getting impatient and ready to abandon his call.

As if Allah sensed this, Aadam, his radio operator, announced, "I have made contact." He handed Faisal the headset.

The excitement Faisal felt at finally speaking to his Mahdi was greater than the elation of taking his first life when he was just a boy of twelve. "*Assalamu alaikum*, Mahdi Abdul," Faisal said into the microphone.

"What? Oh, thank you." Faisal pulled one side of the headphones off his ear so he could hear and in a loud voice he declared, "Their operator is getting Mahdi Abdul now."

Aadam nodded acceptance.

Faisal pushed the headset back into place and waited. The other line almost immediately clicked and beeped, and the polished voice of Mahdi Abdul boomed into his ears. "Yes."

"*Assalamu alaikum*, Mahdi Abdul," Faisal boomed back. "It is an honor to speak with you. I am Faisal Shahzad, the acting commander of the Arizona Regiment. We were on route to Mount Weather when we were ambushed by an American militia group, killing our commander and most of our men. I was able to take our remaining forces and counterattack, killing many of their militia."

"He took a quick breath before continuing as he'd rehearsed this. "We are about to mount a last counter offensive and kill the remaining militia soldiers, finally bringing victory for you and in honor of those martyrs who have been killed."

Another quick breath. "My question to you, Mahdi Abdul, is, what are our orders after we have killed these infidels?"

Faisal pressed the button on the transceiver, allowing the Mahdi to speak. He did not want to wait for Aadam to do this and risk missing the Mahdi's reply. He gave Aadam a thumbs up sign.

Faisal's mind played out many possibilities of what his Mahdi would say to him. Of course he would be congratulated. Then, he wondered if his Mahdi would like prisoners or would like the heads of some of the infidels. Perhaps his Mahdi would ask Faisal to lead more warriors into even greater battles. He could not wait to hear what his Mahdi would say to honor him, their martyrs, and their greater purpose of establishing the Islamic Caliphate in America.

The delay was long on the other end, but Faisal was sure it was worth every moment of the wait. Finally, Mahdi Abdul answered, "Mr. Shahzad, you are no longer authorized to engage any US militia."

Faisal's face must have twisted into something grotesque, because Aadam raised up his hands and shoulders as if to say, "What's going on?"

Inside, Faisal felt as if he were shot in the stomach. He could not have heard this correctly, could he?

"Repeat, do not engage," his Mahdi stated more adamantly.

Faisal panicked. He did not want to stop their attack, even though his Mahdi just ordered him to stop. He had to do something.

"Instead," Mahdi Abdul continued, "take your remaining men and immediately report to me at Mount Weath—"

Faisal reacted. He punched in a new channel on the transceiver and then the connect button, severing the Mahdi's signal.

"What happened?" Aadam asked, understandably perplexed by Faisal's behavior. "Why did you change the frequency?"

"I meant to disconnect," Faisal lied. "The Mahdi congratulated us and said he would pray that Allah would protect us in our final attack. Now, pack up the radio. We must go now." Without warning, Faisal stood up from his chair and whistled at his other three men to complete their final tasks, while he considered the repercussions of his actions.

Their chairs were whisked away, along with the table

and the radio, his men running them to their convoy truck. As Faisal marched to the front passenger seat of the truck, it was started up.

As they moved forward, he watched as two of his men set flame to a large pile of rubble, the remnants of what they didn't use.

Fueled by gasoline, the blaze raced around the camp before they had left.

Watching the bonfire's growing flames dance in his side mirror, Faisal considered the tale he would need to tell Mahdi Abdul to explain what happened. But that worry was for after they had achieved victory. Only after they secured the victory would he tell his Mahdi, and then only face to face.

Chapter 12
Greenville County Jail

National Guard, Joakim

She stumbled toward them, clutching her belly. Looking like a very attractive... *zombie?*

As if picking up on this, Yannick whispered into his friend's ear, in a Bela Lugosi voice, "She's coming to get you Barbara." He giggled at his joke.

"That's not funny," Joakim huffed. Together, they had probably played thousands of hours of Resident Evil, and killed millions of zombies before the power went out. That was fun. This was serious.

"She wants to eat your brains, Joak." Yannick grabbed his friend's arm and pulled him toward his own gaping mouth, while he mimicked the snarling noises all zombies made.

Joakim punched his friend with his free arm.

But then both men stopped their kidding and stared at the approaching woman who wore very little: just a satchel around her chest, form-fitting shorts and a red sleeveless t-shirt.

It's a white covered in red, Joakim thought.

"I think she's actually hurt." He pointed. "Look, blood."

Sure enough, the woman approaching them, now only

feet away, was dripping red drops of what looked like blood. A lot of blood.

The woman groaned a weak-sounding, "help."

She looked up, her eyes meeting Joakim's.

"Help me… I've been shot," the woman groaned.

She let her hands fall away from her belly. In response, volumes of red blood spurt from a ragged opening, just like in a Quentin Tarantino movie.

Joakim reached out to her just as her knees seemed to buckle. She flopped forward, but he saved her from hitting her head.

He looked up at his friend, who backed up a step, as if he really expected this obviously dying woman to rise up as one of the undead at any moment and attack them.

"Help her, Yann."

Joakim laid her head on the drive and put his hands on her belly, applying pressure to her wound, just like they were taught. The warm squishiness of it made his own head swim, and he started to feel queasy, like he might hurl.

"Yann, come here," Joakim pleaded, momentarily prying his gaze away from the woman's soft face to see why his friend wasn't helping.

Yannick appeared to be no longer worried about a zombie attack. He was now looking up; his face held a frown.

"What-ya-suppose-dat is?" Yannick asked, his head tracking something.

It made a buzzing noise, like a drone.

When it came into view, just above them, they could both see it was in fact a drone… One of them fancy quadcopters too.

It banked toward them and then passed over their

heads and kept ongoing, as if it didn't pay them any mind.

Joakim looked back down at the woman, who he could feel through his hands, had gone from practically lifeless to active again. He almost expected her to be one of the undead, except—*You're now wearing a gas mask?* His brain asked.

"What da hell," he said and then coughed.

He clutched his throat with one sticky hand and covered his mouth with his other, knowing already that they had just been poisoned by that drone.

"That—*cough-cough*—bitch," Yannick croaked and then tumbled over behind him.

"Sorry," the woman said to Joakim. She stood up, appearing completely fine, even though blood was still seeping out of the jagged tear in her shirt.

It was all fake. She fooled them.

"Why?" Was all Joakim could ask, before he too fell over, and everything went black.

Lexi

"The two front guards are down." Lexi stated. "I'm headed in."

"Copy that, Lexi. The rest of your team is approaching from the east and west. Hold up for them at your designated entry point."

"Copy," Lexi said back, amazed at the quality of the

sound in her ear from the hearing-aid-sized device. She wondered how her voice sounded from the microphone attached to her neck.

From her satchel, she pulled out the stun gun Smith had given her and jogged toward the front of the building.

So far, Smith's plan appeared to be working. None of them liked the idea of walking into a fight with weapons that didn't fire bullets. But Smith insisted that they not shed any American blood, if it could be avoided. All of them were against this, arguing that military or local authorities who had chosen to side with the enemy, had become the enemy.

In the end, Smith stood his ground—so to speak—and because he was providing them the way in and all the intel, they reluctantly went along with him.

She could see Samuel and Gladys approaching from her left; Jonah and Moondog were dashing in from a field on her right. All were wearing gas masks like hers.

Lexi made her way around the left front corner of the building, working her way to the side entrance, where she found Samuel kneeling in front of a door, planting charges just as Smith had instructed.

Gladys was on the other side of the door, holding three flash-bang canisters. Slung to her chest, a baton launcher like the one all of them carried, except Lexi. Each shot was called a Sponge Baton that delivered blunt trauma to its target. Intended for rioters and unruly crowds, their launchers' targets would ironically be police officers and military service personnel.

Yeah. She decided then that she was glad they were using the non-lethal weapons. Each of them had holstered pistols too, but these were to be used only as a last resort.

Gladys nodded at Lexi, and Lexi nodded back at her. They were ready.

When Samuel was done planting his explosives, he pointed for Lexi to move away, further to his right, around a corner of the building. He pointed to the opposite side for Gladys.

"Slim here. We are in position at the side entrance." His voice was as clear as if he were speaking right in her ear, beside her.

"Jonah is in position at the front entrance."

"Axe is in position, in the van, out front."

"Blow your charges on Slim's count," Smith said, again as clear as the others, even though he was miles away. "Remember, no blood if you can help it. Aim for the body. Grab Frank and the Senator, and then get out."

"On my mark," Slim said. "Three-two-one."

Loud pops sounded, followed by a heavy clank—presumably the door falling to the ground.

A series of muffled bangs followed from their flash grenades going off.

"Go-go-go," hollered Slim.

Karnack, Texas

Longhorn Detention Center

The men and women of the Texas Irregulars crashed through the simple wooden gate, with Boomer McKenzie leading them through in an Army surplus truck. His militia had happily requisitioned this from a group of ICA troops they had fought and stopped days earlier. They had a more important mission now: they were going to rescue the men who had been offering hope to their fellow Americans on the radio, especially when their situation had been looking pretty bleak. They were going to free Lieutenant Grimes and Gunny Sergeant Aimes, of the American Freedom Network.

"Don't stop," Boomer said on his radio to Rob, his second, in the hummer behind him. "Do not fire upon anyone, unless you are returning fire."

"Read you loud and clear."

Luckily, so far, they didn't have to return fire. They had lost so many lives to the real enemy, the last thing he wanted their militia to do was fire upon any of his fellow citizens. Even if they had chosen the wrong side.

So far their plan was working flawlessly. If you could call it a plan. Getting through the gates was going to be the easiest part of this operation. The next part was sure to be difficult.

They had very little intel, relying heavily on Pyro Pete's short time at Longhorn when it was an ammunition surplus storage facility many years prior. It then became a bankrupt developer's dream, offering preppers an off-grid home. Now it was being used by the government as a detention center, where each munition bunker was a nearly impenetrable jail cell, with twenty-four inches of hardened concrete, made to withstand the direct hit from a bomb. Making matters even more difficult, there were dozens of these bunkers spread out along the three-thousand-acre grounds. Which one housed Grimes and/or Aimes was anyone's guess. They would need to get lucky.

Boomer brought their Army troop carrier to a halt in front of the first five bunkers. Toward each, Pyro tossed five separate home-made smoke grenades. That way, if there was a potential for shooting, the shooters were hopefully less likely to shoot at what they couldn't see. Each grenade made a *pop*-sound and hissed out thick white smoke, just as promised.

"Great job, Pyro," Boomer shouted. "Now hop on board the Hummer and hit the next set of bunkers."

Pyro was smiling ear-to-ear as he was once again able to show off what he was good at, making explosives. Since leaving his job at this base, he'd been working at a bank. Then, twelve days ago, God decided he needed to do something different. He was finally doing something he was skilled at. He dashed to the Hummer, knapsack stuffed full of smoke bombs over his shoulder, taking up the passenger seat.

"First unit, move out on me," Boomer yelled. "Second and third units, follow Pyro in the Hummer."

As he heard the trucks drive away, Boomer rushed toward the smoke of the first concrete bunker with a sledgehammer in hand. He was hoping the hammer would be all that was needed to open each steel door. As a fallback, the surplus truck had an acetylene torch... *Which should have been unloaded here.*

"Damit!"

"What is it," a nervous voice barked back from someone in his unit.

"Nothing. We're all good."

Boomer approached the first bunker's door, choosing it over the other four at random. He lifted the sledge, intending to beat the unlocked latch into submission.

It's unlocked?

He handed the sledge to the next man and pointed to the next nearest bunker.

The latch came unhooked easily and he was about to pull on the door when a thought came to him. *This was too easy; it must be a trap?*

Dale County High School

Porter and Wallace

"Here he comes," Porter whispered, his back to the fence, only inches from Wallace, who was facing out.

Wallace didn't utter a peep, acting busy with her watch, on a knee.

Just as Tweedledum was about to pass Porter, Wallace dropped her watch. It rolled a foot out of the cell and in front of the guard. "Shit... Oh, sir, would you mind, please?" Wallace asked, still on a knee.

Tweedledum, reached down to get the watch, smiled and said, "Sure, cutie." He snatched it from the floor, gave a quick glance at it and then offered it back, toward one of the spaces in the chain-link.

"Here we go," Tweedledum said, flashing a smile, darkened by several missing teeth. He gingerly pushed the watch and part of his hand through the fence so that she would take it. Only she didn't.

Instead, she grabbed his hand with both of hers and yanked him toward her.

Porter had already spun around and lightly pushed a pen knife against the man's wrist, being careful to not sever anything. Yet.

"Don't say a word," Wallace said in a hushed tone. "Or my friend will cut your radial artery and I will continue to hold on. You will bleed to death in seconds, long before anyone could come to your aid."

Tweedledum was wide eyed, his facial muscles electric. But after a few breaths, he got down on both knees. "I'll do what you want."

"Your keys and your silence," Porter said, focusing on not cutting this man. He'd prefer not doing what Wallace suggested.

"Okay, just don't kill me. I'm just doing this for the food and because they threatened to cut off my family."

"No worries, Tweedledum," Wallace said. "You let us go without making a scene and you can keep on spending your thirty pieces of silver."

"I'm no Judas," Tweedledum said, surprisingly remembering his Bible.

"Whatever. Keys, through the fence, just like the watch." Wallace waited until the keys were dropped before she moved.

"You got this?" she said to Porter, who with one hand, took grip of the guard's wrist away from Wallace, while maintaining pressure with his penknife with the other.

"Got it… And you better not move, buddy, or I'm liable to slip."

Wallace snatched the keys and her watch from the floor and advanced to the gate of their paddock. When she found the right key, she whistled to the other prisoners. They followed her out.

Wallace appropriated Tweedledum's rifle and pointed it at him. "Into the cell with you. Remember, not a sound, or this time I'll shoot."

Porter released the man, who stood up and lumbered toward the gate they had just walked through. When Tweedledum walked in, Porter locked the gate and joined Wallace.

"That was easy," Porter said.

"We're not out of the woods yet. You take point. I'll keep an eye on our prisoner, to at least make sure he keeps quiet until we're out of here."

"Copy," Porter said, marching to the front of the line of the one hundred and fifty or so prisoners. He looked back at them. "Okay, follow me," he whispered.

"You're not going to shoot him, are you?" asked one of their fellow detainees to Wallace.

"Not unless he gives me reason," Wallace snapped matter-of-factly.

At the exit door, Porter stopped. He wasn't sure what he should expect. One or two Marines. More? He just didn't know. And with no weapon but his penknife, if he alerted anyone to their escape before Wallace brought their only weapon to bear, they would be finished.

It was the Achilles' heel of her plan. If they're stopped at the door, they're done.

Okay, here goes nothing, Porter thought to himself, hunkering down low before the door handle.

He twisted the handle and opened the door quietly, but it didn't matter. When he saw what was in front of them, he knew nothing he did would change the outcome.

He stood up straight and gawked.

Chapter 13

Meer

"This tribunal and execution will have a bigger audience than the Super Bowl and it will be the only thing playing on television and radio. And when our cameras focus in on each of the traitors being hung, everyone will see it or hear it or spread the word to anyone who could not. That is when everything will change for us. After tomorrow, all living Americans will fear this government. With that fear, comes total power..."

The Chief of Staff of the Army, fidgeted in his chair, overtly showing a discomfort at some part or perhaps all of what Meer was sharing to his Joint Chiefs.

Upon seeing Meer had stopped speaking and was drawing his full attention, the general straightened himself in his seat and cleared his throat. "Excuse me, sir. Am I to understand that you plan on executing not just the two traitors here, but immediately after this, you are also planning on televising the hangings of the other examples in four other locations?"

"That is correct, General," Chairman Meer grinned because until that moment, he suspected the General was going to ask something indicating he was wavering on their cause. Though all his Joint Chiefs were hand-selected, he was having some doubts about a few of them lately. But this general appeared to be on board with his question.

"As you know," Meer stated, "the main tribunals and subsequent executions will be televised at eighteen hundred hours, tomorrow, July 16th. Then, exactly five minutes after the Senator and the Major are executed, one of the next executions will be televised, followed by the another, each following five full minutes of the cameras focused on the traitors swinging by their necks."

"Sir?" announced the Commandant of the Marine Corps.

Meer nodded, "Yes."

"Sir, my Marines have fielded many reports of calls by citizens to prepare for a revolution"—All the Joint Chief's heads nodded in affirmation, as if this were a universal problem. "Do you not think that this action will push the American population to the point where a large enough portion of the population might attempt a second American Revolution, as they are saying?"

Meer's response was immediate, as this question was expected. "This scenario has been studied by our strategists and was resolved to be highly unlikely for multiple reasons." He too had heard these reports, but this possibility had already been considered during the conception of his plan for a military takeover of the government. Every scenario assumed Americans could not stomach unconventional warfare at home. Still, Meer was surprised that none of his Joint Chiefs, even though their allegiance had been bought and paid for, had not brought this up before now.

"First, the American population is extremely malleable and subservient when fearful. Look no further than the Covid pandemic for proof of this. They allowed themselves to be locked down, quarantined and even forced to take an experimental vaccination mandated by employers and governments, all for a virus that killed less than 1% of the population, including the elderly and infirm.

"Second, the American population has been frightened into inaction. We saw this when our Justice Department was used by an opposition to go after and convict a former President and many of his supporters and yet, there was very little push back.

"Third, and along the same lines, most of the American surviving population are too busy just trying to stay alive after Farook's attacks killed so many and chaos has taken root in most communities. The last thing they would want to do is take arms against their own government.

"Fourth, and along the same lines of thinking, it's part of the human condition to need to be protected. We are going to offer that protection. We're just making it clear that we will not allow noncompliance.

"And finally, we have the power of the world's greatest military behind us. With the men and women of our military, there is no force that can stand in our way. Certainly not a rabble of unorganized militias, or gangs of American citizens with guns, and least of all a self-proclaimed profit who has already murdered millions."

Meer thought he would be done answering questions after this, but the burly General Metzler and his current Chief of National Guard both had their hands up.

"Go," Meer said in Metzler's direction.

"Forgive me, sir." General Metzler's eyes flitted down

and then back up, surely a sign of disapproval. "Please do not take this as a disagreement, but isn't it a large assumption that our military forces will actually stand up for this? It's one thing to follow orders... that many believe to be unconstitutional; it's another thing to see their fellow service members getting executed for disobeying those orders. And with the AWOL incidents increasing—"

"Do you have an actual question?" Meer interrupted.

The general's face momentarily flashed anger and then back to his usual unemotional self. "Apologies, sir. My question is this: considering all these issues, do you have any concern that we won't have enough of a force to stand up against all of those who have gone AWOL and those who are joining civilians in their calls for revolution?"

Meer only now realized his mistake in choosing this man for his Joint Chiefs. For Metzler to do this, even though Meer was the one to have put this general's career on a fast track, back when he was a lieutenant headed for Leavenworth... Meer could not believe this was the thanks he received for putting Metzler into this position?

It does not matter, he told himself. If this was a question in one of their minds, it was a question in all of their collective minds. He needed to answer it and quash this thinking now.

"That is a logical question, General. But one that we do not have to worry about answering. We already have enough troops who will stand for the legitimate American government; we alone possess the force holding all the armaments and resources of the US Military; and we have already planned for all of this,"—He glared icicles at each of his Joint Chiefs—"Your job is to make sure *your* orders are properly transmitted to and executed by your branch's service members.

"Now, I want an answer from everyone at this table. Are we clear on your orders?"

"Sir, yes sir," they all acknowledged, almost in perfect unison.

Immediately, Meer spoke again. "One final item..." Meer once again made eye contact with each of his Joint Chiefs, before leveling all his attention on his Chief of Space Operations. "I need conclusions now on your search for Farook's doomsday weapons." His CoSO was charged with leading this effort.

"Sir," the man rose from his seat. "Our team has searched locations throughout the United States, spoken to thousands of leads, and so far, found no concrete evidence of the existence of a doomsday bioweapon as alluded to by Mr. Farook.

"Understand that we have not, of course, been granted access to Farook's compound. Plus, we are still exploring all leads. However, at this point, I would conclude that his weapon does not exist."

"Thank you. I agree with your conclusion. However, continue your searching, in the event that there is something there. At the same time, I will reach out again to Mr. Farook to grant your teams inspection access.

"You are all dismissed. We will reconvene one last time before tomorrow's tribunal here at this same time."

"Sir?" General Metzler asked loud enough that he would be heard outside their room, and now standing up his full six-and-one-half feet by his seat. "Do you still want our reports about the mass rejection of orders and AWOLs, especially by noncoms?"

Meer once again scowled daggers at the General. "Yes, if you have them in writing, leave them here.

"You are dismissed, General."

Chapter 14
Greenville County Jail

Lexi

"Get down on the ground," Gladys commanded the smoke, rushing in first, heading her team.

As Smith explained it to Lexi, the flash grenades would disable everyone within the building, disorienting them and making it hard for them to see, hear or shoot. Their weapons, all non-lethal, were for anyone who somehow did not follow Gladys' orders.

"Get on the ground," Gladys ordered once again.

Lexi dashed in right behind Samuel, but lost him immediately in the dense fog. She could barely see her stun gun, held up directly in front of her, much less anyone who might come forward to attack them. Still, she kept her firing arm stiff, ready to pull the trigger.

The fog cleared further inside, just enough that she could see Gladys and Samuel checking different rooms. Each yelled, "Clear" when popping out and dashing to the next room, just as Smith had shown them with the building's schematics.

Lexi followed her instructions too, staying behind to make sure no one else approached them forward or back. Though with the smoke, as dense as it was, she could hardly recognize their shapes, much less anyone further away from them.

She could hear additional call outs of "Clear" further into the station, from whom she assumed was Jonah and Moondog.

They all moved closer to the middle of the station, where Smith said the four jail cells existed. Per Smith's instructions, Frank and the Senator should be in the room after the cells, which was more of an interview room.

Her heart beat like a drum, but at the same time, she was starting to feel a slight relief that they had not had to engage anyone, ever since the two guards that Smith's drone put to sleep.

"This one is empty," said Gladys.

"So is this one," said Samuel.

Lexi ignored her instructions of hanging back, when she saw the last door, Frank's door already open. She rushed ahead to the get a glimpse inside, when she caught the silhouette of someone coming toward her.

She got down on a knee and attempted to acquire a sight picture, yelling, "Freeze" at the same time.

Her finger was on the trigger, and yet the person kept coming toward her.

"It's me, Lexi," hollered back Jonah.

She sprang back up, accepting his familiar voice, and continued into the last room, the one where they were to find Frank and Chase.

"This one is clear too," said Gladys from behind.

Lexi walked around inside. When she saw Jonah and Samuel at the door, she asked them, "Where are they?"

Karnack, Texas

Longhorn Detention Center

Boomer wished Pyro was here to inspect the door for some sort of explosive charge. He had a nose for that kind of thing. Instead, he would have to do it himself.

Meanwhile, Boomer was getting more anxious about the absence of gunfire... from his militia or the guards at this facility. He hadn't expected this either.

Everything felt wrong. But they had gone too far to turn back. He had to be sure.

He gave the door latch and handle a quick glance. There was nothing there to lock the door. In fact, the padlock that appeared to be used for this, was left lying on the ground, opened. It was as if someone had unlocked the door and then just ran off, leaving the door unlocked, but still latched closed.

A muffled voice called out something from the inside, followed by a pounding sound.

Boomer unlatched the mechanism that secured the door and slid the heavy entrance open.

Two men, who looked like they'd been through hell and back, were standing behind the door with smiles on.

"Lieutenant Grimes and Gunny Sergeant Aimes, I presume?" Boomer asked.

"At your service," Aimes said in his familiar drawl.

"I'm Boomer McKenzie, with the members of the Texas Irregulars. We heard you on the radio get arrested. Figured we'd spring you."

"Thank God you came," Said Grimes in his more familiar voice. "One of the guards had come by to unlock us, but must have forgotten to undo the latch."

"Where are they... The guards?" Boomer asked.

"Gone," Aimes said. "Less than an hour ago."

"Any idea why?" asked Boomer.

Aimes braced himself with a hand around Grimes' biceps. "We heard one guard mention that he didn't feel comfortable being a part of this anymore; mentioned that others were going AWOL, too."

Grimes nodded and then said, "Any chance you can give us a lift back to Stowell. Looks like there's a lot to report to our country."

"It would be our pleasure."

Dale County High School

Porter

"What's the holdup?" Wallace asked in a purposely hushed tone from behind the group.

"Check it out yourself," Porter said, turning his head to face her. "There's not a soul out there. The whole place is a ghost town."

She marched to the gymnasium's exit, held open by Porter. Her only words were, "What the hell?"

"I could have told you and saved you all that trouble," yelled Tweedledum from his cell.

Their fellow ex prisoners were already mumbling questions, but this turned their whole group buzzing. Most of them had pushed forward to file outside the exit. Wallace and Porter marched back inside, heading right toward the cell they had just escaped from.

Standing just under the "Fight Warriors!" banner fluttering from the ceiling, Wallace demanded, "What the hell are you talking about?"

"They all left." Tweedledum answered, his arms folded over his chest.

"What do you mean, they all left?" Porter asked. It felt like they were trying to pull answers from a three-year-old.

"Everyone, but me, went AWOL."

"Why are you the only hold out?" Porter again probed, getting visibly angry at this man for being so obtuse.

"I told you. I'm doing this for the food and because they threatened me and my family."

"Okay, I'll bite, asshole. Why did the others go AWOL, not worried like you about repercussions from your superiors?" Wallace sounded just as frustrated by this guy as he was.

The guard just scowled at her.

"Fine, pretty please, asshole. Tell me why they went AWOL, and you didn't? And this time, if you don't answer, I'll shoot you in the nuts."

Yep, she was just as angry, Porter thought.

Tweedledum's scowl continued, but when she pointed his rifle at his neither regions, he spat out a reply. "Well, most of 'em said the President's orders was illegal. Then came our new orders, an hour ago. Everyone was PO'd. Most said they were going home. Many talked about joining the revolution against the government. Our lieutenant said, "If all the non-cons and most of the officers were standing against it, there wouldn't be enough forces to institute the new orders… I just didn't want to risk getting shot for treason, like you were going to be."

"Wait, what?" Porter was less angry now than curious. "What makes you think our fate was a firing squad?"

"This was part of our new orders. A group of five prisoners, which included you two, were to be gathered this afternoon and transported to Fort Moore. There, you were going to be convicted by a military tribunal and then executed in public, so an example could be made of you."

"What example? Why us?" Porter was puzzled why they were going to be executed simply for not following their orders, of which any military court would have to agree were not legal.

"Our traitorous lieutenant mentioned this too. I guess the generals are losing control of the military. Said if it were allowed to continue, it would lead to anarchy. The executions were to prevent this."

Wallace turned away and proceeded to stomp toward the exit.

"Where are you going?" Porter asked.

"I don't know yet, but we need to do something to prevent whatever is happening from happening. Maybe not to us, but to others."

"What do you want to do with this guy?" Porter pointed

a finger back toward the mock jail cell holding Tweedledum.

"Let him rot."

Chapter 15

Senator Marjorie Smith-Valentine

"Hey, lady," a hushed but juvenile voice called out from somewhere in the distance.

Marge jumped, but didn't look up. Instead, she punched Buck's foot, to wake him from his sleep in the bunk next to hers.

"What now, Marge?" Buck said, once again acting annoyed with her.

"Did you hear that?" Marge whispered. Buck had been as useless as he'd been a pain in her ass during their entire incarceration. But he was the only friend she had at this point.

"Over here," whispered the same disembodied voice.

Marge snapped her head toward the register above her and twisted a scowl. "Kid, are you in there?"

"I'm not a kid; I'm a ghost," said the vent.

"Why are you in there, Ghost?" Buck whispered, now sitting up and fully alert.

"Going to help. Who are you, and why are you locked up?"

Marge gave Buck a glance. He just shrugged his shoulders. He was just as helpful in Congress. She guessed it was his way of saying, "Go ahead and tell 'em the truth."

"That is Congressman, Dr. Buck Weston, from Texas. And I'm Senator Marjorie Smith-Valentine, of Virginia. But you can call me Marge. We were the designated survivors of Congress. But somehow, we were abducted by these people, whomever they are. They won't tell us anything and they won't let us out. We can only assume that this is some sort of kidnapping scheme for money or that we are bargaining chips for a prisoner exchange. We don't even know where we are."

Buck jumped in. "So, kid. Now you know our story; why are you speaking to us from the air-conditioning vent? Do you know why we're being held? Do you, kid?" Buck asked, almost demanding as he often was. He was now standing up, with his hands on his hips, staring laser beams directly at the vent.

"How long have you been here?" the Ghost asked, still in a whisper.

"I believe eleven days now, Mr. Ghost," said Marge.

"So you really don't know what happened?" asked the youthful voice.

"We heard there was some sort of attack on American soil," Buck barked, losing any interest in being considerate to whomever this kid was. Buck had the bed side manors of a pissed off porcupine. "We assume these are the people who attacked us. We don't know anything more than that. Spill the beans, kid."

"I'm going to help you escape. Wait right here."

"We're kind of stuck here, kid." Buck sat back down and sighed.

There was a noise, like the crumpling of a giant beer can coming from inside the vent. The kid, whomever he was, had started moving away, inside the HVAC ductwork.

"Well that was interesting," Marge said.

"Yeah, whatever," Buck leaned back, swung his feet up on his bunk and closed his eyes.

Yeah, Buck was worthless.

Travis

Travis didn't have a plan yet. He only knew that he was going to try to help these jailed Congress people escape. He still didn't know why they were locked up or what his uncle wanted from them. But he knew they had some importance to him, or they would have already been killed. It was why he promised to help them: if he could facilitate their escape, it would hurt his uncle. And that made him happy.

He liked the woman, Marge. She was very old, but nice like his mother. He also liked that she didn't take any crap from the guy, who wasn't very nice... Doctor Buck. But they obviously didn't know anything about what happened. Plus, he couldn't make heads or tails as to why they were being held prisoner. Their own thoughts as to why didn't make any sense either.

Travis was hoping the next prisoner would clear up the question of his uncle's interest in these people. It was the cell that Uncle Abdul had come from. So he was hopeful this man would know more.

This time, the man was sitting on his bed with his back to Travis. He was done praying as his prayer rug was put up. The man was simply sitting up straight, hands laying on his lap, while he appeared to be staring at the door.

"Hey, mister," Travis said, once again not too loud, but loud enough that Travis' voice would surely be heard by the man.

The man didn't even flinch. Travis thought the man hadn't heard him, so he was about to repeat his signal to him.

"So, you're back."

Travis froze like a statue.

How did he know I was here before?

Travis was speechless. He started to shiver a little, even though the A/C blower hadn't been turned back on yet.

He chose to ignore the comment and get to the heart of the matter. He wanted to know why this man was locked up and if he should help free him or let him stay in his jail cell. At the same time, Travis didn't want to reveal too much about himself. He was, after all, still a ghost.

The Ghost.

Travis had read part of one of his father's Army handbooks and took an interest in interrogations. An early section talked about establishing a common ground with a prisoner. He knew right where to do this, because he didn't know the answer to how one prays toward Mecca, if you don't know which direction is which. "How do you know where *Qiblah* is if you're locked up in this jail?"

Once again, the man didn't flinch and provided no recognition that he heard Travis' question.

"Is that really the question you want to ask me, Abdul-Aziz? Wouldn't you rather know why your uncle has locked me in this room?

Travis forgot how to breathe.

It wasn't bad enough that he knew who Travis was, but Travis now knew exactly who this man was.

It's Sal.

Now, Travis was shaking like a leaf caught in an ice storm, unsure where to land.

There was no reason to stick around here for one more second. To do so would be terrifying. Travis was found out and surely Sal would tell his uncle he was still alive so that he could get out of jail, for whatever the reason he was there.

Get out! Now! his brain yelled. He knew he should. He only had to head for the exit right now. Then he could be gone, out the top exit, before his uncle sent the psycho back after him.

But a thought occurred to him, holding him in his place.

If Sal intended to turn him in, he wouldn't have let Travis know that he was on to him. Sal needed Travis for something... something more than just getting out of his uncle's jail.

He found his breath again, and started to settle down, even though his heart felt like it might rupture in his chest.

Sal continued. "You want to run right now, but if you do, it would be a shame to let your uncle know that you're alive, after everyone, including your uncle, thought you were killed by Hassan." The whole time, Sal remained seated, as if he were having a conversation with Travis right across from him.

"But," Travis began, "you wouldn't do that, because you need me for something, and not just getting out of that jail cell."

Sal stood up, turned and faced the vent. His face looked like the last page of the scariest horror novel he'd ever read: scars that crisscrossed his face like a soccer ball, now seemed colored in dried blood and his eyes were blacker than total darkness. Travis vividly remembered those eyes when they met at his uncle's camp. Even behind the protection of the vent register, Sal was more terrifying than he remembered. As Sal stared back at him, Travis felt as if the man's eyes could somehow pierce the darkness, like some nocturnal predator, seeing its prey was ready for the taking.

"Your uncle said you were smart, and I can see he wasn't wrong. Let me tell you a story."

Chapter 16

Abdul

Nine separate live video feeds played on the walled big-screen TV behind him. They revealed the current state of the lives of his followers, who were praying, working, and doing all the things that they should be doing.

It was as he would have expected, and he gathered much solace from witnessing this. It was what he needed to calm his concerns.

Everything appeared to be working again, as if Allah had truly reached inside their complex and set things back on the right course once more.

Allah... guided through Sal, he thought.

Sal understood what actions were needed to get his followers back in line. He always had a good sense of what needed to be done...

At that moment, he decided to give Sal complete absolution, even if Sal did not seek forgiveness from his Mahdi.

Yes, Abdul thought. After the hangings tomorrow, when he had taken public command over the American government and its military, Abdul would reinstate Sal as his Deputy. Together they would institute the American Caliphate. Despite Sal's conduct, he had earned the right to be at his side.

Abdul felt good about the decisions he had just made and the actions he had taken last night. They would soon force all living American residents, their government and their military back in line.

And it would start with the tribunals.

Just as Sal recommended, there would be tribunals, followed by the public hangings, all broadcast on national TV and radio. Whether the public witnessed it firsthand, or heard of it directly from those who witnessed it themselves, all Americans would learn to fear him even more.

He repeated out loud the Quranic verse speaking of this understanding. "It is only those who have knowledge among his slaves that fear Allah."

Fear always equaled power and control.

But fear alone was not enough for the Americans. Recent generations were not use to the hardship that had befallen all residents now. So he would also show them mercy, in the form of food and medicine.

Once they had witnessed his majesty as their supreme ruler, for many in living color, they would be given a simple choice: submission to his rule—and the care that would come from their submission—or misery and death.

Surely they would choose submission over death, he told himself.

He was feeling much better. Perhaps he would not have to end it all as he had planned.

He checked his watch, which showed only one set of numbers: the countdown. One way or another, in less than thirty-six hours, his path, as well as this country's path would be set in stone.

But waiting for that time to come was almost too difficult for him.

He could not just sit idly by and count down each minute. Tomorrow late afternoon was still a long way off. He needed more. Perhaps if he heard an update on the setup of tribunals...

He snatched up the pristine receiver from his new phone, replaced by Salman minutes ago, and dialed zero.

When Salman answered immediately. He requested a connection with Meer.

It rang once... twice... then on the third ring, the other end simply said, "Meer."

"This is Mahdi Abdul Farook. Give me an update on the tribunal plans for tomorrow."

"Oh, it's you," said Meer. "Yes, of course. Everything is going as planned. The traitors, that is Senator Chase and Major Frank Cartwright, will be transported here later today. As you had requested, at nineteen-fifty hours tomorrow, the audience of at least a thousand people will arrive. We offered food supplies to everyone who comes, payment, if they only watch the proceedings."

"That is an excellent idea, Colonel," Abdul cut in, liking this method instead of forcing people to attend as he had first suggested.

"It is Secretary, Mr. Farook."

"What is that?" Abdul asked, somewhat taken aback at being corrected by Meer.

"My title is now Secretary Meer, just as yours is now Mahdi Abdul Farook to your people instead of Imam Farook or just Abdul Farrok."

Abdul felt his blood begin to boil.

Meer continued without waiting for a reply to his rebuke. "Then the proceedings will start at twenty-zero-zero. We will have what looks like a brief military tribunal, followed by the rendering of the verdict of guilty, followed by the two men being marched from their seats, situated in front of the crowd, to the gallows. Once there, they will be hung by their necks until they are dead.

"After letting them swing on their ropes for a full five minutes—so that it is impossible for viewers to turn away—I will read your proclamation, letting everyone know if they do not follow, they will face penalties like these two.

"Then at twenty-fifteen, the next hanging will take place. This time it will be a group of five of our military service men and women..." There was talk in the background, and Meer said something about being on the phone.

Abdul spoke up. "Secretary, have you instructed the President to attend?"

"Yes, she will be there, along with her cabinet, the Joint Chiefs of Staff, members of the media, and the bussed in public. However, I don't think you should be there."

"What?" Abdul couldn't believe his ears.

"Yes, I think it's the wrong time to show yourself, as you are known as the leader of the group responsible for the terrorist attack. Your introductions should come later."

Abdul was doing everything he could to tamp down the words that demanded the immediate release from his mouth. The impetuousness of this man, telling him what he should or should not do.

"That, Secretary Meer, is up to me and not you."

"Very well. You already know my feelings."

"Yes, I do."

"Next, Mr. Farook, I need to have some of my men inspect your premises for your threatened doomsday bioweapon. We need to verify that you do not possess such a device to calm everyone's anxiety here."

Abdul puffed out a long, audible breath before speaking. "First of all, Anton Meer, what makes you think I do not have such a weapon in my possession? Second, what makes you think I would allow your people into my premises?"

"Wait... You mean you *do* have a bioweapon? This is not a fictitious threat?"

"Not only do I have a bioweapon, but in..." Abdul glanced at his watch, which was still counting down. "In less than thirty-six hours, if I do not stop it, the whole world will come to know I'm in possession of this bioweapon... That is, those few who live through it.

"Is that clear enough for you, Secretary Meer?"

"Yes, Mahdi Abdul. Yes, it is. Thank you. I must go now to make further arrangements, in the event of your attendance tom—."

Abdul didn't listen any further. He slammed the received down—careful not to damage it this time—cutting off the call.

Abdul just about had it with Meer. He only needed to hold back his temper until tomorrow. After tomorrow, he would be fully in control of this country and would no longer need either Meer or Khan.

Perhaps then I will hold my own personal executions...

A gleam spread across Abdul's face as he imagined shooting both Meer and then Khan.

Would not the Americans like to see that on television?

The gleam turned into a full smile. He allowed this, even though the exercise stung his cheek, still healing from Suhaimah's knife wound.

He found his attention drawn back to the closed-circuit TV feeds and one in particular he hadn't been watching in a while, only because he had been so preoccupied by much planning lately.

He clicked on the screen labeled POTUS' Room.

Just as he had for many years in other locations, and especially lately since he had made her President and remanded her to the Presidential bunker, he enjoyed watching her in her bedchamber. She was usually alone.

Besides just not having the time, the last few days he had lost interest in watching her as she rarely changed in front of his camera. For whatever reason, she preferred changing in her lavatory lately.

This time his interest was piqued because she was not alone.

President Khan was at her little desk. Her Chief of Staff, Shareef, was sitting behind her in the cramped living space. They both appeared to be dressed for meetings, even though this was a private bedroom rather than the conference room, which was where their business was supposed to be conducted.

Both women stood, and Khan mouthed something toward her entrance.

Walking inside, past the camera, was a tall man that Abdul immediately recognized.

He turned up the volume.

President, Abbie O'Neal Khan

The man had to duck slightly to fit under the doorway. "Madame President," he said in his throaty voice, and stepped inside.

"General Metzler, thank you for meeting with us on such short notice," Abbie smiled and beckoned him to sit at the chair opposite her little writing desk, which barely fit in her cramped living quarters.

"I'm sorry I couldn't accommodate you in a location which is more comfortable, but privacy is my biggest concern right now."

"If this is good for the President, it's good enough for me." His eyes went from Abbie to Evie, who was sitting directly behind her on a small metal chair, and then back to Abbie.

"Behind me is Evelyn Shareef, my Chief of Staff."

"General," Evie said with a small nod.

"Ma'am," Metzler said with a returning gesture.

"We… well, I asked you here to talk about your loyalty and your place in this administration."

"Madame President, I'm afraid I don't understand. My loyalty has always been to the United States, regardless of my station or position in its government."

Abbie twisted her forehead and, when she thought she understood the true meaning of his words, she relaxed.

"I'm very happy to hear that General..." She hesitated, and then decided to go for it. "I am aware of a plot to take over the legitimate government and I wanted to make sure which side you were on. Can I count on you to do what is right, not for me or Secretary Meer, but for the country and its citizens?"

Metzler's wiry brow converged into a giant hedge and then snapped back to his otherwise nondescript self. In perhaps the two times she had met with the Joint Chiefs, this man never showed a lick of emotion.

He took a quick breath and then stated, "Madame President, you do not have to worry. When it is time, I will do what is right."

Abbie was satisfied with that and was sure that this was the best she would get from a man who was obviously very careful with his words.

That's one more on our side, she told herself.

"Thank you, General," Abbie said, hesitated, and then turned and glanced back to Evie.

Evie sat up more erect in her chair. "Ah, General. Do you plan to be at the tribunal tom—"

"—What I think my Chief of Staff wanted to ask you was whether you or anyone else has yet identified the bioweapon threat?"

"Madame President, I believe we have far greater issues to concern ourselves than an empty threat from a murderer of millions who has already told many lies. However, Madame President, if you wish to get a more detailed report, I suggest you check with General Howard, the Chief of Space Operations, and the person who has been tasked by Secretary Meer with that specific investigation.

"Was there anything else you needed from me, Madame President?"

"No, General. Thank you once again for coming."

Chapter 17

Abdul

Besides not having been given authority to conduct any Presidential business on her own, much less in her private room, Abdul was shocked at Khan's gall to be plotting against Meer, and therefore against him. As he watched the General leave, Abdul scrutinized what Khan and Shareef were going to say next. He was very happy he had set up this camera, even though it was for his own personal pleasures. Further, this meeting confirmed to him that both women thought that their conversations were protected in Khan's chambers.

There was a disturbance outside.

Abdul shot an angry glare at his office door for the interruption, before returning his attention to the monitor.

He pointed the switching device at the screen and punched up the volume as far as it would go. The women were speaking, but almost whispering to each other now, and Khan had turned away from the camera, to face Shareef, so he couldn't read their lips.

The argument just outside his door got louder. He could hear it was between his deputy, Ali and someone else.

Abdul swiveled in his chair to bellow out a coarse warning when the door flew open. Striding through the doorway was Hassan.

Finally, Abdul thought.

Although this was an interruption, he welcomed it. Just then, Abdul decided to ask Hassan to be the hangman for the tribunal tomorrow. *He would enjoy this and...*

To Abdul's surprise, Hassan stopped just after stepping in from the doorway, and appearing behind him was Ali, who had just hollered for Hassan to stop. Ali put a hand on Hassan's shoulder—*big mistake*—and what happened next was so lightning-fast Abdul almost missed it.

Hassan twisted around, his right arm swinging out of sight and then he halted his motion when facing Ali eye-to-eye. The back of Hassan obscured all but Ali's own bulging eyes... first they flashed anger, then shock and then fear.

Hassan whispered something to Ali in Arabic that sounded like, "Teach you to touch me."

Without seeing, Abdul knew instantly what happened. But it was so quick he could not even react, much less stop him. As Abdul had learned years ago, once Hassan had decided to kill someone, the only action that would halt Hassan from his mission was Hassan's own death or the death of his intended target.

Hassan made an abrupt move with his arm and Ali collapsed, in the middle of Abdul's doorway.

Hassan spun back around, revealing the short blade to his *Jambiya*.

Instead of sheathing it, Hassan proceeded to step toward Abdul, with his knife held by his side while glaring at Abdul as he approached. Hassan demanded, "Did I hear correct, Mahdi, that you would kill me if I did not appear in your office?"—his pace to Abdul quickening—"Well I am here as you demanded. But I have decided to no longer take orders from you. I think I will try being in power once and for—"

Abdul delivered the remaining twenty rounds from his AK into Hassan, stopping him mid-sentence.

He had no choice. It was obvious that the man was going to kill him if Abdul had not stopped the killer first. He had to do it...

Abdul threw the emptied AK on top of his desk and dropped himself back into the soothing comfort of his chair.

This was one more example of those he commanded—one of his trusted followers at that—of whom, he had lost control; one more person who decided to stop following his will. "Even though I have been commanded by Allah to lead these people and this caliphate," Abdul barked out toward the two corpses lying dead on his floor.

Already, blood and other bodily fluids collected around them, spreading across the old-asbestos tile floor.

"Did you hear that?" Khan's familiar voice begged from behind him.

Abdul spun his chair one half revolution to stare at the television.

"It was definitely an automatic weapon," answered Shareef.

POTUS

"And it came from inside." Evie stated what they both knew.

Abbie's door opened and Meer breezed in without a knock.

Abbie twisted in her seat to address him, springing up into a stance.

"Was that a gunshot?" Evie asked in an abnormally timorous voice.

"You know it was," Meer said. "It's just a few terrorists exchanging gunfire with our Marines outside this complex. And it's no matter for you two. But that's not why I'm here."

"Why are you here?" Abbie asked.

"You know why I'm here."

"I do not." She meant this. But she felt a rush of anxiety from the gunfire and Meer barging into the only area she had felt somewhat safe in since arriving.

"Were you meeting with some of my Joint Chiefs behind my back?"

Damn! she thought. Somehow he knew, but the how puzzled her. She immediately reasoned it was one of the Joint Chiefs, probably the wimpy one, Padilla, who spilled the beans. "Well yes. As President, I thought it would be good to talk—"

"You thought?" Meer interrupted, one hand balled into a fist, the other pointing his beefy finger at her like a dagger. "You're not here to think. I made that abundantly clear. You are here to follow my orders—"

Abbie attempted to say something.

"—I'm not finished..."

He now pointed his dagger-finger at Evie. "Have you told her about the tribunal yet?"

Abbie rotated on her heels, snapping her head in Evie's direction. Her heart was now pounding like a bongo.

Evie's face instantly lost all definition, and her mouth hung open. It was like she'd had her soul sucked out. She flitted barely a glance at Abbie before returning her eyes in Meer's direction.

"I'll take that as a "no" then," Meer said.

Abbie remained fixated on Evie, who wouldn't even look at her again.

"I'm speaking to you now, Ms. Khan," Meer said, his voice dripping with contempt.

She swung back to face Meer, barely able to breathe. Yet, she felt somewhere inside of her the smallest wellspring of strength.

"Tomorrow at twenty-hundred-hours—that's eight PM in the evening—you will attend a tribunal topside, along with one thousand members of the public and press. There, you will witness two people who will be tried, convicted and then executed by hanging. You will not turn away. You will watch every moment of it. Do I make myself clear?"

Abbie felt like she'd been kicked in the chest. Meer had not only taken full command of this government, but he was also now executing people, and he expected her to watch; to condone this?

She could not.

"Did I say something you didn't understand?"

I will not!

"Well?"

"No," Abbie said with little conviction, as if the word accidentally snuck out of her mouth without her control. She attempted a deep breath.

"What?"

"No!" she belted out, this time like she meant it.

"No, what?" Meer asked. His pointing finger hand dropped to his side as if it had lost strength. He seemed confused by her response. "No, you didn't understand me?"

"No, I understood you very clearly, Mr. Meer." Her courage was building. "I'm saying, "No!" as in No, I am not going to watch you execute anyone. And no, I'm not going to support this action."

Meer just stared back at her, gobsmacked, as if she had reached over her desk and slapped him. Then his steely determination and angry demeanor were back in full force. "You, what?" he screamed. "You think you have a choice? I wasn't giving you one. You are going to go to this thing tomorrow, if I must force you to go there myself?"

Abbie sat back down in her chair, crossed her legs. Then she crossed her arms around her chest, if for anything to hold back its convulsing. "What do you think you're going to do, shoot me?" She smiled at this, letting the creases of this good feeling cement itself onto her face.

In response, Meer's own face contorted, his eye slits shrunk so small they were paper thin. Both his fists balled up. He bared his teeth and growled like a caged animal wanting to unleash its fury on its jailer. Yet, for some reason, he held back. Under his breath, he muttered several expletives she couldn't hear, did an about turn in place and stomped halfway out the door, before spinning back to face her again.

He released one balled up fist and pointed his dagger-finger again in her direction. "Actually, yes, *Mah-damn President*"—he stressed every syllable in a mocking way—"You *will* attend the tribunal as I have requested. Further, you will do what I say. If you do not, I *will* have you shot on the spot. And before you mouth off again to your superior, thinking you have any power whatsoever, do *not* forget this."

He was leaning forward, just inside the doorway now, finger punctuating each sentence.

"I already have complete authority over the government and the US Military. You gave this to me in two of the many executive orders you had signed.

"So you are already out of power. It is up to you to now decide whether you wish to remain alive by doing what I say or if you wish to end up just one more of the many unfortunate casualties from this war."

He then directed his attention to Evie, pointing his finger at her now.

"And *you*"—he jabbed his finger in her direction—"I may just have *you* shot because you can no longer perform a simple task."

He didn't wait for replies from either of them.

He spun around again in place and marched out the door, slamming it on his way out.

Chapter 18

Lexi

They returned in contemplative quiet, feeling once again defeated, even though Smith told them he had a plan. So focused on their inability to save Frank and the Senator, they did not see any of Faisal's men.

Turning off the highway onto the small private road, they found Smith's gate already opened for them.

Lexi let her mind wander, finding this easier than contemplating all their failures and the bleak future which lay ahead. She thought of Bathsheba, hoping that Smith's pet lion had better luck hunting than they did.

It was almost ironic that when they arrived at the front door, Bathsheba was waiting for them.

Samuel idled before they turned off to the roundabout, in front of Smith's house. Moondog swung the van up alongside, while rolling down the passenger window.

"Smith wants you parked in back," Samuel announced through the Hummer's window.

Moondog eyed Bethsheba, who was sitting near the house's entrance. Then he nodded at Samuel. Without saying anything further, he drove off for the rear covered area where the rest of their vehicles were parked.

"Shouldn't we wait until Smith says it's okay?" Samuel prodded Lexi, who was already out the door. She ignored him and trotted a path right for Bethsheba and the front door. She figured at this point, if nothing else got to her, she was probably safe with an animal who looked relatively tame. Besides, Smith didn't seem too concerned for their safety when Bethsheba patrolled the grounds.

She slowed as she approached the lion, extending her palm outward. She'd read that you should not show fear to a lion. Her Uncle Abdul was really the only thing she feared... and losing Travis. This lion, not so much.

"Hi Bethsheba. Aren't you a beautiful girl? Can we come in the door?" Lexi stopped and waited for either the lioness to react, or for Smith to broadcast something over the loudspeaker, as he did when they first arrived yesterday.

Bethsheba yawned, and then slunk down to the ground, so that she was prone. She stuck out a paw and gave a slight moan. *Was she asking me to come to her?* Lexi wondered.

She remembered having a chocolate chip protein bar in her pack and wondered if the ol' girl would like it.

Slow-like, avoiding any sudden moves, she pulled it from her vest, unwrapped it and held it out. "Would you like a treat?" She stepped forward.

"I wouldn't do that," came her father's voice from the speaker over the front door. It was Smith.

Bethsheba crept toward Lexi another foot, and once again stuck out a pad and pawed at the air.

Lexi may have not been an expert with lions, but she knew cats well enough. This one wanted attention.

She continued forward to within a foot of the lion's outstretched paws. "I'll bet your mean ol' owner doesn't give you any attention, does he?" She stretched out further and intended to lay the protein bar on the ground. But before she could, Bethsheba gingerly snatched it from her fingertips and sucked it down.

Lexi gulped back her breaths in surprise. But then said, "Wow, you're quick for an old girl, aren't you?"

Bethsheba rolled onto her back and stuck out both paws.

Lexi couldn't help it. She leaned forward and scratch Bethsheba's ear and head.

Bethsheba responded by pawing the air.

"That's the spot, huh? I knew it. You are—"

Bethsheba rolled back and sprang to her feet, startling Lexi.

"If you're all done playing with the beast, perhaps we could go in now?" Gladys asked, before ducking into the front door, with Samuel and Jonah in toe. Jimmy and Moondog darted inside, immediately behind them.

"I'll be back," Lexi said to Bethsheba. Thanks for getting my mind off things.

Lexi backed up a couple of steps before turning to walk through the door.

Troubling thoughts of this last defeat filled her mind again and accompanied her back inside.

Bookeater

The remainder of the American Eagle Patriots were waiting for them in Smith's library, as was Smith.

They hadn't let up on their grumbling about not being included in the operation to free Cartwright and Chase. Just before their team members arrived, Smith had debriefed them about the operation's failure. Their comments grew to an uproar.

Smith had to excuse himself, both to get away from the mind-numbing din of voices, which was giving him a headache, and to let the team blow off steam. They would need to for what lay ahead.

While in his side room, Smith examined his smart phone's screen. An aluminum arm held it in place to the armrest of his fully connected wheelchair. Through an app he had created, he was able to monitor and control most of the ranch, even when he wasn't in the command center of his Bat Cave.

It was a good thing too, because he had to warn Lexi about getting too close to Bethsheba. The old girl was pretty tame as far as lions go. After all, he trained her to be that way. But she still was a wild animal.

Just in case, he had kept a shock collar on Bethsheba. He'd only used it once, but he was ready to engage it again when Lexi ignored his warnings.

Smith exhaled and removed his finger off the virtual button, labeled "Shock" when he witnessed what happened next. Bethsheba was putty in Lexi's hands.

Noted, he thought.

Smith wheeled himself through the hallway to meet the team at the door of the Library.

"Welcome back," he said and pressed a button to open the sliding doors to the library.

"Follow me in so we can debrief and talk about the next operation." Smith had to yell this out, to be overheard from the loud arguments inside.

"Hey, kids," Gladys announced. "You didn't have to wait up for us." She marched in, receiving several limp backslaps.

"She likes you," Smith said to Lexi, who was marching in through the doors last.

"Guess my animal magnetism works on animals, too," she quipped.

Smith followed her in and shut the doors.

"Attention," Smith yelled, barely above the militia members' turbulent voices.

A loud whistle blared, and it stopped everyone. "Smith has the floor," Slim stated. It was now quiet, and all eyes were on Smith.

"Thank you," he said to Slim, then proceeded to the grand fireplace in the middle of the room. He turned to face the group.

"I'm not going to waste energy on what didn't work, other than to say that they had abruptly changed their plans, and by the time I decoded the communications, the operation had already started... Yes, Moondog."

Moondog had his hand up and looked a little desperate. "Sorry, but I have to take a whiz bad and haven't had a chance since the operation."

"Geez, Moondog," someone said.

"It's alright. Through that door," Smith pointed to the other side of the large library to a bookshelf. He pressed a virtual button on his smart phone and part of the bookcase parted, revealing a room behind it.

"Thanks, man," Moondog said, and scurried to the

room.

"Now, let's focus on the next operation and what is happening tomorrow." Smith detached his smart phone from his armrest and opened a different app on it.

The Water Lilies and Japanese Bridge painting by Monet disappeared in an instant. It was replaced by a schematic overview of a compound that he had studied up on a lot lately.

"Up here," he pointed to the screen, "you will see a layout of our next operation..."

He had their complete attention.

"This is where both Major Frank Cartwright and Senator Chase are being taken today." He used a laster pointer built into his phone to point at a group of buildings near the entrance of the complex. "They will be held here in a security holding area until tomorrow."

"Then, at nineteen-forty-five, they will be led out to this location. There, they will hold a fake tribunal in front of a large audience, including the currently installed President. It will be broadcast to the nation on TV and radio. After when they announce their guilt, they will be walked from here"—Smith made the red light move from one part of a hand-drawn stage to another part—"to here, where they will be hung until they are dead."

"Damn!" Jonah huffed.

"Tell me you have a plan to stop this?" Lexi asked.

A couple of militia members said, "Yeah!" almost at the same time.

"Yes, of course. I have a very specific plan, where we will secure their release, as well as stop Farook's Islamic Caliphate, and then we will install Senator Chase as the new President of the United States."

There was a race of whispers and quiet voices as the militia members emoted about the impossibility of this.

"Quiet," Slim yelled. "Mr. Smith still has the floor. I'm sure afterwords, he will allow time for a robust discussion." Slim motioned toward Smith.

"Thank you, Slim. Yes, after we go through an overview of the operation plan, I would welcome a healthy discussion. Then we wi—"

"Hey, what did I miss?" Moondog hollered from the other side of the library, coming out of the hidden room. A rush of water from a flushed toilet sounded inside. Several of the militia members snickered or shook their heads.

"Cool map," Moondog said, as he stepped quickly toward Smith. "Where is that?"

"Yes, Smith," Gladys said from a few feet away. "You haven't yet told us where this Kangaroo Court is being held."

"It's Mount Weather, Virginia."

Chapter 19

Travis

He froze in place, heart banging against his chest, and as he had done in the past, he remained as motionless as possible. Being quiet was his new superpower.

Almost the instant he heard them, the percussive beats from the rapid-fire shots reverberated in the ductwork's metal all around him.

The complex's reaction was immediate.

Travis studied the response to sounds coming from all around the bunker, doing his best to try to discern what happened and whether any of this was related to him.

Meanwhile, his mind swam with thousands of possibilities: was it a simple execution, as had been conducted almost daily since he was brought here, but not so much lately; could it have been target practice; maybe celebratory gunfire, as so many of Abdul's men liked to do; or was this an acknowledgment to what he had done with Sal?

Am I no longer a ghost? he wondered.

This line of thinking only jacked up his heart rate even further. But the responsory voices told him something otherwise.

Much of what was being said around the complex traveled well through the ductwork. And there was a lot of it.

In fact, quite a commotion seemed to be occurring everywhere in response to the gunshots.

The consensus appeared to be that the gunfire had come from his Uncle Abdul's office: he had killed one or two people—they couldn't get that straight—and that he was very angry about something. No one yet described the origin of his anger. However, because Travis' name—either the one given to him by his parents or by his uncle—was never mentioned, he assumed he was not the cause. Travis exhaled a loud sigh of relief.

He couldn't wait any longer, even though it had only been a couple of minutes: he had little time to waste based on what Sal told him. He only knew that he was running out of it. And much of what happened next depended on Travis being able to find what Sal described.

Travis slowed when he approached his first stop.

Abbie

After she had waited long enough to make sure Meer or someone else wasn't about to pop through her door, Abbie stood back up, walked around her little desk and locked herself and Evie inside. Then she focused all of her ire on the one and only person she had trusted, long before she had become President.

"Alright Evie, let's have it."

Evie remained in her chair, shoulders and head slumped forward, eyes locked on her feet. She barely flinched at Abbie's words.

Like a rusted mechanical hinge, her neck slowly creaked upward until she was looking directly at Abbie. A ghost of a smile almost formed. "I'm soooo sorry, Madame President." Her nasally voice made her sound almost comical. Though none of this was a joke to Abbie.

"This is not the President talking to you, but your long-time friend, Abbie Khan. Tell me what happened."

"It's all true."—she sniffled—"Secretary Meer *did* tell me about the tribunals early this morning. But honestly, I didn't believe it. The thought of holding kangaroo court trials and then immediately executing Americans seemed like too much. I figured he had to be bluffing."

"But why? What would he gain by telling you something like this if it weren't true?"

Evie planted her face in her hands and sobbed.

Abbie didn't stop her. She had already wondered if Evie was against her and had her own agenda, perhaps guided by the likes of Meer or maybe even X himself.

It wasn't that this episode was so horrendous. But, because she had just asked Evie if she had any news about Meer or anyone else, her saying nothing felt like a betrayal of her trust. It hurt, because she thought Evie was a true friend.

Now she didn't know.

Then again, Evie was also threatened by Meer... Still, Abbie decided she would have to be more careful about giving out her confidence to that woman.

There was a buzzing somewhere in the room, but Abbie didn't pay any mind to it because she wanted some answers.

"Give me the details about the tribunals: what are they, who are we trying and why?"

Evie looked up, both eyes soggy, but one—the one she had covered with makeup to hide the shiner she received a couple of days earlier—looked like it was drooping, as if she had suffered a stroke. "Wa-well... I don't know much, other than there will be two very important men being tried. I don't know their names or who they are. Only, that they will be found guilty, and they will be hung in front of everyone... and-and we have to watch. So does every American... It's going to be live on TV and radio."

Abbie fell into the same seat just occupied by the General. With a hand on her forehead, she considered all she had just heard and its timing.

Was it all Meer? Was Meer doing this? But why? What is the benefit of doing a public execution?

When the answer struck her, she was even more horrified. "This"—she whispered to herself—"is how he plans on taking total control of everything: the Presidency, the government, the military and the American people."

She thought about how fearful this would make everyone, and Meer's wicked plan all came together in her mind.

It's a coup, planned many years ago, before she was brought onto the scene by X...

X!

She let her hand fall.

Was X behind everything? If so, Meer is his puppet! She had thought it was the other way around.

Abbie finally looked up and searched the room to find

the source of the continual buzzing sound.

On her bedside table, she caught that her cellphone's light was on... and the device was buzzing.

That meant only one thing: X was texting her.

As if in a trance, Abbie rose from the chair and lumbered the short distance to her bedside table. She intended to snatch up her phone and sit on the edge of the bed. But she had no interest in seeing the truth: if it was who she suspected it was, everything she had believed was wrong.

She snapped out of it, snatched up the phone and sat.

A quick glance immediately confirmed her suspicions.

Multiple texts. All from X, who was telling her to fall in line, "or else."

But how could he know what she had just said?

The first text appeared immediately after Meer had just left. Meer couldn't have communicated to X and then X to her that quickly...

Evie's eyes were glued to hers now, reflecting back her own bewilderment.

Then Abbie understood.

She popped up from the bed and stepped toward the door, scrutinizing every blemish or scuff from top to bottom. Then she weighed what she would have expected to see against any other anomaly along that wall. She knew it had to be there.

Nothing stuck out, at least not right away.

Then it did.

The double switch plate had an abnormally large screw in it... between the two light switches.

She stomped over and squinted, nearly drilling her nose into the switch plate. Her thoughts were confirmed almost immediately. She'd never seen one in real life, but she saw enough secret agent TV shows to know what a spy camera looked like.

Rather than reacting in anger, which would have been rightful, she forced a smile onto her face, as she back-stepped away from it. She wanted to make sure that he would get the full effect of her next action: her absolute response to his texts.

When she bumped up into her little desk, she continued to eye the hidden camera—the same one that had been spying on her the entire time she'd been here, even when she changed clothing.

So that it would be obvious to the viewer, she held up her middle finger and mouthed the equivalent expletive.

After holding that pose for a good ten seconds, she stomped back over while removing one of her pumps. Using the small point of the heel, she gave the camera several whacks, until she saw it was broken.

Chapter 20

Presidential Bunker

Meer

"You have been called here for an emergency meeting, because I have heard some disturbing news of one or more of you congregating behind my back with the President to discuss treasonous actions."

He glanced at each of his Joint Chiefs, followed by each of POTUS' Cabinet members, all sitting around the conference table. Every member had been hand-chosen by him to do his bidding.

All of them, except General Metzler, squirmed in their chairs. The General simply stared back, revealing nothing. Meer knew it was Metzler and at least four others conspiring with the President.

"Well, that stops now. If I catch any of you meeting with the President in private, I-will-have-you-shot."

Meer let that sink in before he continued.

As I suspected, none of this group had the backbone to stand up and be a hero—.

"Wha-What about me?" Evelyn Shereef asked, her voice broken and almost shrill. "I'm her Chief of Staff. Is it not important that I—"

Meer cut her off. "You now report directly to me."

He looked around the room again. "Any other questions?"

This time General Metzler spoke up. "What about Farook?"

"What about Farook?" Meer spat back, tiring at Metzler's verbal gymnastics.

"You stated long ago your intentions of taking control. So this is not a surprise. We all agreed to be here, knowing we've made our bed with the devil. What I'm asking is regarding Abdul Farook. Because as far as I know, he's still claiming to have a bioweapon which would kill many of the remaining survivors, including us. So, I ask again, what are you going to do about Farook?"

"Simple. I'm going to have him executed too. He will be arrested at the tribunal, which I have confirmed he will be attending. We will make sure we have overwhelming forces here, so that his so-called Peacekeepers won't be able to respond. Then we will round him up, and his Peacekeepers, and we will execute all of them there as well.

"As to his bioweapon, aside from Farook's protestations otherwise, I am certain it is a fake. So once this terrorist is put to death, we can focus our energies on remaking America into the strong military presence it needs to be in this world."

"Haven't you forgotten someone?" General Metzler again interrupted Meer's thinking.

"Who are you referring to now?" Meer snapped.

"I believe the General is referring to the President. Won't she cause us trouble?" This came from Divya Bharti, the Treasury Secretary.

"No, the President will not be a problem any longer. She

has already confirmed with me that she knows that I am in charge, and she will remain the figurehead we need her to be, until we no longer need her."

"But how will you ensure this?" Metzler asked.

Meer drilled into him, wondering if this question was sincere or just Metzler's way of getting further under his skin.

"I know this to be true, because I issued the same threat to her that I did to each of you. She, like all of you, wished to remain alive after all of this is over.

"Have I made myself clear?"

Meer made sure every person in the room gave him a verbal acceptance, especially Metzler.

"Okay, unless you have any other objections, I'm going to have the President escorted into the room, so we can review the details of tomorrow's tribunal. I want to make sure everything goes as planned."

Meer punched a button signaling the Marine guard posted at their door. Almost immediately, he appeared inside.

"Go get POTUS."

Mount Weather Area B

Abdul Farook

Abdul turned the volume off and tossed the controller onto the desk he had stolen from its previous occupant. It clattered off his AK, skittered across the wood-laminate top and fell to the floor, on top of all the contents he had just pushed off of it.

This was his breaking point.

Both President Khan and Secretary Meer were openly plotting against him. He had given them everything. Without him, they would be nothing. They probably would have already been dead.

It was time to stop this, even though the timing was a day sooner than he had wanted.

This is not a problem, he told himself. He would make sure they would fall in line now or he would eliminate them and everyone else. He was ready for it all to end.

Abdul sprang from his chair and snatched up the AK. Before slinging it, he checked the breech to verify there was a round in the chamber. He had just reloaded it but wanted to be sure.

It was ready.

A quick step to the door, he found his guard, Mohammad Number Two... Abdul wondered if he should call him Mohammad Number One now, since he had just killed the man's older brother, also named Mohammad, the first of his two door guards.

Mohammad wasn't as startled as Abdul suspected he would be because he had his ear to the door. This Mohammad also knew better than to open the door without being told, after learning his brother was killed for doing just that. "My Mahdi," he said with a reverential bow.

That is the simple obedience I should expect from everyone, Abdul thought.

"Mohammad, please go and summon my Little Mice. Tell them to meet me at the big meeting room. After you have done this, release Saleem from jail and have him also meet me at the same big meeting room. Is that clear?"

"Yes, my Mahdi," Mohammad said with another bow. He dashed off through the hallway, on a direct route to where all his Little Mice were housed.

Abdul went the opposite direction.

He marched straight to the elevator.

The door opened, and he strode in. After inserting his key and giving it a quick turn, he pressed the D button. The door slid shut at a maddeningly sluggish pace, and the elevator hesitated before moving upward.

The thing was obscenely slow. Only after entering it did he remember he should have taken the midway stairs.

Checking his reflection on the door's polished interior surface, he realized he did not look well. Being Mahdi to a new nation was taking its toll. He had not been with either of his wives in two days, nor spent any time with his children.

The images of both Suhaimah and Abdul-Aziz came to mind. The pain of these thoughts caused him to close his eyes. All his muscles tightened in response.

When the door opened, he practically erupted from the elevator's chamber into the hallway. His Little Mice were already waiting for him, twenty steps away. Each man was armed and ready, though he suspected he would not need them.

He had not expected to ever need them here. But he did now. At least one or more people were about to die—though he hadn't decided who it would be. Their presence was only to ensure he was not one of the dead.

Abdul marched past his Little Mice to the guard posted at the door.

"Let me in," Abdul demanded.

The guard turned his head, the polished silver and brass symbol on his white hat glinted from the fluorescent lights above.

Abdul found the symbology prideful of an eagle standing on the earth, with an anchor through it.

So typical of Americans. As if they were the protectors of this world.

The guard stepped aside, while opening the door for him.

"Sir, you may go inside."

Travis, The Ghost

Just before his next target, Travis stopped at the vent opening to the long hallway. There was a commotion there that drew his attention away from his nearby destination.

There, outside the entrance to a room he was pretty sure was the big conference room he had accidentally hopped into. It was where he had first met Lynn, the pretty older woman who was so nice to him, even helping him to escape... *How long ago was that?* He wondered.

It felt like many days, but Travis reasoned it was only

one... *or was it two?*

An argument had started below.

There were several men, all dressed like Abdul in long thobes, each with shouldered rifles. Other than differences in their heights and weights, they all looked the same: same outfits, same beards, same nasty demeanor. One was arguing with a guard who wore a white hat and a cream and blue uniform. Something about why it was necessary for them to go inside with their Mahdi.

Travis braced himself.

That meant that Uncle Abdul was in the next room.

Travis tilted his head up to double check the location of the vent that led into that room.

He waffled at first and then decided he had to see if Abdul was, in fact, there now.

In a flash, he was sliding his knees across the ductwork's metal surface, his new makeshift pads softening each stretch.

When he was only a few feet from the vent opening, he felt and heard the loud bang of a rifle shot.

Chapter 21

President, Abigail O'Neal Khan

Before Abbie entered the conference room, Secretary Meer had already begun presenting his plan for the tribunals. He barely paused in between syllables to point her to her chair next to Evie.

The details were even more horrible than Evie had described.

When he itemized what the execution would look like, Abbie glanced over at Evie, but her friend was transfixed forward, eyes vacant and she was trembling as if she were sitting inside a meat freezer and not the warm conference room.

Abbie returned her attention to Meer, who was now focused on her as he delivered the timing aspects of the planned televised event, including her role.

She stared past him, logistically considering her own plans instead.

Despite his death threats, Abbie knew that Meer still needed her, otherwise she would have already been silenced. Permanently. She planned to use this to her advantage.

And because Evie was also threatened by him, she believed her friend would in fact assist her as well. If she had truly gained the trust of a couple of the Joint Chief's and Cabinet members, she might have a chance to wrestle control back. But with the tribunals set to take place in less than thirty-five hours, she had to hurry.

There was a muffled noise at the far door, and it opened.

Abbie expected the muscular Marine, who was usually posted at the door, to enter. Instead, an older man in Arab clothing sauntered inside.

At first, the man was turned away from them, addressing someone in the hallway, so she didn't recognize him. But when he rotated back toward them, she was thunderstruck.

Was it really him?

She stood and in a voice that lacked all surety, she said, "X?"

Everyone, whether they were sitting at their seats or standing like her and Meer, were initially silent, as if equally dumbstruck.

The only sounds were of the men outside of the room arguing with the Marine, and the deafening sound of her own heart thumping out a beat that made her think of a countdown.

All at once, the room became excited when they noticed X was carrying a rifle.

Abbie was more agitated for another reason. Because it was at that moment, everything clicked.

This was the man who had picked her up from political failure and put her into the place that allowed her to become the President today. Until her ascension to the Presidency, X had been little more than a quiet benefactor. That's when she started receiving texts from him—which she had begun to wonder if somehow they were from Meer and not X—threatening her.

But this man, standing before her, albeit a little less polished looking, was definitely the man she had met so many years ago. This man, who was even more threatening with a rifle, was the man she knew as X.

X snatched his rifle from his side and aimed it at the ceiling, ceasing the room's clamor instantly.

"Some of you,"—he said in the voice she remembered vividly—I have already met." He looked directly at her.

She was sure this is what a heart attack felt like.

"But none of you know me by my real name, I am Abdul Raheem Farook, the leader of the group you now know as the Islamic Caliphate in America, and Mahdi to all of the Muslims in America."

Abdul

When he first spoke, he drilled into Khan to gage her reaction. He had been relishing this moment for years.

Those pretty eyes of recognition and understanding, lighting up in an instant.

He had high hopes for Khan. Besides being a Muslim, she was the perfect figurehead for his remake of America. She was molded into the political figure she had become and, other than a few minor problems, she had been the perfect servant. But her role was not supposed to end with Abdul's ascension to complete power.

His intention was to be the spiritual leader of his people, which would eventually include all Americans when Sharia was ushered in. He was not supposed to be the face of the country's politics. That was supposed to be her place.

But to now see her acting independently and in complete defiance to his demands. Even offering a crude response to them... He felt certain she would die as his example.

When he announced his true name so that all the men and three women in this room would not be confused, Khan did what he expected. She backed away from the table, uttering, "Nooooo." She tripped on the chair and fell into it.

Meer held a hand up. "Is this necessary?"

Abdul pointed his rifle at him.

He really wanted to kill Meer, for many reasons. Most of all, for Meer believing that he could have Abdul arrested and then hung at the very tribunals that Abdul had set up.

But Meer also had a purpose. He was the perfect military politician, worming his way to a higher station than his actions or abilities should deserve. Yes, he was smart, but more than that, he had no morality, which made him perfect for being in place to make sure the government—especially the military—followed Abdul and did what Abdul desired.

So, Abdul resisted the desire to make Meer pay, instead continuing with what he came here to say.

"Regardless of whatever fantasies you tell yourself..." Abdul directed this at Meer, but it was also intended for everyone in the room. "There is only one person in charge right now and that person is me."

Meer flashed confusion and Abdul knew why: Meer didn't understand how Abdul knew that Meer had been conspiring against him. Abdul had never let on that he had cameras everywhere.

Then the smooth lines of recognition spread across the Secretary's smug face. He sat down, and Abdul felt pretty sure he would not say another word.

"Several of you have been conspiring against me, following your own agendas. But there is only one agenda, and that is mine.

"What you may not know is that I see everything that goes on in this complex. So, I have heard each of you say and do things here and in private which are in opposition to my will."

Abdul looked at everyone. Each person responded by tilting their eyes downward when he glared at them. He knew Meer had given a similar speech, but he needed to know that each and everyone understood what he was saying.

This would determine who he would shoot.

"You *will* follow me and submit to my will from this point forward. To prove to me that I should not kill you, you will first pledge your loyalty to me, right here and right now. Then you will tell me what you have done in the past to plot against me. If you do not give me your pledge and admit your sin against me, you will die right here."

Abdul swept the rifle barrel across the room. Some ducked under the table, others, like Khan and Shareef looked like their souls had been drained from each of their tortured bodies. But a couple of them, like Meer, remained where they were as if they were daring him to do it.

Yes, several of you may die today to make the others fear me.

"And if some of you believe you can pretend to give me your fealty, all the while you continue to plan against me, let me warn you.

"First, I can see right through you. This is a gift Allah has given me. I can always tell when someone is lying to me.

"Second, unlike what Secretary Meer has told you, I *do* currently possess a doomsday weapon. In a short time, if I do not disable it—and I am the only one who can—it will release a massive infectious disease into the sky. At the same time, other locations around the United States will do the same. The bacteriological vapor which will infect millions, who will spread it to others. With a seventy percent mortality rate, most, if not all of you will die. And so will the last remaining hope of America.

"I am telling you all of this to let you know that you only have two choices: submit to me now and forever more or die.

"Now, tell me first of your loyalty to me and then your sin against me. If you say anything more than this, I will shoot you."

Abdul pointed his rifle first at Ramon Padilla, a useless hire who Meer said was always "morally flexible." Abdul didn't expect anything but submission from him.

"You are first." Abdul held the rifle under an armpit, one finger on the trigger, the other gripping the hand guard. He clicked the select fire switch all the way down to "D" or semi-automatic fire.

"What do you mean me fir—"

Bang.

Padilla's head whipped back, sending a ten-foot cloud of red mist behind and around him, some of it landing on the two people sitting to his left.

Travis

He shimmied as fast as he could, until his face was buried against the vent register, looking out across the long room with a conference table below him.

Some of the men and one of the three women were crying. He recognized her as Lynn, the nice woman who had helped him escape.

Another woman had an arm around her and was consoling Lynn.

Near the far end of the table, one of the men, whose face and bright blue business suit were covered in red—*It's blood*—was mumbling something to Uncle Abdul, who was pointing a rifle in his direction.

"Speak louder," Abdul demanded.

"Oh God," the man blubbered.

"It is Allah, not God," Abdul corrected.

Travis' eyes grew wide when he saw behind where Abdul was standing, further away, was a dead man. The man's gore was all over the wall.

Another man, seated in between the dead man and the blue-suited man, looked catatonic. His face was also covered in rivulets of blood which ran down his cheeks and off his chin.

"I pledge my loyalty to you and only you," said the blubbering, blue-suited man. "And although I didn't directly conspire against you, I allowed myself to get pulled into a conspiracy perpetrated by those two"—he pointed at Lynn and the other woman—"the President and the Chief of Staff, who were trying to get me to join forces against Secretary Meer and you."

The man buried his head into his hands and whimpered about not being shot.

Travis turned his attention on the two women Blue Suit had tattled on.

The one he didn't know must be the President. Lynn, who he was guessing was the Chief of Staff, was still crying, but looking up.

It was her turn next.

"Ms. Shareef," said Abdul.

Lynn stood up from her chair, ripping away from the female President's comforting arm.

She wiped away at her eyes and her demeanor changed to the woman he had witnessed: a woman who stood in defiance.

Travis wanted to yell out to her; to not do something stupid. Just say what he wanted to hear and live to see another day. But it was obvious she was not going to do this.

"I pledge to you, in Christ's name, that I will never submit to you or any other false God. You are nothing but a terror—"

Abdul pulled the trigger several times.

Lynn's body danced for just a moment and her face partially exploded as Abdul's rounds ripped through her.

The President screamed.

Travis uttered a loud, "No!" and then puked all over himself.

But he didn't dare move.

Because just when he lost the contents of his stomach, Uncle Abdul directed his gaze up the very same vent opening Travis had been staring back from. Abdul held his gaze onto it as if it were the most interesting vent he'd ever seen.

Chapter 22
Mt. Weather

Travis

This time, he didn't care what he felt like or that the stench of his own puke was so strong. He moved like lightning. He had even less time now.

Because Travis felt sure now that his uncle suspected he was alive and back in the HVAC ductwork, he had to find what Sal had asked him to find and he had to do it now.

There were over a dozen other potential locations Sal had outlined to him. Thinking he had a lot more time, Travis had agreed to go down and search the lower floors first and work his way to the top floor, just below the surface. Since the top floor had the prime location of what he was looking for, he decided to go there now. Hopefully he'd get lucky and find it. Then he could get out of the ductwork and hide until he met up with Sal at their designated meeting spot.

At the end of the horizontal ducting he was in now, he found the vertical stretch of the return duct that went straight down into a void and then vaulted upward to a grill which opened up topside. There was only a faint twinkle of light from the sky, three floors up. Though the last floor looked longer. He only needed to go up two floors.

Without hesitating, Travis spun around and stuck his feet out first while he worked his way into the vertical return air shaft, letting them dangle over the abyss below.

He had come up with a method to vault himself up more safely and he was both anxious and nervous to try it out.

This time, his feet were covered in duct tape some of which included the sticky side out. With less chance of them slipping, he put one foot on each side of the vertical shaft wall in front of him. Stretching his arms out, he pressed with his hands, also lined with duct tape, against the two walls on either side of him. Then he lifted himself out of the horizontal ducting and backed up against a vertical wall.

He was completely suspended by his feet and his hands above the blackness below.

"It's working," he praised himself.

Now the moment of truth. He pushed with his legs and hands, lifting his trunk upwards a few feet. While keeping his feet steady, he repositioned his hands up, held while he lifted his feet.

"Only one and three quarters floors to go," he told himself.

Abdul

Abdul was now officially the supreme ruler of America. Tomorrow, he would make it official.

After showing his seriousness by killing two members of the government in front of each of them, they all offered their loyalty and asked for his forgiveness and mercy for the conspiratorial sins they had committed against him.

Abdul didn't care if any of them were sincere or whether any or all of them hated him. His preference was to be feared by everyone.

Abdul left the room, finding his Little Mice and the Marine guard where he had left him.

When Abdul had shot the first member of the government—he already forgot the man's name—the Marine burst in, no doubt to fulfill his mission to protect the President. Abdul's Little Mice followed in behind. But he didn't need any of them, so he told them to wait outside. And there they remained, just a bunch of unnecessary appendages.

Running down the hallway was one of the two men Abdul had wanted to see. Mohammad Number One—he had decided to call him this now—arrived, out of breath and harried.

"My... Mahdi" He doubled over, hands on knees, trying to not pass out while he huffed and puffed.

"Where is Saleem Hafeez?"

"That's... Why... I ran. He's goah..."

"What? What are you trying to say?"

"He's gone... He escaped."

"What?" Abdul screamed and let loose a barrage of fire from his AK into the ceiling.

Travis

The additional gunfire only made him move faster.

In a little over ten minutes, Travis had scaled both stories and was safely inside the highest subterranean floor in the complex. The next long span up led outside and to his freedom.

He was tempted to leave now, but if what Sal had said was correct, there was nowhere he could have gone, even if he could successfully escape Mount Weather. He had to stay underground and do his job, even if it meant he might be discovered by his uncle or even get killed by one of his uncle's henchmen. He was doing this for his sister, Lexi, and his godfather, Frank.

After catching his breath, Travis flipped around, off his back onto his knees and began to shuffle forward, recalling that he had to pass eight side vent openings before he'd find his target. If he was lucky, he would find it right away.

Unlike the ductwork stretching along the hallways of floors below, this one had vents in each side of the ductwork and one below. The side vents emptied into rooms on either side of the hallway, above the doorway entrances to those rooms. The one below allowed airflow into the hallway.

Because each lower vent was the ceiling above that

hallway, he had to be as quiet as a mouse when he moved over each vent. If someone were to walk by they would certainly hear him passing overhead.

At the seventh set of vents on either side and in the floor, Travis heard the scuffling of shoes on linoleum. When he looked down, a guard passed bye, did an about face and marched down the hallway in the other direction. After a couple of minutes hovering over the vent, another guard—*or is it the same*—passed by, spun around and proceeded in the other direction. He moved forward, but much slower now.

At his targeted eighth set of vent openings, below him was a guard, standing in front of the door opening. He was not moving, but marching by him was one of the marching guards, or perhaps the only one. That meant that this room was probably the correct target, as it was being guarded by two or three of Abdul's men.

This also meant that he couldn't easily get into the room using his old kick-in-the-vent-register or he would be heard by the outside guards.

Travis peered into the side vent leading into the guarded room. It was dark except for a single flashing light about thirty feet away.

He repositioned himself, again careful to not make any noise, with the guard directly below him. He had to get a better look.

Screwing his eyes into the flashing light, he could see it wasn't flashing after all. It was blinking numbers.

One number, then another number, and then another.

Squinting more so he could see them, he read each one:

26:00:15
26:00:14
26:00:13

Chapter 23

Faisal

"Commander," Samir said into his hand-held radio. "We have surrounded the enemy's property, as you have advised, from the west side. My men are spread out from its front gate, along a fence line—which is easily breached—to the back of the property, where there is a small house. There are several vehicles parked behind the house, three of which look like the trucks belonging to the American militia who escaped. Finally, I have just witnessed the return of the white van and members of the militia enter the house. Can we move forward?"

Faisal clicked his radio, while signaling with a forefinger in the air to Hamza, who was in the vehicle beside him. "Thank you, Samir. Hold for Hamza to cover the east side of the property. I have just sent him to the gate. When he is in place, I will give the go command."

"Yes, sir," Samir answered.

Faisal watched Hamza drive away in the American's truck with five of his men. That makes twelve warriors who will be surrounding the infidel's property, closing in. Once Hamza sets up his men, the enemy will be surrounded. Then Faisal will take his remaining two men and drive through the front gate with the convoy truck, starting the attack and blocking any possible escape.

His men had been salivating for the attack to proceed. But when one of the enemy's vehicles had escaped, Faisal had made them wait for its return so that their victory would be complete.

Soon his men would be in place, and they would have victory.

Faisal was already savoring the taste of the upcoming slaughter.

Bookeater

"You will not be going in alone, like you did at the jail. This operation will be a massive one, led by multiple teams made up with not only other militias but also members of the US Military. All of you will be in one team, with Slim as your team leader, who will report to a military unit in your designated area. Each team is assigned a specific mission task and at specific points of entry"—Smith pointed at the map of Mount Weather on his big screen monitor—"and all communication will be running through me from my command center, here."

"Slim, here are your specific mission orders and your meet up location. At least ten others from another militia will be joining you at your meet up." Smith handed Slim the orders he printed before they had returned from their failed mission.

“Please tell me...” Lexi stood from where she was seated on the floor, releasing herself from Slim’s hand hold. “...Our mission is to free Frank, Senator Chase and get Travis, right?”

“Not to worry, Lexi. That is your ultimate mission, but I thought you’d like to partake in the killing of Abdul Farook as well.”

Lexi looked at first horrified by this revelation and then nodded and said under her breath, “Okay. Thanks.”

“Yes, your team will first incur at this point, where you will be joined by members of the first...”

Smith’s attention was diverted to a warning light that flashed on the big screen. It could only mean one thing.

Smith tapped his small phone screen on his wheelchair's right arm rest.

“Ahh, what does that mean, Mr. Eater,” Moonbeam asked from the back of the room.

Smith ignored him, tapping another virtual button on his phone, which then changed the big screen. It was a live camera of Smith’s fence line, about a half mile from the house.

“What are we looking for?” Jonah asked.

“Intruders.”

Samir

Using field glasses, another gift from the American militia, Samir studied the back, side and front of the house, where he saw no change. But there was movement to the south of his location, off to the side, where one of his men should be waiting for his signal to start the attack.

Each of his men were spread out at points behind the enemy's fence line. Just far enough away to make sure the property was covered, but not too far that each man couldn't see the next man on the line on either side of him. The attack signal from Samir would then be sent down the line. Hamza was to have done the same when his team was in place, which he had just confirmed. They were only waiting for Commander Faisal's announcement that the attack had begun. They were not supposed to move before this.

So, it was a surprise to see any of his men crossing the fence line before he had given the signal.

Samir risked his low profile to stand and signal his man to stop.

The man continued to move past the fence, toward the house, as if he were operating solo without any command structure.

With full intent to run over and stop his man, short of shooting him for insolence, Samir put a leg through one course of the barbed wire fencing, using his rifle to separate the strands. He stopped midway, when he saw another movement.

This movement was not something human. It was fast... It was stealthy... It was a lion.

Slim

"Is that..." Lexi started to ask. She didn't have to finish, because Slim knew it was Smith's lion, Bathsheba.

Even though his first impression was that Bathsheba was old and probably not too threatening, they all watched as this apex predator came out of nowhere and tackled the intruder who had just broken through Smith's fence line.

The camera's microphone picked up the man's scream, before Bathsheba stopped his outcry with one massive bite to his throat.

A gunshot rang out and Bathsheba darted away and out of sight.

One more shot.

Smith brought up another camera, showing a similarly dressed Jihadi, taking aim with his rifle and shooting.

"Oh no," Lexi screeched. "Run Bathsheba."

"I think we have larger problems," Gladys said. She pointed to one of the pictures within the big picture of the man shooting on the bottom of the screen. Smith must have been of like mind, because he enlarged it to make it the prominent video feed.

It was a map of the property with two red pulsating lights below the house and now a third one at the gate, followed by multiple red lights surrounding the property. The name of the video feed was Security Breach Overview.

"What does that mean?" Moondog asked.

Jonah answered first. "We're under attack."

Chapter 24
Mount Weather, Virginia

Abdul

"Where is he?" Abdul roared at the jailer, who disappeared into the jail upon seeing him coming.

"I-I do not know, my Mahdi." The jailer halted near Sal's cell door, pointing with a wobbly finger toward its handle. "As you can see, the door is locked, just the way I left it."

Abdul, his chest heaving from running and his head thumping from his adrenalin-fueled anger, scrutinized the jailer, wondering how stupid the man thought he was. "Are Mahdis now expected to see through solid doors?"

The jailer jolted forward, realizing his oversight, and unlocked the door.

Abdul opened it and took a step inside.

"As you can sa-see, the jail is empty."

Abdul ignored the man, his eyes busily scouring every square centimeter of Sal's jail cell for clues as to where he might have gone.

He could not find one.

Sal's Quran was sitting on his bed, his prayer rugs in their proper place, his bed pan hidden and covered under his cot.

There was nothing out of place.

Because of the similarities between this escape and the one by his son, Abdul stepped up onto Sal's bed to more closely examine the air vent. In Abdul Aziz's case, the vent cover had been replaced without the screws. However, with this one, the screws were intact. Untouched.

That could only mean one thing.

Abdul bounded off the bed and centered all his attention on the jailer, who backed up away from the door as if struck physically by Abdul's glare. "There is only one way Sal left his cell, and that is walking past you."

The jailer was backed up to the wall. "No, my Mahdi. No, I was paying attention. There was no way—"

Boom-boom-boom.

A *screech* erupted from the next room.

Abdul advanced toward the twitching body of his former jailer, feeling at least a little satisfaction in shutting up the man's miserable drivel.

He reached over to the dead man's hand, yanking from it the ring of keys, and proceeded over to the next jail cell.

While he sorted through the keys, trying to find one that fit, the whimpering sounds grew. They were coming from within.

The fourth key turned out to be the correct one, and so Abdul unlocked and opened the door to find his two other prisoners, former members of the previously discarded government.

The woman backed up against a wall, her fear appearing to be overwhelming to her. The man sat with his back up against a wall, feet up in bed. It was the same position he had been the last time Abdul had seen him.

He peered up at Abdul and said very casually, "Are you going to execute us now?"

Abdul wasn't sure about this one. He either had a death wish or he just did not care.

"I may not execute you if you tell me what happened to the man in the next cell." This was a lie, as Abdul planned to have both executed in the quiet tomorrow, after he was sure he no longer needed them. At this point, they were probably superfluous bargaining chips, doing nothing but feeding off of his mercy.

"Well," the man swiveled his legs up and off the bed so that he could more directly face Abdul. "As you can see, we do not have any way to see outside our jail cell unless the door is opened. However, we can hear everything."

"Buck, don't," the woman whispered.

"About ten minutes ago, I heard the door to the cell near us open. There were two voices mumbling to each other. I even had my ear on the door, and I can tell you there was no way to hear what they said or differentiate who each speaker was.

"Then I heard the door close and some footsteps, walking away from our door... Well, that's it. I walked back to my bunk and went back to sleep until I heard you execute the inept jailer."

Abdul studied the man. As best as he could gather, the man was telling him the truth. But Abdul also knew that many politicians were adept liars.

Abdul glared at the woman. "Is what he said the truth?" Abdul pointed his rifle at her, making her squirm even more.

"Yes-yes, that's true. I was just afraid you wouldn't believe him, because I knew we couldn't tell you anything useful."

Abdul nodded once and walked out, slamming the door

and locking it shut. He figured correctly then: the jailer must have been asleep when Sal and whomever helped him escape walked out of the jail. That meant he was looking for two people, a traitor and Sal.

Abdul exited the jail, finding Muhammad Number One waiting for him in the hallway. He was liking this Muhammad more and more: the man seemed to understand when to stay out of the way and when he was needed.

Feeling a little more at ease, because there were only so many places Sal could go, he breathed out a sigh and said, "Okay, Muhammad, did you hear everything that was said by the prisoners?"

"Yes, my Mahdi," Muhammad replied immediately, without hesitation.

"Good. You are now my Deputy. Your first duty is to get everyone to carefully look for and find Sal and his conspirator—of course we do not know anything about this traitor, other than these two must know each other. Do you understand my instructions?"

"Yes, my Mahdi."

"Excellent. Report to me in one hour with an update or less if you have found him. Now go."

Muhammad bowed and then scurried off.

Abdul hoped he could find Sal. More than anything, he wanted to ask Sal, who was about to receive the keys to Abdul's kingdom, why he would choose this path instead? If only he could find him and ask him this.

Sal

To anyone who might have seen him, he was just another worker in a blue jumper, covered in dirt. Sal glanced to his left and then to his right before stepping into the small closet, where he had stored a few things for this very event.

He opened the door and closed it behind him, engaging the handle lock in the dark.

When he found the light switch, he flicked it on and immediately grabbed some of the cleaning clothes from a middle shelf and tossed them on the ground, distributing them along the bottom of the door to hide evidence of the light being on. He kept hold of one of the clothes and then examined himself in the dusty little mirror clinging to a wall above a small chair.

Sal wiped away some of the dirt from his face and hands that he had collected while moving through the ductwork.

He had to hand it to the kid. The boy was industrious and fearless. He would have made the perfect successor to Abdul, if Abdul had not been so corrupted by his own power, making him obtuse to the people he so desperately wanted to conquer.

Abdul would ultimately fail. Sal was as sure of this as he was about anything in this life. He loved and respected the man, but he could not stand by now and allow him to senselessly murder millions of more innocents when he did fail.

Like Abdul, Sal had originally thought that their plan to conquer America would succeed, because Sal also believed that its citizens would ultimately submit to their rule, and to Allah. So Sal's advice to bring fear through public executions and then offering mercy would have been sound, for most peoples of the world. But not for Americans.

He realized this early after they had struck at the heart of America. Abdul did not. This was the primary reason why he had conspired against Abdul.

Sal understood quickly that Americans would not submit, no matter how much pressure they applied. It was because they were different than most citizens of the world. Aside from their Christian roots, there was another even stronger religious fervor that was baked into most Americans' DNA: the desire for freedom.

Abdul and Sal's attempt to remove these freedoms, instead of forcing them to submit, would only incite them to revolt. They had seen multiple examples of these days ago. But Abdul ignored them. Now, these signs were obvious to everyone, including many of his own followers.

What Sal had not counted on was Abdul's plan to employ a doomsday weapon.

They had discussed such a weapon. In fact, Abdul had been searching for and attempting to purchase mass-destruction weapons for many years. However, these tools were part of a greater plan for conquering a people. To use such tools out of simple vindictiveness was against everything Allah had taught. It was not their way.

Then Abdul admitted that he had already obtained and

deployed this weapon, setting it up on a countdown, and that he planned to allow it to go off if he did not get his way, like some obstinate child. Sal knew he had to find a way to stop him. He prayed for this.

Abdul Aziz was the answer to his prayers, proving that Allah was on his side once again.

He stood motionless, gazing one more time at himself, but looking past his lifetime of scars. Enough surface dirt was removed that he would not arouse suspicion, which was the whole reason for this exercise.

Sal reached into a bottom most shelf and pulled out a bag he had stored there in the event he had to leave. It was part of his nature to plan for every possibility.

From the top of the sac, he snuck out a radio. Turning it on, he entered in the frequency and then clicked the transmit button three times. He waited a full minute before again pressing the button three more clicks.

After four times of doing this, he received his answer. Four clicks back.

Sal turned off the radio, but rather than returning it, he clipped it onto a loop on his waist and explored his pack for food.

He was going to have to wait here for several hours before he could take further action.

Chapter 25

“Trespassers Will Be Eaten"

Faisal

“Beware, they have a… *al'asad…* a lion fighting for them now. It attacked and killed one of our men; maybe two… I just heard another dying scream. I tried shooting the beast, but it was too quick. Beware my brothers!”

Faisal pushed the radio up against his ear because he thought he was not hearing right: a lion… two more warriors down? “Faster!” he barked at his driver.

“Commander,” the driver said. “I cannot go faster, or I may lose control of the truck.”

As if to prove his point, the wheels of their convoy truck skidded off the road, but then grabbed hold and threatened to send their top-heavy vehicle sideways.

Faisal held on, as the driver course corrected with a grunt, and they were back on their path. They *were* going as fast as they could.

“Good driving, brother… There!” Faisal pointed forward.

Up ahead was their target, a small house where Samir said the enemy infidels were hiding.

Lexi

"Follow me, everyone," Smith bellowed. "Let's get you suited up with your weapons and radio equipment." Smith had put his wheelchair into a speedier gear, as he zoomed through the group and out the library door.

"Shouldn't we get out of here?" Gladys asked, scurrying to keep up, just behind Smith to hear his answer.

"Come on," Lexi insisted, pulling on Slim's hand which again had found its way into hers. She gave a final tug and let go when he was up. She dashed in Smith's direction, wanting to hear what he said.

"We will be protected from any type of attack they attempt," Smith hollered with his head half-turned so everyone could hear. "Please, quickly follow me."

As he said this, something happened which Lexi didn't at first understand. But then it became very clear.

Loud mechanized sounds, followed by *thuds* and it seemed as if the inside lighting was suddenly dimmed. Ahead of her, down the shotgun hallway leading to the kitchen, she could now see what was occurring.

Some sort of sliding shutter closed with a *thump*, cutting off the outside light, just before she turned to run downstairs into... What did he call it? *His Bat Cave*.

"I don't know if you understand these people," Jonah shouted to be heard among the *thud*-sounds and din of footsteps and voices. "I've dealt with them firsthand. They are ruthless. They will burn this place down and everyone in it before they can chant, *Allahu Akbar*."

Jonah turned at the bottom of the stairwell, already following Smith and Gladys through the two doors—both open—into his Bat Cave.

Lexi heard Smith's response. It was something like, "Mr. Price, I have a few tricks up my sleeves too."

She couldn't help but think though that they were in fact racing to reach their tombs.

Faisal

"Ram it!" Faisal cheered, beating the dash for punctuation. The driver responded, but not verbally.

They hopped up onto a gravel circle, which was the center of a roundabout drive, that they were bisecting. Their target ahead was the dwelling's front door.

While the engine of the old US Army truck roared, Faisal noticed two things which seemed off to him.

The first were the dwelling's windows, which previously appeared to be reflecting the fading sunlight back at them through color-accented trim. Now it seemed as if the windows were gone, replaced by horizontal slats of the same color as the house.

The second thing he noticed happened so quickly, he could not warn his driver in time, nor could his driver respond before it was too late.

Round black tubes rose from the ground, similar to long pointless fangs encircling the house like a giant open mouth. Rather than waiting to consume them too, these appendages became an immovable barrier, keeping them out.

The truck's brake drums screeched, but they could barely slow the two-and-one-half ton truck.

They hit the black teeth at sixty.

The truck's driver and Faisal were catapulted through the windshield and almost into the door of the house, both landing at odd angles.

The driver's neck snapped, killing him instantly. Faisal landed on his right shoulder with a crack, and his head smacked the concrete stoop, knocking him out.

Lexi

"Shouldn't we engage them? We have more than enough firepower." Samuel begged Smith.

She agreed with him. Using a few of Smith's rocket launchers would be more than enough to take out these jihadi pukes. The rest could be polished off with a few sprays of their automatic weapons, all of which had to be far superior to their enemy's old-world AK's.

"You have much more important tasks ahead of you, Mr. Slim," Smith responded as he checked Lexi's tactical vest to make sure it fit properly. "These people are as insignificant as fleas."

"True, but these fleas bite hard and carry diseases," Gladys responded, always offering a dose of her humor during the tensest of situations.

"True, Ms. Gladys. However, I promise none of us will get sick from these fleas. More important is the chief parasite at Mount Weather. That is where you must focus all your energies." He looked up into Lexi's eyes. "You good, soldier?"

"Yes," she responded. She had to admit, it *did* feel good. Real good. She twisted her arms back and forth to verify she had complete mobility.

"What about a radio check?" Slim asked.

"We'll have to do this while you're on the road. Time to mount up," Smith said, before spinning in place and racing out of the gunroom. "Bring your weapons and ammo and follow me," he said this already a room away.

All eleven of the remaining American Eagle Patriots, now looking more like a polished military unit than a militia's common patchwork of nonuniformity, double-timed it out of the gunroom. They followed Smith, who had disappeared, off the side, into his vast server space.

At the far wall, he waited until they caught up. They saw him pointing at a door that was swinging open, just like the Bat Cave's main entrance. "You'll exit here. This leads to a tunnel, terminating right up into the area you've parked your trucks." He was blocking their way so they couldn't leave before he was ready.

"A few quick actions you need to follow when you exit.

"First, Mr. Price, if you would take up the rear and be sure you secure the exit hatch. Once you close it, the automatic lock will engage. Just smooth the sand over it so that it's not too obvious where your exit point is."

Jonah nodded and said, "I've got that."

"Second, Ms. Gladys, if you'd take point on the exit off the property. You will probably have to engage one or two of the jihadis near the rear of the house. And certainly, when you all have left in your vehicles."

"Sounds like cake, Mr. Eater," Gladys said, smiling at either her use of Moondog's previous reference or because she liked the prospect of shooting some more terrorists. Probably both.

"Third, Mr. Slim, have your team take one of the two trucks and you take up the rear in your Humvee since it can take enemy rounds as you head out."

"Yes, sir," Samuel said. Lexi could tell he was taking this all very seriously.

"Finally, who will be driving the lead truck?"

"That would be me, Mr. Eat, I mean, Smith." Moondog glared first at Gladys, indicating he understood her little dig and didn't care for it, then back at Smith.

"Fine Moon... dog." Smith looked like he was making a mental note. Perhaps it was just to say his name correctly from this point onward.

"When you exit around the last building, head for what will look like a block wall under the big tree in back. It is not a wall. It's an optical illusion—"

"Seriously?" Moondog asked.

"Yes, using light refraction, as governed by Snell's law, I've set up a series of mirrors so that its refractive index closely match the surrounding medium, causing the light to bend..."

Smith could see Moondog's eyes had already glazed

over. "Sorry, TMI. When you see this, even though your mind will want you to lay on the brakes, don't. Hit the gas and you'll go through an opening that jogs left and on a little dirt road in the valley, which will meet up with the county road on your map. Do you understand?"

Moondog smiled and said, "Gotcha, Mr. Smith. You've done some sort of scientific voodoo shit with a brick wall. I'll drive right through it and take the little road in the valley onto road you showed us in your map all the way, and then on to Mount Weather where we will finally send these ragheads back to their so-called paradise and their doe-eyed virgins."

"Amen to that, Moondog," Smith said. "Alright, I think you are all ready to go."

He paused and glanced up momentarily, as if he were seeking inspiration or saying a prayer. "Okay, I'm going to say what Major Cartwright said to me and to Lexi's father, just before we went into our operation... "Eyes open, stay frosty, and bring everyone home. You got that?"

They all verbally agreed.

Lexi couldn't help to shake the nagging feeling that their operation might end up like Smith's, where one of them gets seriously hurt or worse.

Chapter 26

Hamza

"They're escaping through some sort of secret passageway out of the ground," Hamza roared into his radio. Then he ran as fast as he could the other way.

"Where are you, Hamza?" Samir asked.

"East end… of property… getting to truck… before they escape."

Hamza had dropped off each of his men along the way, spaced out as Faisal had requested, finding a driving path along the edge of the fence line. When he spotted the house, he parked out of sight.

Good thing. He now needed the truck as their new commander destroyed their only other working vehicle and led them into another trap.

The radio chirped. "Hamza, I have sent two men around to the back of the house to see if they can slow down the infidels before they are able to escape again."

This rubbed Hamza the wrong way. "Why not you, Samir?" He jumped into the truck and started it up.

"I'm attending to Commander Faisal. He is unconscious. Also, we are about to light the house on fire and burn anyone hiding inside."

Hamza didn't respond. He knew it was up to him to stop these dogs before they ran away again.

There was some gunfire on the other side of the hill separating him from the back of the dwelling. He groaned at this and mounted the hill. Ahead of him was the razor wire fence. Gassing it, he braced for it, hoping that he had enough force to break free.

The crash into the fence and the grating sounds of it clutching onto the truck were deafening. It held for a millisecond, lurching him forward. Then it snapped, releasing him. He reset his sights on his already moving targets in front of him.

One or more of their warriors were firing at the infidels' two vehicles attempting to escape once again. He would not let this happen, but they were almost out of range.

Hamza saw an opening: a set of bushes before a patch of gravel; they were headed towards this. He stabbed the gas pedal, and the truck immediately responded.

Based on his speed and their route, he would miss the first truck, but he would definitely hit the second one.

A large rock pounded his left front wheel sending him off track. He wrestled with it, finally regaining control and repointing it on a slightly different trajectory.

When he hit the bushes, the truck rattled and lunged him forward. But it slowed him just enough that he zoomed past the rear of the second truck, missing it by less than a meter.

Again, he jammed on the brakes to regain control, while redirecting his course forty-five degrees so that he was back on their gravel path. They were now a solid five seconds in front of him and already no longer visible, obstructed by a large building.

Once more his foot mashed the accelerator, even though he couldn't see where the white gravel path would take him.

Leaning, Hamza pulled on the wheel to navigate around the building, holding firm to make sure he didn't slide sideways.

Wall?

He tried to stop in time, but it was not possible. The brakes locked, and he braced for impact.

Somehow his truck sliced through the wall, which in an instant had disappeared. He squinted when he passed under a tree, not understanding. But he was free, so he stomped again on the accelerator. At the same time, he struck something invisible.

To his shock, he watched himself go through the windshield and sail over what looked like black teeth, then the sky, and then boulders. He hit face first.

Bookeater

Smith punched a button in his control panel and the south emergency exit bollards retracted.

He couldn't really see what happened to the driver, but he could see the mangled truck and its opening in the windshield where the driver had sling-shotted through. He couldn't imagine the driver made it. Regardless, he was not a threat to his team anymore.

Smith spun in his chair to face his main console and check in with his team.

"Comms check. This is a comms check," Smith announced into his boom microphone. "Please call off based on the number on your vest, starting with who has number one, Lexi, and then the next person until everyone makes sure your comms are on."

"Broadmoor here. I hear you loud and clear, ah Smith?"

"Just say, base. And if you want to acknowledge without saying anything, especially if you have to keep quiet, just click your mic."

Lexi's mic clicked.

"I've got number two. Price here. Hey, base, can I ask if we have any followers?"

"It looks like you're clear. Now, number three, please check in..."

Everyone checked in, confirming their mics were working.

"Alright folks. Your rendezvous is at zero five hundred tomorrow. Find someplace close to there to catch a zed or two. But make sure you are in position before then."

"Base, this is Broadmoor."

"Go ahead, Broadmoor."

"I don't think I thanked you for all that you've done for us..." Her voice cracked a little and it seemed obvious she was tussling with her emotions. "...and for my father. I'm sure Frank and he were proud to serve with you. You're a Godsend, Matt."

"You're welcome, Lexi." Smith cleared his throat.

"Alright, since Broadmoor brought God up. Here's my prayer to each of you...

"May God bless you and keep you... the Lord make his

face shine on you... The Lord turn his face toward you and give you His peace."

"Numbers 6:24-26. My favorite. Ah, this is Moondog. Thank you base."

"Thank you all. Until the operation begins, let's keep radio silence. Have a good night. Tomorrow's a big day."

There were multiple clicks on the radio.

Smith smiled and spun around again in his chair to give himself a commanding view of several scenes outside. He was already enjoying the show. But then when they did what he expected, attempting to set fire to the house, he was beaming.

"Okay, now it's fun," he said to one of his screens.

Faisal

Faisal woke up in the back of a truck with several of his men sitting around him. They were moving.

Hearing voices, he looked up and saw an albino with blue eyes hovering over him. This was not the view he expected when he died. So it was instantly obvious that he had not gone on to Paradise. At least not yet.

"Commander Faisal, can you hear me?" Samir asked. Faisal blinked at the foggy view that shook from their movement. He blinked again and saw more than one Samir.

"Yes, I am alive," Faisal answered. "What has happened?"

"Sir, six of our men are martyrs..." Faisal first thought was that they were the lucky ones. "Many of the infidels escaped for now in two trucks."

Faisal grunted both in anger and pain as his head and shoulder hurt.

"What about... House?"

"We set it ablaze before we left."

"Good... Wait, you said escaped for now?" Faisal's question came out weaker sounding than he wanted.

"Yes, before the trucks had driven off, I had planted a tracking device in one. It was one of the many gifts they had left us from the camp. We are tracking them now."

Faisal wondered but had difficulty asking the question. He just wanted to sleep. Finally, he was able to articulate it. "Where... we going?"

"We're headed to Mount Weather."

Faisal closed his eyes, assuming that when he opened them again, he would either see Allah or his Mahdi Abdul.

Chapter 27

Mount Weather, Virginia

Frank

They arrived at their destination blindfolded and disoriented, which, as Frank knew, was their captors' intent. Still, he was able to gather one important fact.

Based on their length of time in the vehicle, the sound of the SUV's engine, and the cooler temperatures he felt when the driver exited the vehicle, they must have gained a little elevation. Otherwise, he was fresh out of guesses as to where this place was or why they were there.

Senator Chase and he remained quiet for most of the trip from the sheriff's interrogation room to wherever they were now.

A new rush of air flooded in when his door was opened, and a beefy hand plucked him out of the back seat. In the process, his blindfold was nudged up just enough that he could catch a glimpse of his surroundings. It wasn't what he expected.

The sky was a burnt orange color, so the sun had already set. They were parked near several buildings, all of which looked governmental: function with no ornamentation.

He turned his head slightly to the north, trying not to

alert his keepers that he had some limited vision. A giant antenna tower rose up out of sight nearby, with several other buildings in the foreground.

He was led around the back of their vehicle so that he now caught the view east, and another giant tower and several dishes pointed to a valley below. Further around, a building had a FEMA emblem on a sign. Next to this, a placard read, "Communications." Then it struck him.

We are at Mount Weather.

"Come on," insisted someone pushing from behind. Frank didn't resist.

He corrected his head a click forward and saw Chase was in front of him. Further, to his right, back toward the west, was something else he hadn't noticed at first glance... He crooked his neck further to make sure he was seeing it correctly.

Covering most of a large open area, like a sports field, there was what looked like a prefabricated amphitheater, with a center stage, in the middle of which stood...

He had to squint back the fiery light silhouetting it to be sure his eyes were not playing tricks on him. They were not.

Center stage was an elevated structure with half a dozen nooses dangling down from a giant wood beam.

They're gallows.

"Hey, this one can see. Hold up," announced the guy behind Frank. Undisciplined hands grappled with his shoulders, one connecting directly with his week-old bullet wound. A dagger of pain rocketed through his nervous system. His body's friendly reminder that he was still alive, though he was getting mighty tired of those reminders.

Those same hands let go and readjusted his blindfold. Just before his vision was once again concealed, Frank caught one last glimpse.

There were multiple ICA trucks parked in front of the building that appeared to be their destination. Surrounding the building were dozens of ICA soldiers, each carrying a rifle.

"Keep moving," ordered the same voice.

FEMA Communications

Jamal glanced at everyone in the communications center's main room. Most were seated at their assigned stations. Jamal was not only focused on the people, but one specific terminal.

He noted the station number 62. He was familiar with this one, but needed one more confirmation that it was the correct one: he had had his hands on all of these terminals multiple times. He also needed to confirm no one was presently at that station's terminal. If someone was, they might notice what he was about to do. If that happened and he was caught, he would be shot or beheaded.

Finally, he checked that all the workers, most especially his supervisor, were occupied. They were and that meant he had a couple of minutes before anyone noticed he was gone and investigated.

Jamal popped out of his chair and, while attempting to make as little noise as possible, he darted out of the room, hurrying toward a door opposite the main communications center.

He glanced behind to confirm the center's guard was in fact there, but looking away from him, for now.

Slowing just long enough to catch a glimpse out the parking lot facing window, he saw two blindfolded, older-looking men being marched to their brig. He was guessing those were the men Abdul was going to hang tomorrow. But he did not have time to linger.

Once there, Jamal double checked in all directions of the hallway and center entrance before opening the door. He stepped into the darkness and sealed himself inside.

He had been in this room dozens of times and knew it well enough, he could have done this in the dark. With the click of a penlight, he had ample vision to expedite his work while not calling attention to anyone who might walk by.

He opened the dusty panel after locating it right where he remembered. A pre-1960's box of fuses which were never upgraded to breakers even when all the new communication equipment was added in the 1990's. He had witnessed the transformation as a lowly IT student studying at a local American college. He paused.

A sneeze burst from him before he could suppress it.

Better move, he told himself.

All the fuses were numbered to correspond with the station numbers. Finding number 62, he yanked out the fuse, closed the panel door and turned off his pen light.

With any luck, no one would notice until long after tomorrow afternoon, when it would not matter.

He held his breath and listened for any movements outside.

It sounded good.

Jamal opened the door and stepped out into the hallway. At the opening to the center's main room, his supervisor was standing, arms crossed, staring directly at him. Beside him was the center's guard, on the opposite side of the doorway.

Sucking in a breath, Jamal closed the door and walked toward his supervisor.

"*Assalamu alaikum*, sir," Jamal gasped, while attempting to march right by him as if this was part of his normal duties.

"What were you doing in that room?" the man demanded.

Jamal looked up and, fighting his nervousness, he said the first thing which came to mind. "I made a few modifications to the station's grid structure to ensure the modulation of multiple broadcast indices did not overwhelm our available bandwidth tomorrow when we attempt to simulcast radio and television broadcasts on multiple frequencies all at once."

He held his breath after tossing out that completely BS answer of nonsensical gobbledygook. A word salad of technobabble that would have made a Star Trek fan blush. However, he was counting on his supervisor's minimal knowledge about what he or all the other techs did in this center. If his words sounded legitimate enough, and because he had proven himself many times to all his superiors, they should be acceptable enough to pacify this fool.

His supervisor's forehead wrinkled, and he screwed his

eyes into Jamal's, who held as steady as his shaky knees would support, while waiting for a reply.

"Very well, continue."

Jamal returned to his station, noting the time. He did what he was asked to do exactly five minutes early. Just one final act of treason left.

At his terminal, he quickly logged back on and found the secret channel he shared with the only other man he trusted.

As rapidly as he could, knowing his supervisor would appear behind him at any second, he typed, "Done." Then, he closed that window and brought up his overall monitoring window onto his main screen, showing the status of all of FEMA's communication networks at High Point Special Facility.

Heavy footsteps lumbered behind him. After a minute of burdened breathing, his supervisor grunted and plodded away.

Jamal sighed and returned to his normal duties, waiting for the proverbial shit to hit the fan. He would not have to wait long.

Chapter 28

High Point Special Facility, Area B

Travis

As the seconds ground by, Travis was sure that the combination of waiting, and his imagination were going to be the death of him. There was nothing he could do to temper his worst fears.

He paced his storage room, sucking on another protein bar, even though he wasn't hungry.

Think, Travis, think, he coaxed himself.

After confirmation of the existence of a doomsday weapon—which Sal said would kill at least fifty percent of the surviving US population—inside this bunker complex, and that it was going to go off in less than twenty-five hours, he wondered how was he supposed to just wait here and do nothing with this information?

Sal said he would help once Travis found the device's location. Well, he did that...

Now what?

He did what he was tasked to do. So how could he just wait around here until their meeting at six o'clock in the morning? That means he would have to do nothing for the next ten hours, while their certain doom clicked closer by the second. And by six, they'd only have fifteen hours to stop it.

As if his nerves weren't already being stretched past their breaking point from this monumental burden, one that he alone had to bear, they snapped each time another hail of gunfire erupted almost every half hour around this complex.

He gulped at a new realization.

What happens if Sal is not there at their meeting? What if Sal gets caught, what would he do then?

It's not like I can tell anyone: I'm the Ghost.

He stopped pacing, his brain twisting at his newest progression of thought.

Why not? Sal never said don't do anything, only what to do.

That's when he decided to do it.

Going through his steps of self-assessment, he reexamined his knee and elbow padding. Checking his tools first, he then attached the belt he had already modified for his waist size. Finally he put on his gloves.

The Ghost is ready.

Using a chair he'd set up against the back most shelving unit, he paused at the reflective rear of a stored piece of equipment on the third shelf. Its chrome finish was almost mirror-like, giving him a more clear view of his face.

He flashed the only non-black part of his body at the image staring back at him. But he decided his teeth were still dirty too from lack of brushing.

Later. The Ghost has too much work to do.

It took over an hour of monitoring the guards before Travis decided his next course of action.

The most important takeaway: At no time did any of the guards go inside the room with the flashing countdown clock. So, he reasoned that if he could get inside without calling any attention to himself, he should be fine to examine the device completely. If he could do that, maybe he could figure out how to disable it within the next twenty-two plus hours.

With any luck, the hardest part would be not alerting the guards to his presence.

No longer could he do his Ghost Kick, loudly knocking the register out and onto the floor. So he figured out a solution to that too.

From his tool belt, he worked two pliers at opposite ends of each slat, twisting inward, until the slat popped out of the vent register. Taking out four slats gave him a large enough hole for the next step.

When he looked through the tools in his storage room, he'd found a cool right-angle electric screwdriver. It was simple enough to use, but eminently harder when trying to dislodge a screw only by feel. After the first screw popped out and into his hand, the second one was easy.

With the register free, it was effortless for the Ghost to stow it away in the ductwork and slither out as quietly as one would expect from an ethereal being like him. He couldn't help but smile at this thought. Yet, when he turned on his mini flashlight, his smile slid away.

There was nothing in the room he could use to get back up into the vent.

Some ghost…

Well, inspect the device first, he told himself. If he could stop it or find a way to stop it, he could figure a way up and out. After.

When he first heard about the doomsday device from Sal, he assumed it was some sort of bomb, like in thermonuclear or even dirty. He never questioned how a bomb one hundred or more feet under the earth would be able to kill fifty percent of the American population. Until now. And after scrutinizing the device with a flashlight, he understood it even less.

Travis would never claim to be an expert about nuclear devices, but he'd read lots of books about nuclear war and understood the basic engineering of them. At least he knew enough to know this didn't look like any nuclear weapon he'd seen or read about.

The apparatus itself sat in the middle of an otherwise rectangular, empty room. His brain told him it looked like a large air compressor. From the vent wall, a power cord was plugged in and snaked into the back of this thing. That made sense. It was the cylinder on top that seemed odd to him.

What looked like round ducting rose up and connected with what appeared to be another vent register. Under closer inspection, Travis could see the vent register was gone, and the ducting was taped to the register opening. Now he was curious.

No longer convinced it was a bomb—because everything in him told him it didn't make sense—Travis now wondered if it was some sort of chemical deployment device.

Then he caught the symbols.

Right below the count-down display, changing every second, were three clear tubes, each of which appeared plugged into the unit. On each tube was a yellow and black biological hazard symbol.

The meaning of all of this came crashing down at once: this device delivered something biological, which was being pumped directly into the complex's HVAC system and then presumably outside so that everyone inside and out could be exposed to it in such a way that fifty percent or more would die.

Travis bit back the bile in his throat. He never could have imagined that his uncle—or any human, for that matter—could be this monstrous. But none of that mattered. He needed to find out how this device could be disabled.

And he needed to do this in 22 hours, 36 minutes, 14 seconds… 13… 12…

Chapter 29
Stowell, Texas

Grimes

The equipment was different, though it all looked functional. Better even. There were a few pieces of military hardware too, of which he was only vaguely familiar, and a new computer screen to boot. It was all part of the "big surprise" his new and old friends had set up for him.

Grimes turned to face all their gleaming mugs, many of whom he'd just met, but all reflecting back the joy and appreciation he felt.

His new friends from the Texas Irregulars, who freed him and brought him back to Stowell, told him about this on the way. They also told him and Aimes what was going on around their area.

Evidently, after the National Guard unit had arrested Grimes and Aimes and then destroyed their equipment, everything changed.

Military officers and even more non-coms were going AWOL and gathering, often with militia groups, to discuss the next steps they might take against the illegitimate government that was colluding with the ICA terrorist organization.

The US Army Reserve in Beaumont became the gathering point for Southern Texas. It was decided that establishing and strengthening communications among military units and outside sources was primary. Because Grimes' and Aimes' American Freedom Network was down, that was their starting point.

Beginning with the two-meter and Citizen's Band channels, they resurrected AFN's recorded broadcast, adding their own request for military and militia members to come to their Army Reserve unit for further instructions. Everyone else, outside of their area, were directed to Channel 9 on their CBs to get local instructions.

Then they set up the short-wave transceivers and re-supported the antenna tower. Added to this was a thousand-watt amplifier. Though to Grimes, much of this effort at reestablishing their short-wave transmission capabilities seemed less important at this time because of the enemy's ability to jam all of their signals.

The last additions were the two unfamiliar military radio transceivers, from which supposedly new intelligence had been coming in via a source deep inside the government. Grimes hoped one of his new friends would shed some light on this newest revelation.

The room had turned quiet, and Grimes realized that they were waiting for him to say something. But for the first time in his life, he felt unable to speak. He was not only overwhelmed by the outpouring of support from his brothers and sisters in the military, but by civilians he'd only just met. If he were a crying man, he would be balling now.

He beamed a wide grin and then said, "I'm at a loss for words. I really don't know how to thank all of you."

"Our best thanks is that you get back to work," announced an unfamiliar voice at the back of the crowd filling his radio room.

"Make way," said the same voice.

There was a slight murmur from the gathered masses. Slowly, several moved out of the room and in came a young man Grimes didn't know.

"Army Radio Specialist Clinton Stamp, at your service, sir." The young man saluted, and Grimes saluted back.

"Are you responsible for all of this, SPC Stamp?"

"He done all of this, Bob," said Wilbur McCullum, a long-time townie and neighbor he hadn't seen since the terrorist attack. Wilbur was a pain in his backside when he first erected his fifty-foot antenna tower.

Grimes held out a hand, and when firmly shaken by the young man, Grimes said, "Well then, thank you especially. Now, if you could help me figure out some of the military hardware, I'd be greatly appreciative."

Without answering, Stamp moved in front of Grimes, past the complicated-looking military transceiver to the newer Kenwood, and flipped on the switch. Unlike his older tubed unit, which took a couple of minutes to completely warm up, this one flipped on immediately, unleashing a flurry of voices from his speakers.

"Later on the new toys. I wanted to call to your attention to a change, which is huge."

Stamp punched in a frequency and then reached over the monitor and pressed the base mic's button.

"Stamp here. We have the package. Confirm receipt of intel I sent over earlier. Over."

"Message confirmed. Over and out."

Stamp looked up at Grimes and smiled. However,

Grimes didn't understand what had just happened... Then it clicked.

"Where's the jamming signal?" Grimes asked, eyeballing the antenna tower out the window and then the equipment to confirm the 40-meter frequency on the display and then Stamp. It didn't make sense. Any short-wave signal from this location had generated an instant jamming tone from Mount Weather, which overpowered AFN's broadcasts. It was the reason why they had to turn to the HF bands, even though their ranges were so much shorter. But there was no jamming signal now.

"That's correct. I just noticed this before you arrived. I had this confirmed with another Army station at Corpus Christi. We believe the enemy has, for some reason, stopped jamming. Which is why we think you should restart your AFN broadcast while you still can."

Grimes was already ahead of him, parking himself in his wooden chair—rebuilt after being damaged, this time with ample cushions—and he pulled the microphone over to him.

"But before you start, you should know this." Stamp handed Grimes a folded piece of paper.

Grimes opened it up, glanced at it and flashed a look of astonishment at Stamp. "Is this true?"

"It most certainly is. I'll share more with you after your broadcast. You know what you need to do, right?"

"Already ahead of you, son."

Grimes did a one-eighty in his chair, muttering, "I just need Gunny..." He examined the group, expectantly gathered around, listening to everything being said.

From outside in the hallway, there was a little bit of a commotion, followed by, "You don't think I'd miss this?"

Once again, a few people parted and moved into the hallway, so that Gunny, Logan Aimes could come in. He was accompanied by another welcomed surprise, Aimes' wife Susie.

Susie, who had been recovering from a stroke and suffering from Parkinsons, so she was the last person he expected to see, much less helping her husband inside the radio room.

She and Aimes grinned at Grimes, and he returned the smile back. Words weren't necessary.

Aimes pecked Susie on her lips and found the seat next to Grimes. "Don't you think it's time for the revolution to start?"

"Just waiting for my wingman."

Grimes mouthed the frequency to Stamp, who punched it in. The room grew quiet as everyone, including Grimes and Aimes anxiously awaited the next long awaited AFN broadcast.

Grimes punched the mic and began speaking.

Wallace & Porter

"This is AFN, back on the air to tell you, my fellow Americans, that the revolution begins tomorrow."

Several cheers erupted at AFN's newest broadcast.

"Turn it up," Wallace yelled from a seat positioned with others on the altar of what was the First Baptist of Virginia, but now was their operations center.

The speakers squealed and then boomed. "—is now back on the air, but we don't know for how long, so I'm going to make this broadcast brief."

"That's my dad," Porter said. "I can't believe he's still alive." He gleamed at Wallace, who grabbed his hand with hers in an overt display of PDA, something she said she never did.

"Yes, our revolution to take back our country from the terrorists and the fake government will begin tomorrow.

"First to you, all of those in the military or with public authorities who have accepted your illegal orders from this illegitimate government. It is still not too late to join us. I urge you to do this immediately, because by tomorrow it may be too late. If you do not join us, we will consider you the enemy.

"Next, to every able-bodied man or woman out there, we ask you to turn on your CBs to Channel 9 and look for instructions on what to do next.

"There are military units and militias convening as we speak, discussing plans for multiple operations being conducted tomorrow, all to take back our country.

"I cannot say for certain that we will win these battles. In fact, it is likely that we will lose some of them. But I can say this, with certainly. Because we are fighting for the same freedoms that our founding fathers fought for roughly two-hundred and fifty years ago, we will win this war. But we need you if we are to succeed.

"So please gather your weapons, which you've hidden, tune into Channel 9, and find out where you will participate in the next and hopefully final American Revolution."

Before the radio was turned off, a chorus of cheers rang

out from the thousand or so men and woman from all branches of the military and a large contingent of citizens, including many from local militia groups.

Wallace released Porter's hand, and she stood up, holding her hands in the air to silence everyone.

"Can everyone hear me without a microphone?" She hollered.

A dozen yelled back, "We hear you, First Lieutenant."

She found this interesting because she was wearing only an olive T and cargo pants, all donated, but no markings or indication of rank.

"Okay, as some of you know, I am First Lieutenant Lucy Wallace. Like many of you, I was recently arrested for not accepting my illegal orders from this illegitimate government that is colluding with the terrorist enemy who attacked our country. They killed millions, including hundreds of thousands of servicemen and women who were saran gassed at various military bases. Well, all of that stops tomorrow.

"As that broadcast indicated, the revolution to take back America begins tomorrow, and we have a huge roll to play. With several other units around five states, we will be taking the fight directly to the enemy's new home base.

"Tomorrow, we will kill the head terrorist and overturn this illegitimate government based at Mount Weather, Virginia."

July 16th

16:16:58
16:16:57
16:16:56

Chapter 30

Radios All Over The US

"Greetings, America on this day, July 16th, which will be remembered as the beginning of the Second American Revolution.

This is Lieutenant Robert Grimes of the American Freedom Network, broadcasting to you live—for now.

"Before our signal gets jammed again, I am making the following plea... Every able-bodied citizen of the United States, whether civilian or member of any military organization or any public authority, please go to Channel 9 of your CB radio to get local details on how you can serve your country on this special day. We need you now.

"Here is an update...

"Our illegitimate government, which colludes with the terrorists who murdered millions of Americans, is holding mock trials today in multiple locations. They plan to find guilty and make an example of several Americans, including a retired US Army Major who has valiantly fought against the terrorists, and a current US Senator and the legitimate designated survivor, who should be our President. Our illegitimate government plans to hang these individuals in public, under the guise of treason, all to scare you into submitting to their tyranny.

"John Locke, known as being the father of liberalism—back when that meant the belief in liberty and the rights of individuals—famously stated the following:

""Whenever the Legislators endeavor to take away, and destroy the Property of the People, or to reduce them to Slavery under Arbitrary Power, they put themselves into a state of War with the People, who are thereupon absolved from any farther Obedience...By this breach of Trust they forfeit the Power, the People had put into their hands, for quite contrary ends, and it devolves to the People, who have a Right to resume their original Liberty."

"Thomas Jefferson one of our forefathers and the co-author of the Constitution that had bound our republic for two hundred and fifty years until our current government ripped it up, has been attributed as saying, *"If a law is unjust, a man is not only right to disobey it, he is obligated to do so."*

"Well, a government that plans to take away the lives of men and women who stand up for injustices against their citizens is the epitome of unjust law, and each one of us is obligated to make a stand against this. And that time is now.

"As Jefferson famously said in a letter about revolution...

""What country can preserve its liberties if their rulers are not warned from time to time that their people preserve the spirit of resistance? Let them take arms... The tree of liberty must be refreshed from time to time with the blood of patriots and tyrants."

"It's that time, my brothers and sisters of this great country. We need you to join us on this monumental day, when we take back our country from the tyrants and terrorists who have killed millions and have stolen many fundamental rights from our remaining citizens who have survived.

"Their reign ends starting today, this Second Revolution Day.

"Please go to a CB radio and turn to Channel 9 to find local details on how you can serve your country..."

Chapter 31

Just Outside of High Point Special Facility

Lexi

15:10:01

Sleep once again didn't find Lexi, as her imagination raced through every possibility of what might take place today. Adding unnecessary fuel to this nervous fire was a decision that would likely cost her her life. She would tell them right now.

Three-and-a-half miles to the north of their target, they were reviewing a map of High Point Special Facility, or what was commonly called Mount Weather Station. Samuel and Gladys had spread it out over one of Blue Ridge Regional Park's picnic tables.

"If you need me to act as bait, I can do that."

Both Gladys and Samuel gave her surprised looks, but then Gladys nodded and said, "That's not a bad idea. Hopefully it won't come to it."

"I don't like it one bit," announced Samuel. "Putting Lexi within the clutches of that crazy terrorist is a bad idea, no matter how you propose it."

"No, hear me out, Samuel." Lexi put her hand on his.

"We'll follow Smith's and your plan, but if we need to get close to Abdul or to draw him out in the open so that one of us can take a shot, why not?"

"Because you might get hurt in the process," Samuel stated.

Lexi glared at him. "Look. My primary goals are to kill that sonofabitch and rescue Travis and Frank. I do not care what happens to me in the process. I want to live, but if I die ridding this universe once and all of that plague, I will happily give up my life." She really did feel that way.

"Let's call Broadmoor's idea, Plan B and table it for now," Glayds said.

Samuel nodded.

"Bogies headed our way," announced Jonah on their comms, from just north of them.

"This is base. They are friendlies. A Lieutenant Wallace is leading multiple units from the Army, National Guard and Marines. She will go over today's operations plans with you."

"Roger base," said Samuel. "And Price, can you flag them over to us?"

"Will do."

Porter

Wallace and Porter exited their Hummer and were greeted by several people dressed in pricey paramilitary clothing.

"Didn't know BlackStone was part of this op," Porter quipped. "Or should I say, BlackStone's misfits; get a load of Dueling Banjos."

Wallace glanced at the man sporting a ZZ Top beard over a fully equipped M4 and then said, "Smith says they're top level for a militia, and there's a young woman we are supposed to talk to as well."

"Yeah, but how much do we know about this guy, Smith?"

Wallace was about to answer, but then noticed the youngest of the group coming to them. "I'm guessing this is our contact."

"Lieutenant Wallace, I presume," asked the lanky guy, who reminded Porter of a surfer more than contract military.

"Yes, and this is Corporal Grimes," she answered.

"I'm Samuel Horton, but everyone calls me Slim. Grandma, who is my number two," he signaled in her direction. "Moondog, who you passed. And this is Lexi Broadmoor."

"Ahh..." Wallace nodded. "So you're the one Smith says we should meet. I assume that's because you are somehow related to Major Cartwright?"

"That's my godfather," Broadmoor said. "But more likely it's because, my uncle is Abdul Farook, the head MF-ing terrorist, who wants nothing more than to get his grubby hands on me and make me his third wife... But that is something we might be able to use to our advantage." Broadmoor looked over to Samuel, who was giving her a curious look.

Wallace swallowed her words and then nodded. "Well

that's a lot to take in, but you're right it might present us with an additional opportunity—oh, good, you have a map of the facility," she motioned them to the map they had stepped away from to make their introductions.

Another five of Slim's militia, all dressed in new paramilitary gear, wandered in from different points and crowded around the table.

Wallace snatched a red marker, evidently already used on the map, and on the four sides of the map she began writing. First, the number one, circling it, followed by number two, three and finally four. "We have four points of attack against High Point, each led by a different contingent of our military, militia and civilians.

"I am leading Team One, which includes several units of the Army, National Guard and Marines, coming in from the north. Number two is led by one of several seal teams, who have already started the march up the thousand-foot eastern elevation of this mountain. Number three and four are mechanized Army units that will come in from the south and west.

"As you know, our team has been charged to stop the hangings and safeguarding the two men they intend to hang. Then, if we have a shot, to take out Farook.

"Just before the start of the scheduled tribunal, we will enter the facility through the Old Blueridge Rd. Gate here." She pointed at this road on the map. "This should give us easier access than say the main gate. We will wait there until Teams Two through Four engage the enemy. That's when we will strike.

"Slim, my military unit will take both the lead and the post, with your militia unit between us. Together, we will double time it to the temporary tribunal bandstand they've set up here." She drew a box in red on a large open field near one of the several helipads. "Our units are only to engage the enemy if they try to impede us. When we get to the band stand, we will identify and secure Cartwright and Chase."

She glanced at each of the militia members.

"This is where we might meet heavy resistance. Though because this is televised, we also don't believe their troops will chance hitting civilians. For that reason, we also will not fire upon any of them until we are fired upon.

"It is your unit Slim that will go directly to Chase and Cartwright and secure them. My units will be providing support and protection around your perimeter. We will be the shields for Chase and Cartwright, as well as your militia. So you should not have to fire upon anyone, unless it is absolutely necessary. And Slim." She looked directly at him. "This place will be full of civies. So, please no cowboy stuff."

He nodded.

"We will also have drone support, and we have two imbeds inside the facility, who will guide us to Cartwright and Chase to escort them out of the complex. If we get a shot at Abdul during the operation, we will take it. Otherwise, we will assess our chances on the ground.

"Any questions?"

"Yes," Broadmoor jumped in. "Aren't you forgetting my brother, Travis?"

Wallace gave Porter a side glance, before taking a breath and giving Lexi her attention. "Our current intel from inside the bunker is that... Well, that Travis Broadmoor, also referred to as Abdul Aziz by Farook has been... killed in an accident."

Broadmoor expelled a grunt, and moved away from Wallace, as if she had been shot. Her lower lip dropped open and began quivering. She tapped her throat. "Base, come… in," she said, her voice cracking.

"Base, damn it. Come in," she called again, now sounding more firm.

"Base. Yes, Broadmoor," said their comms, and by everyone's reactions, all heard it.

"Did you know about Travis?"

"Lex—" Their signal went silent, but it appeared Lexi was still receiving. Smith must have quieted everyone's but Broadmoor's comms, so that he could have a tough talk with her.

"Noooo," she cried out. "It's not tr… It can't be…" Her hands covered her face and she sobbed. "Why didn't you tell m…"

She turned away from them and sobbed quietly.

Slim started to walk in her direction, but she held up a hand, stopping him.

Wallace turned away from Broadmoor and started to say something, but then Broadmoor shook her head, marched back to the picnic table and stated, "I want into that bunker. I want to verify that my brother is dead."

"Lexi," said the ZZ Top throwback, they called, Moondog. "I'm sorry for overhearing and for your loss. You probably didn't know this, but there's almost seven-hundred thousand square feet of space down in what the Fed's call Area B. And that's a best guess. It would take you hours to search that place if you had 100% access, and I'm guessing the ragheads won't give you full access."

"I agree with Moon…"

"Dog, as in Moondog."

"Right, Moondog is correct," Wallace stated in a pleasant and not her usual dispassionate voice. "It's not about only the size, but the access. You won't be anywhere near the eastern and western entry points. And even if you were, we expect strong resistance at those points. We have to trust that if our intelligence is wrong, that your brother will find his way out."

Broadmoor's shoulders dropped as if led weights were dragging at them. "Fine," she said, "but if you let Uncle Abdul get away, I'm going in myself, and I will kill that *Ibn al Kalb* with my bare hands if I have to." She marched away from the group, garnering a few pats on the shoulder from her fellow militia members.

Chapter 32
Area B, Level E

Abdul

14:50:33

Today was going to be his day, regardless of the insignificant troubles they had experienced.

Sal had not been found yet, but Abdul's Little Mice were watching over him and his other guards were protecting the critical parts of the bunker's infrastructure. So Abdul was not worried. All would work out per Allah's plan.

The only two things that would make this day perfect were if Abdul Aziz were still alive and he could finally have Suhaimah.

After considering himself and his wounds in the mirror, Abdul gave a nod, and his female servants slipped his newest gown over his head. It was created for this very day. A white silk material, interwoven with golden threads and actual gold embellishments around the neck, sleeves and down his front. On his breast were the first few words of *Surah An-Nisa 74: "To anyone who fights in Allah's way, whether killed or victorious, we shall give a great reward."*

He looked himself over, liking its bespoke design, crafted last month in preparation for this very day. It was a perfect way to usher in the new caliphate on television. The world would see him as the new ruler of this land, and all would bow to him.

So many before him attempted to conquer this land, but only he would succeed. Yes, he would be victorious. He felt it and relished this moment when it was all coming together.

His face soured for a second or two. It was still possible that he would not succeed. It was why he set up and deployed the doomsday weapon. This was his insurance that no one would interfere with his plans. It was the reason that he had the device designed to be impossible to disable without him present. This prevented anyone from making an attempt on his life. He was pretty confident that this was the reason why he would succeed.

Americans would rather give up everything out of fear of losing their lives. Whereas he and his followers, knowing rewards awaited each of them even if they failed, had no fear of death.

He felt sure that after the tribunal had concluded and the men were hung for the world to see, he would say a few words to cement his authority, and that was it. All would submit to him then. Only after this would he return to the device's secret location and turn it off.

He had almost thirty minutes to get to the primary elevator, go down one level and turn off the device. Plenty of time.

Of course, if the people didn't comply or attempted to stop his tribunal, he would not stop what had to happen. Either way, he and his followers would earn their reward.

But he chose to believe he would be victorious, allowing

that thought to wander onto his face, even though it stung.

"Are you happy with this, My Mahdi," asked one of his female servants.

He ignored her and let his smile take over. It was his day of victory.

In a few hours, he would have most of what he wanted, and by then, no one could stop him.

Chapter 33

Area B, Level B

Travis

14:48:25

Only a few minutes after six in the morning, Sal finally burst through the locked office door to find Travis waiting for him.

Sal locked the door, grabbed the chair Travis had used as a step stool, and walked over to Travis, who was sitting on the floor, with his back against the room's far wall.

He'd been waiting at this same place for hours, chewing off all nine of his fingernails in the process. Now, he was so tired, he was practically delirious.

"I can't stop it," Travis spat out, followed by tears. "It's impossible to stop this."

"You found the device?"

"And it's going off in less than fifteen hours." Travis stood up so he could face Sal, who remained in his chair. "I know it's biological and not nuclear, but I don't understand how this device, buried underground, could kill fifty percent of the US population."

Travis wiped at his tears with the sleeves of his jumper

and sat. He was too tired to stand.

Sal waited until Travis was still and in his seat before answering. "This device is only one of twelve total devices set up around the country. When this one goes off, sending a biological cloud inside and then up and into the sky, it will infect everyone within twenty miles. Then the cloud will spread out and the infected will infect others. The mortality rate is above seventy percent.

"This device will also communicate the same command to another eleven devices, spread out throughout the US, telling them to do the same thing.

"The infection will spread everywhere across this country and within thirty days, at least half of those alive now will die from this infection."

"So we're all doomed?" Travis asked rhetorically. He already knew the answer.

"Not unless we can figure out how to stop the device."

"Well, you cannot. I looked at everything: disconnecting the power, but there appears to be back-up power; pulling out the biological cannisters, but they are permanently locked in; breaking the cannisters, but that would just spread the contagion early; moving the device, but there is a trigger switch on it that will go off if it is moved even a little; there are other triggers on it, which probably go off if you try to disable it in other ways; and so on. There is only one person who can turn this device off and that's my uncle, Abdul."

"I do not doubt your intelligence, but how can you be sure that only Abdul can disable the device?"

Travis stuck his thumb in the air. "Because only Abdul's thumb print is acceptable to the machine. When I tried to use my thumb print, it threatened to go off if I tried any other thumbprint other than the, 'owner of the device.'" Travis used the forefinger and middle finger of each hand to demonstrate he was quoting what the machine said.

"And we know he's the owner of this machine..."

Travis began tapping the toe of one foot on the ground, eyes now drilled into his knees. He flashed back a reckless look at Sal.

"I just thought of something. One thing didn't make sense, but with what you said, now it does. There's a coaxial cable coming out of the device and going into the ductwork, which best I can guess, goes down to this floor, Level B."

Sal responded quickly, "It must go to the Area B Communications Center, which is about fifty feet from here."

"I wondered if it was something like that. But then you told me about the other devices. So, here's my idea: could you shut down all communications from Mount Weather out? That way, if this thing goes off in fourteen-plus-hours, it cannot communicate with the other eleven?"

Sal got up from his chair, crossed his arms, turned and walked toward the other end of the room.

Travis watched him as he returned, stopping a few inches from where he was seated. "Yes, I can do this. But I may not have to. I think I can stop this device, too."

Travis gave the man with the horrible scars a stern examination. "How could you do this... Unless..."

"Yes, you understand." Sal stuck his thumb in the air and with his other hand acting as if he snatched it, like the missing thumb joke he used to play on his sister. "Seems only fair for his taking one of yours. Consider it my gift to you for all that you have so bravely done."

"But what if you are not successful... Ah, getting his thumb?"

"Then you must leave this place. The rest of this country will be safe from the other devices, but most everyone within twenty miles, or more, will die. Unfortunately, that would include your godfather—who is an excellent warrior—and any others in this area. But that is only if I do not succeed in getting Abdul's thumb."

This time, Travis bounded out of his chair as if he had been sitting on something hot.

"I am happy to see you are leaving now," Sal said.

"I'm not leaving." Travis halted beside Sal. "I'm working on another back-up plan in case you are not successful getting my uncle's thumb. Can you tell me where the instruction manuals are for this place? All government projects like this one have instructions detailing all its functionalities and fail safes. I just need to read what they are and maybe if there is one that would..."

Travis leaned over to Sal's ear. It was probably foolish, but he had this horrible feeling that this place like everywhere else around the bunker was bugged, which was another reason why he could not have all their lives depend on the success of Sal's plan to get Abdul's thumb and take down communications. He had to find a backup.

So he quietly told Sal what he was looking to do.

Sal nodded and agreed that was a good idea and stated that he did not know how to do what Travis was asking.

"So," Travis continued, whispering, "where are the manuals on this place?"

Sal thought about it for a full minute and then responded, "There are a couple of manuals in Abdul's office on Level E. But I do not advise going there, because of his heightened security. And I cannot be sure that he would have what you're searching for.

However, I believe all the manuals you want are in the vault, in the basement, Level G. There is no one there, so you should not have any interference.

Chapter 34
Area B Communications

Saleem Hafeez

14:05:17

At just before 07:00, a man in a worker's blue jumper sauntered up to Area B's Communication Center's two guards, as stealthy as a cat about to pounce on two canaries.

The first guard didn't even see Sal slash him twice, sending him to the floor, writhing and unable to call for help.

The second guard thought the first had slipped. Sal came right at him so quick he couldn't react before it was too late. Sal had him spun around, a bloody knife up against the guard's throat.

In Arabic, Sal whispered, "You will live if you do exactly what I say. Nod your affirmation, brother."

The guard nodded.

"Press the button."

The guard complied, while Sal moved his knife away from the man's throat and pressed its tip against his trapezius so that its presence was known. "Look at the camera and tell Salman it is important to let you in."

The guard spat out a flurry of words, and surprisingly Salman buzzed open the door.

When Sal pushed the guard through the doorway, Salman was in his chair, spinning around to face them. His expression changed from annoyed to surprised.

Salman attempted to spin back around, intending to swing his arm over and onto the center's big alarm button. Sal was already there, clasping onto Salman's arm before he could.

"I would not recommend that, Salman."

"Mr. Hafeez, I thought you were under detention," Salman said, his voice steady and clear. "What can I do for you, sir."

"Look at me Salman," Sal demanded.

Salman repositioned himself so that he could. But Sal spun around and in one quick motion, threw his knife across the room. The second guard had just put his hand on the exit door, intending to leave, but Sal's knife found his back first. The man collapsed to the floor.

"I told him he would live if he followed my exact instructions. Now, it is your turn."

Sal gave Salman his full attention.

"Call Mahdi Abdul and tell him that you have Suhaimah on the phone right now, but he must come to the Communications Center to speak to her.

"Do this now."

Salman nodded and picked up the hardline telephone receiver in front of him, while punching one of dozens of buttons beside the receiver. The button's light turned green.

Sal moved quickly through the partially opened door,

and drug the dead guard inside. Then while keeping his eyes on Salman, who was already speaking to Abdul and repeating the words given him, Sal secured the door.

Salman hung up the phone, as Sal rolled up a chair toward him in a nonchalant manner. Sal sat and drilled his eyes into the man, who remained calm.

"Thank you for not resisting. What did he say?"

"He is coming right now."

"Very good. Next, I want you to shut down all outgoing radio, television and phone communications and data transmissions going out from High Point Special Facility to the rest of the world."

Salman gave Sal a slight head tilt and squint, as if he did not fully understand his clear statement. "I am afraid, Mr. Hafeez." Salman expelled a long breath. "This is simply impossible to do from the Area B Communications Center. This type of thing must be done at the FEMA Communications Center, topside, in Area A."

"So you are telling me that you cannot physically shut down this facility's communications from here; you have to do this from the Area A Communications facility?"

"Yes, that is what I am saying. And if I attempt to ask someone to do this from there, they would have to first get the Mahdi's approval, which we know will not happen."

There was a buzz at the door. Sal swung around to glare at the screen above it, displaying who was outside.

It was Abdul.

And with him were about a dozen guards, along with his Little Mice.

"Let us in Sal. We know you are inside."

Sal spun back around and glowered at Salman, one of

his hands visibly on his resheathed dagger's handle to stress his resolve.

Salman pointed in front and above him...

There, mounted on the ceiling, was a dome-shaped camera... A camera that was connected to the complex's closed circuit television system, which Abdul monitored all the time.

"Sal you cannot escape this time," Abdul instructed the camera above the outside door. "You must let me in, and I promise you that I will show you mercy. Or in ten minutes I will have the door opened and you will feel my wrath.

Sal turned away from the monitor, ignoring what Mahdi Abdul said. He knew he was dead in five minutes and so he better not waste his time. He had two calls to make on his radio: two chances to save the American people from an unnecessary calamity. That was assuming the boy was unsuccessful.

Chapter 35

Area B, Brig

Buck

13:45:29

Buck was just about to rip Marge a new one as she wouldn't shut up with her incessant stories and trips down memory lane, when their door opened, shutting her up instantly. But it wasn't someone he expected.

A psycho midget, who looked like he was shat out hell's anus, appeared inside their doorway. His presence made Marge shriek and Buck hold his breath.

The devil dwarf stopped just long enough to examine each of them, his Frankenstein-like, electrified hair bobbed with each head turn. His eyes were the only flashes of whites coming from a face caked in grime. What were white surgical bandages wrapped around his elbows, knees and feet were so sullied they looked as if they had come off an ancient mummy. But the half-pint's voice was the most surprising.

"You need to leave now," said the familiar voice from what was obviously a child and not a midget.

"You're the Ghost, aren't you?" asked Marge.

Only then did it hit him: the kid from the vent. He nodded his affirmation of this.

"Here, I tried to guess your sizes. Put these on over your clothes," said the diminutive boy.

"What the hell happened to you... Ah Ghost?" asked Buck. The kid had a story, and he wanted to hear why he looked like such a wreck. Buck could even see, under further examination that some of what he thought was grime was dried blood.

"There's no time. Put these on," the kid ordered, holding one blue jumper out to each of them.

Marge took hers and started to wiggle herself into it. Buck grabbed his. "Fu—" he cut himself off before he could utter the word. "What the... hell did they do to you, boy?" Buck asked, pointing at the kid's missing digit.

"Oh my," uttered Marge, as she caught sight of the kid's maimed hand. She zippered up the front of the jumper, accentuating her figure. "How do I look?"

"Too much like a woman," said Ghost, but it'll have to do." He glared at Buck. "Put yours on now, unless you want to stay here until your death in a few hours."

Buck didn't need any more coaxing.

"Are they-they going to... execute us?" Marge stumbled to ask.

"They're going to execute everybody, if you don't let me finish."

"Please continue, Mr. Ghost," Buck cajoled, while he zipped up his jumper.

"Here's how you escape out of Mount Weather—"

"—What? Wait, Ghost. You mean we're at Mount Weather?"

Ghost shook his head and blew out a puff of air before

continuing. "Okay, listen to me and do not interrupt."

They both nodded.

"You are being held captive by a terrorist group called ICA inside Area B, a bunker under Mount Weather, Virginia. They have taken over the country and killed over a million Americans. They control the American government, of which you are only two of the remaining three survivors. In just over thirteen hours, a bioweapon, located two floors up, will go off, sending up an infectious cloud which will kill over half of everyone who comes in contact with it. You need to leave, okay?"

Buck and Marge remained silent. Shell-shocked.

"Okay, you need to wait here for forty minutes. Then, exit this jail, turn left and walk fifty feet to the stairwell. Proceed up to Level A. Exit, turn right and walk to the end, where there should be a crowd of others all waiting for an elevator. Some will be wearing blue uniforms like you. Do not look directly at any of them, especially you, Senator."

Ghost saw Buck's Cub's cap on the bed. "Senator, put that on your head and tuck in your hair. No one can see that you're a woman. In fact, wipe off any lipstick and apply any dirt to your faces to make you look like workers."

"So, at ten this morning, or about forty minutes, you will be part of a group of workers and troops that will be taken up to the East Portal Exit. Once outside, if you see an opportunity to escape, take it. If you cannot, you'll be bussed to a primary area topside. Sneak away there. The worst case is you could remove your blue jumpers and try to blend in with the crowd that will start coming by five tonight.

"But I wouldn't wait around that long. If I were you, I'd

try to get out before the bioweapon goes off and kills everyone here."

Ghost didn't wait for a reply. He turned and proceeded back out the door he'd come in.

"Wait," Marge insisted. "Aren't you going to come with us?"

Ghost turned to face Marge. "Nope, I have work to do. It's up to me to save the world."

He left.

Buck glanced at Marge and Marge back at Buck, before Buck scurried after the kid.

He looked down one hall, toward what looked like an exit, and then the other way, which only had two doors. One clicked closed.

Buck bounded to the door, threw it open, and searched for the light switch. There was a clank-sound at the back of the room, but Buck's eyes couldn't get a fix in the darkroom.

Finally, when he found the light switch, the kid was gone. And there was no sign of him in this storage room.

Perhaps he is a ghost.

Travis

He had a long way to go, so he tried not to think about it, or the two people he tried to save.

It felt somewhat fruitless to even try, and at the end

of explaining it all to them, he wished he had just left them inside their jail cells. But he couldn't when Travis had decided to do what he planned next... Assuming he could do what he planned.

It just felt wrong to let these two die. They didn't do anything. The rest inside this place... he had no problem with them dying.

Before Travis knew it, he had arrived. The middle vent, which shot up into the darkness, to how many levels he didn't know. It also went straight down to his next destination: Level G, the ground floor.

If Sal was correct, he would drop down four floors and head to a vault with all the government manuals describing all of Area B's construction. If it was there, he hoped to find the one about the ventilation system and how it was controlled.

Travis squinted against the darkness, flicking on his flashlight and training it below.

There was a trickling noise that sounded distant. But then its sound disappeared when the blower kicked on.

More important, he could see the floor at the bottom of the HVAC system's vent. Below that was the Level G's hallway.

Travis took a breath and then started to lower himself down, working his feet into the vent's ridges to support his weight.

Slowly, he worked himself down one level. Then another. But when he lost his footing and then a handhold, he slipped.

It was so quick.

He was flying.

His stop was sudden. He slammed against a metal vent

at the bottom. Then he was flying again.

This time he hit something solid and unyielding.

He was staring straight up and saw his flashlight roll out, drop and hit him in the shoulder, where it bounced away.

Surprisingly that didn't hurt.

He tilted his head toward the flashlight and saw it float and then sink... In water.

When the light blinked out. So did he.

Chapter 36

Stowell, Texas

Lieutenant Grimes

13:42:54

One of the two encrypted military radios sounded off and ARS Stamp flew into the room from Grimes' guest bedroom.

"Good afternoon," Stamp said, his voice as sharp as if he just had a cup of coffee, even though the kid was snoring just moments ago.

"Sleep well?" Grimes asked.

"Oh, man. Two hours' rack time. Just what the doctor ordered. Thanks," Stamp said, while maneuvering around Grimes' desk, to the small seat in front of the encrypted gear. He put on his headset and tapped in his code, mumbling something to Grimes that wasn't heard.

So far, Stamp had been rather short on details about his sources. Only that he had a few pretty high up in the government and at least one source inside Farook's ICA group.

"Yes, I'm here," Stamp told his headset.

He nodded, as if whomever he was talking to could see

his affirmations.

"No, I haven't heard from my source yet." Again he gave a nod.

"Okay, yes. But I'm trying to be careful, because my source is under close scrutiny. And I—" He halted mid-sentence, finishing with another nod.

Stamp's shoulders sunk a little.

"Okay. I'll contact him right away and I'll update you then, sir. Stamp, out."

He coded something else into the keypad with one hand, simultaneously pulling out a standard keyboard on a sliding shelf. With a forefinger from each hand, he pecked out a message, which appeared on the radio's screen.

He then uttered a small sigh. While keeping his eyes glued to the screen—probably for a response. He huffed under his breath, "Come on, chime in."

Area A Communications

Jamal

Once again, his contact sent him a private encoded message, generating a red dot by a Messages icon on his screen. Jamal did not dare to open it.

His supervisor's shadow passed before him. The man's clumsy footsteps shuffled past, on his way to the bank of terminals manned by most of their comms team.

The message light flashed again, indicating another transmission was sent by his source.

Jamal waited and was about to open his coded messages when his hand-held radio pinged. The volume was at its lowest setting, but it was still far too loud.

Unlike the teletype transmissions, which he could read on a screen, this was a voice transmission. And because his source could not wait, Jamal decided to risk it.

He glanced over to his supervisor, who was now on the other side of the room and engaged with another technician.

It was now or never, he thought.

Jamal slipped out of his chair and soft shoed his way toward the center's exit.

As if on cue, his supervisor's head popped up and, like a beam from a flashlight, both eyes were directed right at him. Jamal mouthed the word, "bathroom" and pointed in the direction of the facility's restrooms.

Although this was his destination, his gestures were not exaggerated as his stomach was turning somersaults from all of this cloak and dagger stuff.

Again the radio beeped, while he was striding to the men's room. He answered with a "Hold on," as he pushed through the door and did a quick check of the stalls to make sure he was alone.

He was.

"Yes," he said, putting the radio to his ear.

"Forgive me for the direct call," Saleem Hafeez said. There was no one else who called this private channel, so there was no need for identifications, especially on the chance that someone may overhear. "I need you to disable all communications going out of High Point Special Facility, whether they are radio, television, or data. I do not have time to talk, because I'm about to be arrested."

Jamal took a quick breath and thought about his words before swiftly responding. "I am sorry, but that is impossible. Just stopping the jamming terminal was a big enough risk. But stopping all communications, if I could do it, would alert everyone. There is no way I could get away with it quietly."

He had hoped that would be the end of it, but Saleem continued, "I am sorry to ask you this, as you have been so loyal to me and our cause. But I need you to stop all outgoing communications from this facility. Mahdi Abdul intends to set off a bioweapon which will kill everyone here. I was unable to stop this. But if communications are not stopped here, at least fifty percent of the remaining US population will also die. If we stop communications, we can save most everyone else. Either way, you and I and everyone here will die today. But you must do everything you are able to save millions more, many of them innocents."

Jamal's response was immediate. "Yes, sir. I will do my best, though I will probably be unsuccessful, as there is no way to do this without alerting everyone."

He was surprised at how quickly he accepted his death sentence.

"Thank you for your sacrifice," Saleem told him.

The radio went silent, and Jamal turned it all the way off. He stood on top of the commode and slipped the radio up and through one of the ceiling's hanging tiles, depositing it up above. It was where he also hid a satellite phone, he had used twice to communicate to a CIA man he'd been feeding information.

The easiest thing would be to call the CIA and have them bomb the center, but that probably wouldn't work. He would have to do something more direct.

Stepping down and pacing himself toward the exit, Jamal thought about his options. There was only one.

His quick plan was to steal the weapon from the guard posted at their door. All he knew about hand-to-hand combat, he learned from the movies. But maybe today he'd get lucky. After all, the guard wouldn't expect an attack by one of their nerdy techs.

This was his only choice, because he would need a weapon if he were going to force everyone at the center to stand back while he shut down all communications systems. Then he would use that weapon to destroy the five or so primary terminals that controlled all outgoing communications. But first, he had to take the guard's rifle.

Jamal held at the bathroom door, allowing his mind to go through every possibility of what might, and probably would go wrong from his efforts. Just getting the rifle away from the guard seemed an impossible task.

"I am dead anyway, so just do it, Jamal," he urged himself.

He yanked open the door and rushed through, head down, thinking about his first move, then the next, then—

Jamal stopped and looked up.

The entrance guard was right there in front of him. So was his supervisor and several other guards. All the guards had their guns pointed at him.

Somehow, they caught him before he did anything.

For just a fleeting moment, Jamal considered rushing the closest gunman. Maybe they'd miss him with their first volley, while he overpowers the one, getting his gun...

Instead, he gave up, thrusting his arms into the air.

"I always knew you were a traitor," his supervisor stated with a pretentious smirk.

Chapter 37

Area B Communications

Saleem Hafeez

13:40:40

Sal was almost out of options. He held out a small sliver of hope that Jamal would have an answer. But as Jamal had said, there was no real way he could shut down communications, before being stopped. Sal had one option left, and it too was a long shot.

He entered the frequency to the other private channel he used and pressed the call button and asked, "Are you available?"

While waiting for an answer, he shot a glance at the viewing screen above the door. Abdul was no longer visible and there were only a few guards there now, with their backs to the door.

General Metzler answered. "Can't talk," he said in a low voice.

"Alright," Sal responded. "Can you listen then?"

Metzler clicked his radio twice, indicating he could. Sal guessed he must be with others in a meeting, or that others were close by so Metzler could not talk out loud.

Sal described in as few words as possible what the problem was and what he hoped Metzler could do. He knew Metzler couldn't answer back. So, Sal signed off and turned off his radio.

He gave another glance at the screen above the door, half expecting Abdul's guards to be breaking it down as it was long past his five-minute deadline. What he saw instead was completely unexpected.

General Metzler

Metzler turned off his radio and slipped it into his briefcase, next to his useless Sat phone. He sat down hard and glanced at the others and then the clock on the wall. With each tick of its second hand, he felt the weight of the world build up on his shoulders. All he wanted to do was keep his family safe and live an easy life, which was why he went along with Meer; why he always went along. But if what Hafeez had told him was to be trusted, the fate of most United States citizens might be entirely up to him.

It was only a few days ago that he even knew of Saleem Hafeez's existence. His radio chirped and Hafeez contacted him, asking him to communicate on a private channel. Once there, Hafeez said he was aware that Metzler had been conspiring with others against Meer. He said only that Metzler needed to be more careful. When Metzler heard that Hafeez, Farook's formally trusted soldier, was arrested and about to be executed for treason, Metzler didn't expect to hear from the man again. Now this?

Hafeez's statement sounded credible based on Farook's previous bioweapon threat. When Meer so easily discounted its existence, Metzler thought there was more to the threat. Then there was Farook's explosion of anger upon hearing Hafeez was able to escape. Hafeez also told Metzler other details he knew, including that Metzler was able to communicate with someone from outside the bunker. This was why Hafeez was reaching out to him: to use Metzler's contact to stop HPSF's communications to the multiple bioweapons around the US, all set to go off at the same time.

Because Hafeez failed, Metzler was their only hope to stop High Point from communicating to other weapons around the United States at twenty-one-hundred hours.

He wished he could have asked Hafeez more questions, but others were listening and would hear his side, and he just didn't trust any of them.

Metzler wiped away a bead of sweat with a wrist. He took off his jacket and set it beside him on the empty chair holding his briefcase.

This was unfamiliar territory for him, a man who never took off his bespoke suit in public nor took any benevolent action. He was choosing now, after a long and selfish life, to wear the suit of a hero. It was more uncomfortable than a new pair of shoes. But there was no one else.

What was needed of him could not be any clearer: he had to get hold of his contact and tell him to shut down communications from this complex, otherwise most of the US population dies.

Metzler's man in Virginia had just told him of a massive military operation to reacquire High Point Special Facility in a matter of hours. Surely they could find a way to take down this facility's communications at the same time. There was only one way he could think to make contact.

The problem was Metzler's Sat phone did not work from anywhere in Area B. Getting outside was now impossible as he, the rest of the Joint Chiefs and Cabinet were sequestered under lock and key until sometime after nineteen-hundred hours, when the East Portal gate was scheduled to open again as it did every day, twice per day. Only then would he and the others be escorted out of the bunker and brought topside, where they would be taken to the tribunal. That would be his only opportunity to make his call, assuming he could get away from the others.

Nineteen-hundred hours was therefore the earliest he could attempt to make that call. Until then, he would have to wait... for almost thirteen hours to pass.

He glared at the clock, watching each second tick by slower than the previous one.

Saleem Hafeez

They were gone. No Abdul. No guards. No one was outside the door.

Sal paced over toward the exit, thinking he was not

seeing this correctly. But when he was directly below the monitor, he studied the screen and there was no one. This was something he had not counted on.

He assumed Abdul and his men would break in and then arrest him or shoot him on the spot. But there was no reason for their disappearance. Unless it was a trick.

Just then he remembered something Abdul had said about this room and the Presidential Bunker: they were both nearly impregnable.

Perhaps they could not break in as easily as I had thought.

And that meant it was a trap. Abdul's guards were probably waiting just outside the door, ready to spring when he left.

Sal picked up both guard's weapons and pointed one of them at Salman. "Okay, you are coming with me."

Salman had been watching from his seat the whole time and now surprised, he rose up and out of his chair, reluctantly walking over.

"You are not going to shoot me, are you Saleem?"

"No. Just keep following my orders and I will release you. Now open the door, step outside it and tell me what you see."

Salman thought about it for a moment, before pressing the door lock release button. It buzzed and clicked, indicating the lock was disengaged.

He turned the doorknob and pushed, but the door barely moved. Again, he tried, only this time he used both hands and grunted while pushing. The door moved only a millimeter or two. Salman gave Sal a perplexed look.

"It will not open," he said and stepped away.

Sal motioned for him to get away from the door, so that he could try.

The same thing. It was as if something big was blocking the door.

"They have left us in here to die," said Salman.

Sal feared he was correct.

Chapter 38

HPSF Emergency Operations Center

Main Entrance

2:57:07

The first buses arrived just after six in the afternoon.

They were coming to Mount Weather for a variety of reasons: some actually wanted to see the executions; many were there for the free medical care, as some needed medicine or treatment badly; but all came for their promised allotment of one month's worth of food. To receive this, they only needed to attend the tribunal and hangings.

They had started lining up as soon as it was announced on television and radio hours earlier. There were multiple pick-up points given, including one as far as Pittsburgh.

Abdul did not want to take any chances at making the crowd look big, so he arranged for earlier than planned pick ups at all the locations. Image was going to be most important for this event.

The hundred-fifty or so people were directed off their buses and led to a temporary facility, where they were inspected again for weapons and any other contraband.

Some of the better-looking ones were cleaned up and given new clothes as they were going to be placed in plain view of the television cameras. The rest would be placed where only the broad view cameras would see them in the distance. Some looked so awful, they were rejected and put back on the bus, to be discarded like they would the trash. Everything, down to how they were organized in their chairs, was prepared for its presentation.

Almost two hours before the tribunal was set to begin, the first few members of the selected audience were placed in their seats. There was nothing for them to do but sit and wait, so they began to talk to each other.

Metzler

An hour earlier than what was told to them, the door opened, and they were ushered out into the hallway.

"Where are you taking us?" Metzler asked. One of his many worries was that Farook was going to execute them anyway.

"You are going to your seats at the tribunal now," the guard said, while pointing down the hallway toward the elevator.

"But the tribunal is not scheduled for two more hours," stated General Howard, the Chief of Space Operations. That man had been complaining to anyone who would listen, for the past several hours, about having to sit and wait during their incarceration.

The others mumbled their disquiet about being moved early. Perhaps they, too, were worried about their fate.

Metzler was ecstatic. This was his chance to get a call out.

"You," said one of the guards to Metzler. "Leave your case here. You must not bring anything with you."

Metzler was already prepared for this, having snuck the bulky Sat phone and smaller radio into the inside pockets of his suit jacket. "Okay," he said, dropping his case in the hallway without slowing, as they all continued their forced march toward the elevator.

Once there, they ascended four floors and exited the long tunnel leading out of what was known as the East Side Portal, on the far eastern side of HPSF.

He had exited and entered this doorway multiple times over the last several days as he preferred the accommodations topside over the meager accommodations in Area B. And yet, each time he walked through the tunnel, he couldn't help but respect the engineering that went into this place.

Dug out during the Cold War, this was one of two entrances to the underground bunkers, or Area B. The east entrance was the one primarily used to house the President and other government officials in the event of an enemy attack to ensure a continuity of government.

Back then, they were worried about Soviet Empire aggression. This time, it was a well organized terrorist group, originally attempting to create its own Islamic empire on US soil. Metzler always suspected something like this would happen. But what was worse than this, or the puppet US Government they installed, was that the ICA's leader was demented enough that he planned a failsafe doomsday device to kill many more if he didn't get what he wanted.

It seemed crazy to not only build such a device, but to activate it so that it would go off only if he didn't stop it himself, and only after he got what he wanted.

Metzler passed a couple of guards who were speaking Arabic. His Arabic was rusty as hell, but he understood enough of their words to decipher what was being said: all their forces were returning to Mount Weather right now.

Panic struck Metzler. Had Farook found out about their plans to invade? He'd communicate this to Smith, too.

It was now more incumbent upon Metzler to make contact. Everything was happening all at once, and he needed to find a way to use his satellite phone immediately.

Now in the sunlight, the surviving Joint Chiefs and Cabinet members were directed out of the East Portal entrance to a bus waiting for them a dozen yards away. This was his opportunity.

There was no way to run for it, as there were several guards following behind him. He would lie and improvise. It was something he'd done quite well his whole career.

Metzler halted and grabbed his crotch. Flashing as much panic as he could muster on his face, he said to the nearest guard, who was already glaring at him for stopping, "Damned prostate. I need to use the head; to take a piss. I'll be quick." Metzler pointed to a bank of porta johns set up near the entrance. Without waiting for a response, he dashed toward the closest one.

Braced for the possibility of getting shot in the back, he winced with every step. Thankfully it didn't happen.

Once the portajohn's resin door was latched behind him, he yanked out the Sat phone from his pocket and dialed his number.

Smith answered immediately.

In as low a voice as he could muster, but loud enough to be heard over the guard yelling outside, Metzler stated, "We have a big problem."

Chapter 39

Just Outside HPSF

Lexi

2:57:05

"Heads up everyone," announced Smith's familiar voice over their comms. They had been waiting for their "Go!" command, hoping it was now coming early.

"ICA troops are currently advancing to Mount Weather from all points. As had been reported earlier, most are driving older model US Army trucks. One convoy is only a mile from your current location, closing in fast."

"Copy, base," Slim said, almost whispering.

"What does this mean for us?" Lexi asked. She remained hunkered down with the rest of their unit of almost one hundred, spread out, only a few meters away from the northern entrance to Mount Weather.

The Corporal calling himself Porter leaned into her. "Assuming they're not wise to our op, we stick to plan and enter in fifteen."

Lieutenant Wallace was signaling for Porter's attention and when he looked her way, she mouthed "spread the word," while making a twirling motion with her finger.

Porter gave a thumbs up and walked toward the closest of their team, keeping low. He proceeded from group to group, pointing their attention north and warning them to watch and listen for incoming ICA troops.

Lexi could already hear the rumbling sounds of large truck engines and heavy tires coming closer. Everyone could, their heads at once turning in that direction.

"Attention all teams," announced their comms. "I have just received new intelligence from a source inside the new government which confirms what our drones are showing: ICA has recalled all of their forces. We do not know if this is in response to our planned attack or it was done for some other reason. I have additional intel to share with each team. Please hold."

There was a pause as several of their team members mumbled something about this latest news. "Quiet," Wallace demanded.

"Attention Team One, especially you, Broadmoor," Smith said, apparently speaking to just their team members who were connected to him. "I have more unsettling news, which directly concerns your team and a change in our mission.

"My source has confirmed that Farook set up a bioweapon underground that is set to go off if he doesn't disable it by twenty-one-hundred hours. If this weapon goes off, it will kill most everyone there on and around Mount Weather and across the US. My source says at least half of all Americans who survived the first attack will die.

"Your new mission is to find and disable this weapon at all costs. To do this, I am sending you to the East Portal of the facility. You will advance there on foot immediately, meeting up just east of the helipad, where one or more Seal Teams are already on location and will be waiting for you.

"Team Leader, Wallace will choose seven members total from your team, in addition to her and Broadmoor, to go into Area B, led by a Seal Team. The remainder of Teams One and Two will provide support for your entry. You will meet resistance; we just don't know how much at this time. Additionally, you will not have comms with base nor anyone outside of Area B during your op.

"Broadmoor, as you had suggested earlier, you may need to use your relationship with Farook to convince him to stop this thing. I don't think I need to tell you how important this is. And..."

The line remained open, but Smith had stopped speaking.

"... Lexi. It's your brother. He is still alive and trying from inside the bunker to stop this weapon. None of Farook's men know that he's alive."

Faisal

Faisal watched the American dogs from the militia at a distance, trying not to move his head much. Samir had him propped up in the truck bed, as his other men were spread out watching the people they had been tracking since yesterday. If only he could stay alive long enough to reap his vengeance.

He knew he was dying, as he couldn't stop shaking nor halt his nausea. His concussion was bad. But as long as they didn't have to wait much longer, they would all get their chance to strike.

They had lost the militia at first, searching all night until his men found some of them sleeping in a campground, and now with their military babysitters. Because there were too many and they were too spread out to do anything successfully, they waited.

When the militia dogs and their babysitters began to move toward the entrance of Mahdi Abdul's headquarters, he assumed they were planning a sneak attack. He also suspected there was a specific reason why they had waited so long before advancing toward the entrance.

A plan started to form.

Faisal figured when the Americans started their advance into the facility, his men would charge them from their flank. This would alert the Mahdi's troops, who would come and stop the American's frontal assault. Then Faisal's men would continue to fire from behind, killing them all.

"Our attack will come any minute, my brothers," he assured his men.

But then the Americans changed everything.

Before Faisal and his men could attack, their targets moved east.

Once again, he would have to wait for their attack. If he did not die first.

Chapter 40

Outside East Portal

Lexi

2:42:38

Their destination looked different than what she had thought. She had seen Mount Weather on a post-apocalyptic TV show once, and the entrance depicted on the show was like a huge bank vault door. In front of them appeared to be plain-looking home with a massive RV garage to its right side and a series of porta potties nearby, as part of a construction project. The RV garage door was open, but she couldn't see inside further than a few feet.

Unfortunately for them, there was a lot of activity. Scores of people paraded out, while others paraded in, including hundreds of ICA soldiers who had just arrived in the convoy they had heard minutes ago.

"Hey," Lexi said to Porter, who seemed to be looking out for her as much as Slim did. "Did you notice that all of those entering are wearing ICA uniforms or traditional Muslim garments and those exiting are not?"

"You know, Broadmoor is right about that," Porter said.

"What do you make of—"

"Regardless," Wallace cut him off. "Commander Thomas of Seal Team 8 just told me to be ready for their signal to move.

"Let's line up, starting with Grimes, Broadmoor and Slim. Then, Price, Sparks, Grandma, and finally Styles. We will be surrounded by sixteen of the finest fighters, whose job it will be to get us into Area B with stealth.

"That means, you will not have to fire your weapons, unless it is absolutely necessary. Any questions?"

There were none.

Lexi wanted to ask Wallace or Porter, both of whom knew combat, if it was weird not to be nervous. She really wasn't, and she didn't know why.

It was only a few seconds later—it felt much longer—when Commander Thomas signaled them forward.

As all of them hurried across the parallel road, Lexi realized that the television's portrayals she'd seen of Seal Teams did not do these sixteen men and women justice. They were as silent as ghosts. Only the members of Team One made noises from the scuffling of their shoes or clicking of their gear. They double-timed it over a green stretch of grass and bushes, and then bisected a helipad to the left of a parking area.

Only after clearing the helipad did the Seals have to use their weapons, quietly dispatching one after another of their enemy, before they could fire off a shot.

A loud boom beside them drew all of their attention, as one of the few ICA guards had raised a rifle. He was struck down before he could take aim at their group, but still squeezed off a shot. This alerted everyone.

Several more rifle cracks rang out from a couple of points in front of them, all directed at them. When one of their members near Lexi grunted and stutter-stepped before regaining his stride, Lexi's breaths became rapid.

From around the corner of the house-like building, an ICA soldier ran toward them, his rifle pointed in their direction. Lexi feared no one else saw the man, as they were directing their fire in front and to their right sides. She pointed her M4 at the man, its optics instantly painting a dot on him, all while she attempted to maintain her pace. When the man fired, she reacted. Several bursts erupted from her weapon and the soldier fell. She took her finger off the trigger and pointed her rifle upward, so she didn't accidentally shoot one of her team members.

"Good shot, Broadmoor," Gladys huffed from behind.

As they entered the garage entrance, Lexi turned her head to look behind her and caught a glimpse of another convoy arriving on the road they'd just crossed. It's soldiers already emptying out the back and running in their direction.

Before she could turn around, she ran into Wallace, who had stopped in front of her.

There was no time for apologies, as volleys of gunfire sounded from their front and back, halting them all in place.

"Advance," yelled the Commander.

They continued their run forward through a tunnel, concentrating their fire in that direction. When they'd first entered, it appeared dark, but as their eyes adjusted, everything was visible, including the dead ICA soldiers who had been firing at them.

In the thirty seconds it took for them to get to the

elevator doors, which were already opened, the soldiers from the convoy had already entered the tunnel, firing their AKs at them.

"Bob, ten-second charge," the Commander stated as calmly as he might say, "Bob, get ten coffees."

Lexi assumed the man who threw a bag out of the elevator toward the oncoming soldiers was Bob. The elevator doors slid closed, cutting off the deafening sounds of gunfire.

They descended, although a lot slower than Lexi would have guessed. All her team members were heaving, except Wallace and Porter. The Seal Team members barely seemed winded. The lone exception was a tall East-Indian, who was holding his side. A small trickle of blood leaked out of his fingers.

Lexi had been mentally counting, and when she hit eleven, she cringed just as the elevator shook from a throaty boom above.

All the Seal Team members had taken a knee and were pointing at what she quickly recognized was another door on the wall to the right of where they'd entered. Each of her team members had followed, taking a knee as well, their weapons pointed and ready.

Although out of breath, Lexi felt fine. She wondered what they were going to do about the injured man, who showed little sign of discomfort. He simply kept pressure on his wound with one hand and aimed his rifle with the other.

When the bunker entrance opened, several of them fired their silenced weapons. But she couldn't see at what or at whom they were firing.

There was no return fire, nor a second volley by them.

This was a surprise, because at least several hundred soldiers went inside the tunnel, and they only encountered maybe two dozen of them.

When Lexi tilted her head so she could take in some of the long corridor in front of them, there were only five bodies. She couldn't help but wonder, *where were the others?*

Abdul

A deep boom reverberated in his head and body, followed by an alarm ringing in his ears. Abdul had been napping in his gold-threaded thobe when his door banged open, and his Little Mice scurried inside. Abdul ignored them and immediately glanced over the feeds of the complex. But he didn't see anything to indicate something had happened. He wondered if he overslept and they were waking him. "What is it?" he barked.

"It's an attack on top. We came to get you to somewhere safe," said the littlest mouse with a high-pitched voice.

"Nonsense. How could I not be safe with you around?" He was in a great mood, despite their interruption. "Besides, there is no place better protected than this bunker. Tell me what has happened."

"We don't know, but there was an explosion at the top of the lift," squeaked Littlest Mouse. "It does not function now."

Abdul turned away from them and once again faced his television screen. He pulled up the video feeds for each of the floors by the eastern elevator and searched for evidence.

On Level E, his level, there were hundreds of his troops jamming the halls and crowding around the elevator. Same on Level D. Level C was quiet. Level B had what he guessed were a few of the exiting Americans waiting for the elevator.

He skipped ahead and attempted to look at the topside view, labeled East Portal Tunnel 1, but it was black, as if there was no feed. East Portal Tunnel 2, which was pointed in the other direction from the entrance, showed another story.

Debris was scattered everywhere, carpeted with large splashes of sunlight. His eyes then resolved that the roof was partially caved in... "Maybe the blast I heard was real, after all," he mused under his breath.

"What, Sir?" asked another Little Mouse.

Abdul ignored him.

It occurred to him that he had skipped Level A. So, he opened this view and immediately saw something peculiar.

Zooming in at one-hundred percent, he could see something that did not belong. Or someone and definitively military.

He manhandled the remote and punched the buttons, which gave him several views of that Level: more than just the one pointed at the elevator.

Several of his guards, who were protecting the device, were down. They looked dead.

Abdul exploded out of his chair.

He punched in the next set of frames, scrolling through image after image to find the one he wanted. Then he saw it.

Several men and women were in the protected room, surrounding his device. They were inspecting it; talking about it to each other...

Abdul turned up the volume to the camera's microphone.

"It cannot be disabled without setting it off," said one man, dressed like the one he had just seen by the elevator.

"I'm looking for options, people," said a woman, who seemed to be in charge.

Abdul huffed his scorn.

"Maybe we should find Travis," said a female voice. "He might know something—"

Abdul dropped the remote and ran out of his office, his Little Mice trying to, but unable to keep up with him.

Chapter 41

Lieutenant Wallace

2:20:15

"Where are you going, ma'am?" asked the Seal Team commander.

Wallace was half out the door, with the rest of her team following. She halted and turned. "I want to tell base that this thing cannot be turned off and the only way I can do that is to either go topside, via the West Portal elevator, which I'm guessing will be protected by a lot more terrorists, or I use their Area B Communications Center, one level down from us, to get word out to base. You got us in; let me do my job."

"Carter," announced the commander, "take five with you and assist the Lieutenant.

"Yes, Sir," said Carter, who signaled five others from their team to follow.

Although Wallace appreciated the Seal Team, she wanted to keep this simple. The last thing she wanted to do was get into a shootout against several hundred terrorists in this concrete coffin. But she relented, because they were running against the clock.

"Fine. Everyone follow me, on the double. Carter, please have some of your men cover our flank."

She raced out of the room and down the hallway without waiting for his answer.

Abdul

He could not believe what he heard and saw. He only could see her back. But that voice was none other than his Suhaimah.

"I am coming my, Shuhaimah," he hollered at the slow elevator, ascending one agonizing floor after another.

His Little Mice were crowded around him, not understanding what he was doing or why, but at least they were silent now. He warned the next man who spoke without being spoken to would be shot.

He just could not believe that his Suhaimah came to him finally, and after all of this time. He did not even mind that these interlopers attacked his bunker, killed many of his men and were trying to mess up his plans: they brought his Suhaimah to him and that was all that mattered right now.

He really believed that Allah was steering him on the correct path, as everything that mattered was going to plan.

Finally, the elevator stopped at Level A. He couldn't wait

for the doors to open.

Lexi

It was obvious to Lexi that Wallace was in superb shape, as everyone had difficulty keeping up with her as she raced down a stairwell, midway through the Level A hallway, and then out, to the door with a placard that read, Communications. She held up.

"What do you make of this?" Wallace asked Porter. He was also breathing heavy, but not as much as Lexi and the other Team One members.

"It looks like a door jammer of some sort," Porter said, as his fingers were already on it, untwisting the butterfly screw at the top of the red device.

"Is that wise, ma'am?" asked Carter, who also wasn't winded. "Perhaps there's a reason why they wanted to lock this door."

Porter halted and glanced at Wallace. She waved her hand at him, and he continued.

"Most likely," Wallace replied. "It was Farook's people who did this. And that means whomever is on the other side of that door is probably a friendly. Besides, we need in there to use their equipment, now."

"Got it," Porter announced. He pulled the device out from the bottom of the door. "Ready?" he asked.

"Do it."

The door buzzed before he touched the door handle. He turned the knob and opened the door so the others could enter.

"Don't shoot," announced a man inside. "I am on your side."

His voice sounded familiar, but Lexi didn't know how that could be possible, as she had never been in this bunker before.

"Praise Allah, you are here," the man said. "But we have little time to waste, we need—"

"Hold on there," Wallace stated, as she walked through the door, aiming her rifle at a man with his hands up. Behind him was another man, hands also raised. Two AK rifles were on the floor beside them.

"Step away from those rifles and the communication equipment. Then we'll talk." Wallace motioned with her rifle for the men to move to Wallace's right.

"I've got two dead tangos," announced one of the Seal Team soldiers. He was leaning down, feeling the pulses of two men who were lined up on the floor, off on their left.

"Those were Abdul Farook's men. I had to kill them, or they would have killed me," said the man, whose voice and demeanor reminded her of someone. She just couldn't place him.

"The equipment won't work for you," said the other man. "After Mahdi Abdul locked us in, the main communications center topside must have jammed our ability to communicate outside of this bunker."

"I am afraid we don't have a lot of time for chatter," the familiar man said.

Then it struck her, and a lightning bolt of shivers shot

down her spine. She backed further away from him in utter revulsion. “It’s you!” She pointed an accusatory finger at him.

“Hello Suhaimah or I would imagine you prefer, Lexi,” he said, his voice calm and reassuring.

While she was backing away, Slim moved in front of her, putting himself in between them.

“My name is Saleem Hafeez, though Lexi knows me as—”

“Sal,” she said in a broken voice. “You’re a murderer and follower of my uncle.” She stomped around Slim, her anger giving her strength now, and again pointed her finger at him.

“I am also a traitor to your uncle, because I would not go along with his plan to murder more innocent lives. And if you do not let me go, millions more will die.”

“You know about the device?” Carter asked.

“Yes, of course. I am the one who told General Metzler, the current Chief of Staff of the Army, who then reported it to your Bookeater. At least I hope he did by now. I suspect you are here because of the report from your Bookeater—odd name is it not, even for an American?”

“So, you know that the device cannot be disabled, except by someone’s fingerprint?” Porter asked.

“It’s Abdul’s, isn’t it?” Lexi asked.

“Yes, and it is his thumbprint. But that is why I need to leave now: I intend to kill Abdul Farook and take his thumb so I can use it to turn off the device.” Sal started to walk toward the door, giving a sly smile at Lexi. His dark eyes connecting with hers.

She pointed her rifle at him. “Stop!” she screamed. “You tried to turn my brother into a monster. You...”

"In fact, your brother freed me from my execution. Last I saw him, he was somewhere in the complex, trying to find a solution to save us all. Remarkable young man."

Surprised, especially at this revelation, Lexi asked, "Do you know where he is?"

"I know where he went. I have been locked in here ever since." Sal continued toward the door.

"Where did he go?" Lexi lowered her rifle.

"He went to the records vault, on Level G. But—"

Lexi turned in front of Sal and ran for the door. She was going to find Travis herself.

Ignoring the multiple pleas from her team members, she dashed out of the Communications room and turned to head for the stairwell, where she intended to run every step down the six levels to where she hoped she would find her brother.

Once in the hallway she halted, absolutely shell-shocked by what she saw.

Chapter 42

Abdul

2:19:27

The first shot came from his Little Mice, proving their usefulness this time.

Abdul ducked against the wall as his Little Mice engaged the American military stationed in front of the room, holding his device. From what he saw on the video feed, there were not very many of them. So he had to get more of his men to retake this room, and he needed to do this now, before his Suhaimah was injured.

A glance at his men confirmed none of them had their radios and neither did he.

He tapped his Littlest Mouse on the shoulder and yelled, "I'm going to get more warriors to finish off these Americans. You and your men do not leave this position. But if you harm Suhaimah, I will kill you myself.

Abdul did not wait for an answer. He dashed for the door, intending to get the dozen or so guards from the sleeping quarters next to Communications.

He had to lift the bottom of his thobe to clear two

steps at a time, and when he saw his exit, he burst out, intending to run the thousand or so feet to the guard quarters.

But he halted to regard the many who were rushing in his direction.

She was in front of them all, coming to him.

Lexi

"Suhaimah, I knew you would come back to me," said the man who was the source of every nightmare she has had for the last eight days.

Only she was different now and he was no longer her worst nightmare. He was still scary, just as it would be with any other evil man who desired to take from her for his own pleasure. But in the end, Lexi knew, he was just a man.

Her muscles relaxed as she remembered her promise to kill him, and she could do that easily now. But she needed him to save everyone else.

A chaotic flurry of voices sounded off behind her and behind Abdul. "Freeze," they yelled behind her. "Put your guns down," hollered the ICA soldiers, who swarmed behind Abdul.

Abdul and she were in the middle of it all.

"Please, Uncle," Lexi said, "would you turn off that device? I know you can."

Abdul let his smile widen, its only resistance coming from the stitching in his left check, where Lexi had stabbed him.

"Of course I would stop the device for you," he said. "But only if you come to me of your own free will." He extended out his arms to welcome her to him.

A million thoughts and emotions flashed before her. *This* was what she had nightmares over. She also knew it was the only way. If she, by giving in to him, could stop this device, millions would live, including maybe even her brother and Samuel.

It was worth giving up her life.

"I agree," she said. With a forced smile, she took several steps toward him.

"No, Lexi. Don't do it," pleaded Samuel.

She continued to step his way, her body on autopilot, making moves that she had pre-programmed into herself so she wouldn't have to think about it.

When she came to within a hair's breadth of his fingertips, which were reaching out for her, a breeze brushed past her. She tilted her head.

It was Sal swooping in between them.

"Greetings my, Mahdi," he said, while plunging a dagger into Abdul's side.

Abdul backed away, looking at Lexi and then Sal and then at his side. Where the fabric was broken, a red blotch grew, spreading up and around his fancy white thobe. He looked bemused. Thunderstruck.

Then he turned, stumbled and ran.

There were cracks of gunfire behind him and behind her, causing Lexi to drop her own knife. It clattered imperceptibly on the floor in front of her, drawing only her attention.

At the last second, she had decided to kill him and let Sal slice off his thumb. It was far better than letting him live. But Sal stabbed him for her.

Gunfire continued, but Lexi remained in her place, reaching down not for cover but to pick up her knife.

When she looked up after sheathing her blade, she saw that several ICA soldiers had fallen, but the clog of them had turned and rushed into the stairwell with Abdul and out of her view.

"I'll finish you off after I find my brother," she told the trail of blood droplets leading into the stairwell.

Chapter 43

Lexi

2:14:53

"Lexi, are you hurt?" Samuel grabbed her shoulders and spun her around, inspecting her like a prized stallion he'd won at auction.

She wrestled free of him and then readjusted her M4, intending to follow Abdul downstairs. Not to finish him off, at least not yet. That would be for later. No, first she was going to the very last floor of this bunker to get Travis.

"Broadmoor," Wallace hollered down the hall. "You good?"

"Yes, ma'am," she responded.

"Okay, let's split up," Wallace continued, marching closer to Lexi. "Carter, I need you and and one other Seal to help me get topside to contact base." Carter nodded and signaled one of his Seal Team members to follow him.

"Corporal," she said to Porter, "I want you and Slim to take the rest of our team and help Broadmoor find her brother. Stay on comms."

"Yes, ma'am," Porter said.

Salman, the man locked in with Sal, cleared his throat. "Let me help you. I have some ideas on how to shut down communications."

"Why should we trust you?" Carter asked.

"You should not," Salman said. I am a follower of Mahdi Abdul and a believer. However, Saleem Hafeez convinced me that this device and the death it will cause is not Allah's way. You can arrest me after I have helped you."

Lexi could see Wallace was about to give it some thought, before replying almost instantly, "Okay, fine. You follow me and start talking."

The four of them jogged in the opposite direction, making their way toward the Western elevator.

Lexi turned back to the stairwell. "Okay, let's go find my brother.

Wallace

They were all surprised that there was no enemy resistance to their three-thousand-foot jog to the elevator. Only one of Farook's men showed himself. Upon seeing the three Americans running his way, he turned and ducked back into his room. It was almost like Farook's people were instructed not to engage them in any way.

Likewise, the ride up on the elevator was adventure free. That's when Wallace became skeptical.

Meanwhile, Salman explained that there were three

keys to shutting down all communications from Mount Weather: antennas, the Communications Center and the fiber optic trunk lines. He explained that the antennas were easy enough to destroy. The Center was hardened but could be destroyed easy enough with the correct munitions. But before this, they needed to destroy the trunk line, and that was a problem. Although they were buried and protected throughout the complex, they were weakest to an attack near the back corner of the Communications Center building. If that corner could be hit, with heavy enough munitions, all other data communications from the facility would be stopped.

Wallace felt confident that this intelligence was correct and desperately wanted to get this communicated to Base.

When the elevator doors opened up to a smaller tunnel than the one they had run through barely thirty minutes ago, that was when they finally found their resistance.

Past the elevator doors to the tunnel opening were hundreds of ICA soldiers being marched toward the entrance. There was no way they could escape without being seen and far too many to fight them off.

She tried her comms on the off chance it might work. "Base this is Team One, Commander Wallace. Do you read me?"

They weren't going to get through.

"I have another way to get topside, which requires a little climbing," Salman offered.

Wallace made a snap decision and closed the elevator doors before the ICA troops saw who they were.

Salman continued while they slowly descended. "Go down one level to Level A. Near the elevator is an air vent which goes straight up and outside. It has a small screen cover on it, which a strong woman like yourself could remove easily. Exiting here will give you a clear line of sight to your repeater antennas for your communications."

They exited on Level A and Salman led them to the vent access, via a small room, a few steps away from the elevator.

Once inside, Salman handed Carter a screwdriver from a shelf of tools. "You get that side. I'll get this one."

Within seconds they had the vent register off and Wallace was preparing to duck into the vent.

"Ms. Wallace," Salman said, "You appear to be a good leader, for a woman."

She suppressed her response, which would have been in anger. As a woman in the military, she was always having to prove her worth. And that pissed her off to no end. This man was simply naive as to their ways, but he was sincere, and he had been enormously helpful. "Thank you, Salman."

At that moment, Salman turned, motioning like he was about to leave them.

"Where are you going?" Wallace asked.

"I'm going to blow up the Area B Communications room. Just in case. Then I am hoping Allah will take me. But first, may Allah be with you." He bowed to them.

He shot a glance upward and then back at Wallace. "Do not forget to focus your bombs on the southeast corner of the Communications Center and to destroy all east and west antennas."

He slipped out the door before they could thank him again.

Wallace stuck her head into the vent and looked up,

willing away her natural fear of heights when she saw the light of day. She now had a plan of attack, given to them by this Muslim man who had taken their side. With the backing of two Seals and a clear line up to where she needed to make her call out to Smith, she knew she had this part.

As Wallace ascended the first few feet, she said to herself. "Alright, Team One, we'll get the communications shut down. You need to do something about that device."

Lexi

Before they made it all the way down to Level G, they had to wait out one gun battle after another below them. An exchange of gunfire would start and then stop almost as rapidly. But after after a pause and then a scurry of movement further down the stairs, another exchange would occur. During each lull, they descended.

At each new level, they encountered one of Abdul's guards. Dead and scattered around the body were dozens of bullet casings. At Level D, they found no one dead, but lots more blood. The majority of the droplets stopped at the exit out.

Lexi didn't intend to stop there, even though she assumed the blood was from Abdul. She took the first two steps down the next level when she heard two muffled voices just outside in the hall, prompting her to stop.

The first voice was Abdul yelling something in Arabic to Sal, no doubt he had been the cause of the gun battles with Abdul's guards.

Sal responded in English, insisting that Abdul, "give him the boy."

Next, a young voice hollered, "Let me go!"

"That's Travis," Lexi hollered back. She raced back up the stairs, out of Porter's hands, who tried to keep her back in the stairwell and out of the hallway. But she burst through.

A mortally wounded Abdul held onto a crazed-looking small person covered in dirt and blood. By any measure, this didn't look like Travis. Although, she was sure it was him by the way he stood in defiance of his uncle.

Sal was there, offering to lay down his weapon if Abdul would give up Travis, even though Abdul had his rifle pointed at Sal.

But Sal continued to bend down like he was going to give up his weapon. "You see, I am laying it down right now."

When it appeared as if Abdul might have taken a shot, the door he was standing beside popped open and a woman dashed out, grabbing Travis and pulling him away from Abdul.

Abdul didn't seem shocked at all by this. And although he wobbled a little at first, he moved fast.

Just as Sal reached to pick back up his rifle, Abdul was gone. The door shut with a heavy *clank*.

"Travis," Lexi yelled. "Is that really you?"

She jogged in his direction, getting ready to throw her arms around him, no matter how dirty he was.

The woman who whisked him away from Abdul let go

of the boy, just when Lexi was there to embrace him with a bear hug.

Instead of replying with a hug of his own, Travis was rigid, holding tight to two large binders.

"Aren't you happy to see me?" Lexi asked.

"Of course," Travis said in a monotone voice. "But much more important, I know how to stop our device from sending a cloud of bacteria into the sky."

Abdul

He fell into one of the swivel chairs and huffed out a long sigh. He had won this small battle but lost the war.

He knew Abbie Khan would leave the bunker when he offered up the child. It was the only way she would let him inside. And once he was inside, there was no way Sal, nor anyone else, could enter, and that meant they could not stop the device. This was, after all, the Presidential bunker, hardened to be almost impregnable.

He was surprised at the time that Meer had left Abbie alone, when he had told the man to remain with her until it was their time to go to the tribunal. He could not even complete that task without treachery. And more maddening was that he would not get to see Meer's death. He had been looking forward to that.

Now it was time to face the facts, no matter how painful

they were: he was going to die here, he would not witness the death of Meer and so many others, the device would go off, killing most of his people and there would not be an Islamic Caliphate in America.

At least he would die with one consolation: after today, there would be no America.

Once most of America's population had died, the pieces of this once proud country would be picked apart by other countries, like vultures fighting over a dead rat in the desert.

At least, he would die here in peace, treasuring that one consolation, knowing that he had caused the downfall of America.

Abdul closed his eyes, not because he was ready to go to Paradise just yet, but because he was tired.

An interior door slammed shut, followed by a grating voice. "Okay, I am done with the bathroom now... Where did you go... Oh, it's you."

The voice was unmistakable. It was that traitor, Meer.

Abdul slowly opened his eyes, just as Meer was reaching for a gun someone had left on the conference table.

Abdul didn't hesitate. He pulled the trigger to his own rifle, ending Meer's traitorous life instantly.

He smiled at receiving this one final gift, before falling asleep for good.

Chapter 44

Frank

1:59:47

They were marched out of their jail cells, fully expecting they would be taken next to where they would be executed.

Frank, Chase and a young Muslim man named Jamal were led through the temporary jail, hands bound behind their backs, toward the building's exit.

The timing felt earlier than when they were told it would occur, but Frank and Chase were ready. They had prayed together, and both were prepared to face whatever was about to be sent their way. They had relinquished control to God, a concept generally foreign to an old warrior like Frank, and someone who had to be in control of everything around him.

For the past hour or so, they'd heard gunfire and an explosion, but they discounted this as celebratory outbursts by their enemy. It wasn't until the building's exit was opened that they realized something was happening. Something big.

Multiple shots by friendly 556s, some autocannon bursts and a couple of booms from what sounded like cannon fire.

When they stepped outside, it was charlie foxtrot. Individual ICA troops were scattering in different directions, as were scores of civilians. All seemed to be in a panic.

Could this be our military, Frank wondered, but he didn't dare say… Until he heard it.

"You hearing that, Frank?" Chase asked.

Frank did. "It sounds like music to this soldier's ears… Mechanized Infantry Combat Vehicles and that means our infantry."

"Amen to that."

Their three jailers seemed unsure what to do next. They remained standing out in the open area of a large parking lot, turning their heads in one direction then another. Frank guessed they were supposed to be taken to the outdoor theater and gallows, about two hundred yards away. But people were streaming out of the stands and away from there.

One of their jailers fell, struck down by what they did not hear or see. Frank instantly thought, *snipers*.

Then the other two fell, leaving all three of them unattended. *And in the open.*

Frank didn't need an invitation. "Let's hoof it," he started running, "to the noise."

"Right behind you," Chase said.

"Thank you, sir," said Jamal, who followed Chase.

Up ahead, coming right at them, were several armored vehicles. They were driving through the compound, seemingly unhindered by the enemy. Behind the vehicles were at least a hundred Army infantry.

Oddly enough, leading the charge of this company was a Lieutenant Colonel.

Most of the dozen or so MICVs drove past them and took positions east of the tribunal field and at various points in a circle formation around what looked to be a center point in the complex of buildings. Each MICV had their 25 mm autocannons pointed outward from their infantry personnel, who were collecting up in the middle.

Frank, Chase and Jamal ended up in the center of the zone of action, when the Colonel marched up to Frank.

"Colonel, I'm Major Frank Cartwright, retired," he nodded towards Chase. "And this is Senator Thomas Chase. And this young man has been trying to help us strike against Farook."

"Gentlemen. HQ said we had a pickup. Damned glad you gents made it this easy for us. " He signaled three of the infantry to cut their bindings. "I'm Commander Dabber, and I am leading this assault on the *Hajjis* who stole our HPSF. You need any medical assistance?" He said this eyeing Frank, who suspected he looked like crap, but at this point he didn't care.

"Thank you," Frank said, rubbing at the rope burn on his wrists. "We're fine. Have you had much resistance from the enemy?"

"Negatori. Like hot knives through butter. Our units have reported less than one hundred enemy around the SF. Our bean counters said thousands."

As strange as this sounded to Frank, since he expected Abdul to put up more of a fight, he was more concerned about their timing. So was Jamal, who had informed them about the device and was now buzzing with nervous energy. "Great news, Commander. However, our big concern, from what our friend Jamal explained, is that all communications must shut down at High Point Special Facility because of some sort of doomsday device set to go off here soon."

"Already received this intel from two sources inside. Our orders are to secure you and the senator, while clearing Area A of the enemy and protecting civilians. The second part of our operations is to take a safe position and destroy all antenna arrays and the Communications Center. You and your friends are welcome to enjoy the show, Major."

"I'm sorry to interrupt, Commander," Jamal had his hand raised. "But you cannot just destroy the Comms Center, you must destroy the trunk lines going out to be sure there is no communication with the other devices."

"And Commander," Frank added, "from what I understand, we don't have a lot of time."

Chapter 45

Sal

1:55:09

"No!" Sal huffed, striking the door with his closed fist. That was it. He lost him and there was no other way he could stop the device.

His own weakness let this happen. The truth was, he could not shoot the boy to kill Farook. The boy was worth saving, but now at what cost?

"Thank you," a woman said. He turned to see who it was. In front of him was Suhaimah speaking to him, with Abdul-Aziz beside her.

"I should have killed Farook," Sal lamented, but I would have hit the boy," he said.

"That's why I'm thanking you," she said.

"Excuse me... Can anyone tell me what just happened?" said another woman in an overly nasal voice. Sal instantly recognized her as the current American female President.

The muffled sound of a gunshot made the POTUS flinch.

"Come on," insisted the boy to his sister. "I need to stop

this thing before it goes off."

Sal had barely given the boy more than a momentary glance when Abdul had grabbed him. But now he could see that he was holding two binders. "Did you figure it out, Travis?"

"Yes, it was as I thought. But because you failed, it's up to me to save us all." The boy looked up at Lexi and then Sal and then some others, who appeared to be American military. "But I will need your help, and we may need more guns."

Lexi

1:22:57

"Seriously, you want me to wear this and carry these manuals?" Travis protested.

"Yes," Sal said very calmly. "As far as they think, you will be a small woman."

Not liking this plan at all, Lexi only half-smiled at seeing her brother in a burka.

She wished that the other members of Team One could come with them instead. But Sal said his plan required Travis and, "one other women, which must be Lexi if they were caught." After some arguing, especially by Samuel, Porter called it and said they would lend support, if necessary and for Lexi to otherwise stay on radio.

"Okay, do we all understand the plan?" Sal asked.

All of them responded, "Yes."

Lexi glanced down at Samuel, Gladys, and Porter, who were in a line against the stairwell wall. Further down were Jonah and the President, standing aside.

"Let's go then," Sal said and opened the door. "Abdul-Aziz, you follow me, followed by Suhaimah."

Without waiting for their acknowledgment, he took off and was out of sight.

Travis shot out the door, and Lexi tried to keep up. But Lexi could only see the two black shapes of her brother and Sal in front of her and not much else.

She had witnessed women wearing burkas before, but never thought twice about it. Now she wondered how anyone could see out of them. Worse, the fabric stunk, like someone's armpit.

Using a hand underneath, she pulled at the mesh she was supposed to see through, bringing it closer to her eyes, which made a big difference.

She could now see the long hallway, and Sal leading them toward the Systems Room a quarter of a mile away. The hall was packed with people. But not just any people... ICA warriors.

Hundreds of them.

Many hundreds.

"Umm," she whispered into her comms. "There are too many terrorists here. Do not come out that door, no matter what you hear."

It was what Sal had warned them about.

But what were so many of them doing down here? She wished she knew. She was very glad that Sal didn't take Travis' suggestion of blasting their way through. That would have been impossible.

Lots of Arabic words were being thrown around, but the ones she caught quite often were "Paradise" and "Martyr." Almost universally, they were chanting, *"Allahu akbar,"* over and over.

Perhaps because of this, most of the soldiers ignored them completely as they walked past. That was until someone grabbed her shoulder, roughly yanked at her, spun her in the other direction and groped her.

She gasped.

Sal's response was nearly instantaneous. He spun like a flash and before the pervert could speak the foul words he had been planning to unload on her, Sal's knife shot up from nowhere and was driven into the man's throat, stopping him at his first syllable.

Sal withdrew his knife slowly out of the man's throat and Lexi was mesmerized by the length of it and the amount of blood that poured out of the man's neck.

The dead man fell to the ground and Sal wiped the blood from his knife on the man's shoulder while yanking his rifle from him.

"Are you alright?" Samuel whispered in her ear.

"Yes," she murmured back. She really was.

Sal discharged a flurry of Arabic at all the other potential perverts and pushed his fake wives along, so they could continue on their way.

There was no more errant hands after this, and the hallway was a little quieter, as if word spread about what just happened.

She didn't realize that they had stopped when she ran into her brother. "Sorry," she said.

"Move aside," Sal demanded, but to whom she did not

know.

"Saleem Hafeez, I thought Mahdi Abdul arrested you," said a man she could now see, but just barely.

"Well, it is obvious I am not as I am here speaking with you, brother," Sal was putting on a show, but he wasn't done.

"Why are you here anyway?" Sal asked. "Should you and all the others not be outside fighting the Infidels?"

"Did you not know?" said the man, leaning into Sal. "Mahdi Abdul has recalled us all to prepare ourselves for Paradise..."

Lexi had to contain herself to keep from gulping in more air at this newest revelation.

Abdul was planning to kill everyone, including his own people.

"But should you not know this?" the man asked Sal. "Unless you are no longer close to Abdul"—the man reached for Sal—"in which case you need to—"

All Lexi could see was that Sal had moved in front of them and did something to stop the man's words.

A thud followed.

There was a jingle of keys and the sound of a door opening and the dragging of a large object. Finally, Sal whispered, "Come on."

The burkas were off and discarded by the door. Wearing one was pure torture. Lexi decided then she would chance it without the burka when they left. If they could leave.

She had already let her team know about Abdul's ultimate plan to kill everyone. Wallace wasn't reachable and she hoped that meant she was out and communicating with Smith. But Smith might never know about this fact. It all made their operation so much more important.

She glared at the door and the body of the guard Sal had killed. What if one or more came in or if someone in the vast System's Room saw them? She needed to be ready while Travis did whatever it was he needed to do.

"Sal," Lexi said, eyeing the two AKs he lugged over each shoulder. "You better give me one of those things. Don't worry, I know how to use it."

Sal hesitated and then slipped off one of the two, still frowning at her. There was no doubt in her mind that the whole concept of a woman using a rifle was unnatural.

He handed it to Lexi, who immediately slung it around her head and then like an expert—at least in her mind—pulled back the charging handle to verify it was loaded.

Sal restrained a smile before turning to Travis, who was struggling with his two binders. "Okay, we are in the Systems Room, where you said we needed to go. Now, please tell us, Abdul-Aziz, what did you figure out?"

Lexi knew her brother well enough. When others looked to him for answers, he would take his time and describe things in such a way that made you feel stupid. Only this time, he didn't do this.

"As I had mentioned," he laid his books down on a slanted table with a scattering of tools on top of schematics and opened one up. "Even if they are successful in shutting down communications, most of the people around Mount Weather and wherever the winds blow and the infection spreads, will probably die. I cannot do anything about the communications, but I can stop our device from releasing its infection outside."

Travis looked up and then at the pages in the open binder and back up again. He picked the book off the table and started walking, looking only at the ceiling twelve feet above and its myriad of crisscrossing pipes and wires, and his binder's pages.

Lexi and Sal followed him, having no idea where they were headed, waiting for her brother to tell them why.

"You see," Travis began again when he seemed to find one or more pipes fit the diagram on a page in the book he was scrutinizing. "This bunker is designed with an automatic lock-down mechanism in the event of a nuclear or biological attack. If its sensors detect one of these events happening, the mechanism automatically engages and shuts down all of Area B's vents and doors, making the entire underground bunker airtight, so that it is impossible for any radiation, chemical agents or biological infections to get in... or in this case, escape."

Travis turned to face them, perhaps to see if they were following along.

Sal jumped at Travis' pause first. "So, if the device goes off here, the biological agents will be locked inside?"

"Well, it should," Travis responded immediately. "Except Abdul already disabled the automatic system." Travis turned back, looked up and now using his finger, traced his path forward. After his finger pointed to the back wall, he moved again, now walking toward that point.

"So, we have to set the mechanism off manually," he

continued.

"How do we do that?" Lexi asked the question she knew he was about to answer, but taking too long to get there.

He stopped before a circuit breaker box, or at least something that resembled one. He turned and faced them again. "Well, actually I will do it."

"Can you open this, Sal?" Travis pointed at a heavy-duty padlock, securing the door to the box.

Sal didn't answer. He searched for a moment, nodded and then stepped over to an "In Case of Emergency" sign above a glass case. Using his elbow, he gave a quick stab to its center, causing all the glass to shatter. He kicked away a few pieces still clinging to the frame and snatched the axe hanging inside.

With one swing the lock came loose. Sal opened it to reveal a large gray lever. Above it were the words, "Manual Containment Switch."

"You see," Travis continued as if this were a planned pause, "Whomever pulls that will be locked inside. And unfortunately, per this manual, everything is set to a timer. So once it engages, none of the vents or doors to the outside world can be opened from the inside or out for 48 hours. Of course, by that time I will already be dead."

Chapter 46

One Click from HPSF Comms Center

1:15:16

The area was cleared of combatants quickly and all civilians had been led away, out of the designated target area. Meanwhile, Army and Naval Seal teams were completing the demolition of the facility's antenna arrays. Everything was going smoothly, even the targeting of the Comms Building.

Because they could not easily penetrate the hardened building with simple munitions and sending in Rangers was too risky as multiple enemy soldiers had secured themselves inside, they settled on a missile delivering multiple shaped charges to its target.

They painted the precise spot on the outside corner of the Comms Center with a laser mounted on one of the MICVs. That way, they could ensure accuracy and the safety of their soldiers.

Within a few minutes, an incoming drone would fire one of its two missiles. Its armor-piercing casing would penetrate the hardened building, delivering its munitions into the building at the precise location. The detonation would melt everything inside and below, including the trunk lines they were targeting.

Now all they had to do was wait to hear the drone had launched its missile and watch the pyrotechnics from a distance.

Faisal

Faisal finally saw their opportunity.

His warriors had to stand by and watch as the Americans killed many of their ICA, and then wasted time escorting civilians out the compound to safety. Faisal already expected their protecting civilians, but he did not expect the complete lack of support from Mahdi Abdul's troops. It was as if they had all disappeared. Faisal had witnessed them arriving in convoy trucks—just like those given to his unit—one after another. Thousands of ICA arrived, but with no action. He just did not understand where all the Mahdi's warriors went.

Attacking such an overwhelming enemy using only his seven remaining men, without the support of their warriors, was suicide without yielding any results to the Mahdi's cause. So once again, against their many protests, and knowing he may die before they could act, Faisal had them watch and wait for many hours.

Then Allah provided them an opportunity.

The American soldiers had cleared out of the area, taking with them all their equipment, except for a tank-like vehicle. It was purposely parked off the pavement, fully operational, and left there for the taking. But that was not the best part.

Faisal's point man watched the vehicle maneuver behind a large building, up on an embankment, and then turn its turret and gun so it was aimed directly at the building. But instead of firing upon it, they turned off its engine and abandoned it. When his man moved closer, he reported a laser light was still operational and its red dot was pointed at a bottom portion of the building. This was proof that this structure was very important to Mahdi Abdul.

He had heard about bombs that could follow a laser beam. This had to be what they were planning. They were going to bomb this building at that exact point.

Faisal decided they would take the vehicle, turn off its laser and move it away from the building. Perhaps they could then use this to better defend Mahdi Abdul's complex against the Americans. But most important was stopping the laser.

Doing this would ensure that they were the few, out of his thousands of warriors, who took action to protect Mahdi Abdul.

"Let's move," Faisal announced to his men, as Samir helped him up and guided him in the right direction.

Six of his seven men jogged into the open field, headed right for their chance to turn this war back into their favor.

Frank

To Frank, combat was often ten percent planning and ninety percent figuring shit out on the fly. So it wasn't at all a surprise to him when their targeting plan went to hell.

"What in tarnation am I seeing?" Colonel Dabber barked on his Comms. He had an acorn sized wad of chew under his lip, which with his idioms and accent would have made him comical if this wasn't so serious.

"The enemy is trying to steal our MICV," a voice said, stating the obvious.

"Let me be more specific for you fopdoodles not paying attention,"—Dabber leaned into Frank. "Great old British word, fopdoodle; means idiot—"why in God's green earth have we not lit them up?"

"Sir?" asked Mr. Obvious.

"Shoot these *hajjis* who think they can steal my gosh-darned equipment and send them all to Paradise!" Dabber hollered, sending spittle onto a private's neck.

"Ah, sir, all our infantry are outside the zone of action."

"Dagnabbit, then, where are my snipers?" Dabber spat, this time turning his head away from the private. He leaned toward Frank and Chase and in a more subdued tone, he said, "These goshdarned fopdoodles are going to drive me to an early grave."

Before Dabber could finish his narration, one of their snipers struck, hitting one of the three ICA soldiers crawling over the MICV. This one was crouching over the laser, attempting to mess with it. The man folded over like a newspaper in the rain.

"Now we're talking," Dabber announced.

"We have confirmation, our bird is off," said their comms.

Before any of them could breathe a collective sigh of relief, another one of the small band of ICA soldiers, this one an albino, jumped up on their MICV and using the butt of his AK, drove it into the laser, knocking its trajectory away from the building, into the parking lot. He hit it once more, before their snipers stopped him with a shot to the head. But the damage was done.

The laser was now pointed directly at them, and then it blinked out.

"Colonel, what's the missile's eta with contact?" Frank asked.

"Private?" the Colonel asked.

"Two minutes, fifteen seconds, sirs."

"You gotta blow it and we need another way to deliver the second," Frank said, signaling Jamal, who sprang from his waiting area he'd been pacing around and rushed to him.

An idea had popped into Frank's head based on the previous conversations he and Chase had had with Jamal in the holding cell next to theirs about their mutual contact. It was time to figure shit out on the fly.

"Colonel, I have an idea."

When Jamal was in front of him, Frank asked, "Jamal, where is that Sat phone you used to talk to Smith?"

"In the Comms Center bathroom ceiling," he answered.

"Is it close enough to the trunk lines?"

The smirk on Jamal's face and his animated movements confirmed that he could already see where Frank was going with this. "No, but if I could get in there, I could move it to the room so you could target the phone properly."

"You don't need to do that. Just tell me where it needs to go, so I can move—"

"No," Jamal interrupted. "It must be me. Only I know exactly where."

"Okay..." Frank gave a quick look around. Not seeing any of the infantry nearby, as they'd been told to clear buildings west of them of any potential combatants, he knew it was up to him to get Jamal inside to the target and back out safely. "We both go."

"What in tarnation are you two talking about, Major?"

"Colonel, I need cover fire so that Jamal and I can enter that Comms building, place a sat phone in the target location, so that your next missile can use that phone as the target. Also Colonel, if you don't hear from operations within fifteen minutes, that means we were unsuccessful. Have them do the best they can to target that building's corner. And keep your infantry out of the zone for their protection, regardless of what the enemy is doing."

Jamal tried to get Frank's attention by pulling on a sleeve. He was more anxious than ever about something Frank had said.

The Colonel responded first. "Major, if you think this will work," he glowered at Frank's knee brace, "we've got you two covered whenever you are ready."

"I'm coming too," said Chase, who also appeared to have escaped the civilian observation area.

"Thanks, Chase." Frank put a hand on Chase's shoulder. "But your most important job is about to begin," Frank responded. Then to Dabber, "Colonel, you need to get this man to safety. He's the next President of the United States."

Frank turned to their target and grabbed Jamal's arm. "Ready?"

Jamal shook his head "no," but then nodded.

Frank readjusted his knee brace and started his best imitation of an old, handicapped man attempting to run fast. It would have been another comical moment to all who were watching, but their situation had now become dire.

Jamal had no problem keeping up, as Frank was the one going way too slow. He just couldn't get his beat-up body to move any faster.

After they were more than a hundred feet inside their zone of action, Jamal spoke, "Ahh, sir, you know my contact may not be connected—"

They zigged around two parked cars.

"—to the Army's drones. If he is not, the drone pilot might not be able to target my phone and then—"

Several shots rang out and a nearby clank told Frank they were the targets. He pulled Jamal behind another parked car, keeping an eye on the MICV, from where he assumed the gunfire was coming. He said to Jamal, "Not to worry. I am certain, our mutual contact, Matt Smith is in charge or at least well connected to this operation. It will work."

Frank saw Dabber used one of their MICVs from a thousand yards away and directed its autocannon fire on the parked MICV that the ICA soldiers were using as a shield of protection. What the ICA didn't know was that their autocannon's munitions were armor penetrating, and the armor on their MICVs wouldn't protect them from it.

They were not even halfway there, and Frank wanted them to continue. So he yanked on Jamal's shoulder to prod him to run as he was speaking.

"I am glad to hear—"

More shots.

They took cover behind another car, right when bullets pinged off its body. These came from the Comms Center building.

Once again, the Army directed their cover fire on the shooter, who must have come out from the protection of the building's interior protected room and set up at a window.

"In case I am shot, so you know, my Sat phone is untraceable. I modified it so that Abdul's men couldn't find me when I transmitted to Smith. But it would be traceable when—"

Frank pulled Jamal up and they were running again.

Jamal huffed out, "Yes, well, if I keep my line open to Smith, he could easily target the open line. So,"—he huffed and took in two huge gulps of air—"it must remain open for this to work."

Frank shot him a glance, then at the upcoming doorway. "Got it. You call Smith and then leave it by the target and then we go."

"Correct." He smiled at Frank. "We might actually make—"

Three *pop-pop-pop* sounds of semi-auto rifle fire were very close. Jamal fell to his knees.

Frank pulled him a few feet further behind the cover of another parked car and examined him.

Dark red bloomed from Jamal's chest. He coughed and looked at his wound while clutching onto Frank. He glared at Frank, obviously aware of his condition and said, "You must… Get phone to northwest room… It's the server room… Go to far northern wall and at Trunk Line Access, call Smith…" His eyes were closed, and he'd stopped moving.

"Thank you, Jamal," Frank said, laying his body gently onto the asphalt. It was up to him now.

He looked for the MICV, where he was certain the gunfire had come from, but it was now behind the edge of the Comms Center building. There was no more enemy fire.

Frank ran the last ten meters directly into the building's entrance.

Chapter 47
Level E

Lexi

57:25

After a lot of arguing, some tears from Lexi, there was finally an agreement. Sal would pull the lever.

It was then that Travis finally showed his emotions, as a wellspring of tears streamed from his eyes and his body shuddered. Lexi figured it must have been the relief he felt from not having to commit himself to certain death after preparing himself to do so. She made a pact with herself then. If they somehow lived through this, she would never disregard her little brother. He was a genuine hero, even if he was only ten.

While she was consoling Travis, his demeanor changed in an instant. He was looking at the clock and she understood it too.

"How in the hell are we going to get out of here in fifty-seven minutes?" Lexi asked. "We cannot go out the hallway."

"I've got this," Travis said. "You just need to follow me and not look down."

"Hang on." Lexi walked over to Sal, unsure of what she would say. Finally, "I don't know why you're doing this or... how to even thank you. So, I'll just say, thank you."

Sal didn't react. But he said, "We all die, Lexi. It's what we do with our life that is most important. Make sure you and your brother do not waste this opportunity.

"Perhaps we will meet again.

"Allahu akbar."

He turned away, got down on his knees and continued chanting, *"Allahu akbar... Allahu akbar."*

Frank

Without any enemy fire directed at him, Frank didn't slow at the entrance and dashed inside the building's blasted out door way. He gave a quick check past his rifle's iron sites, in both directions.

No one. Just debris.

The Comms Center room was closed, as Jamal had said it would be. When he saw the Men's room across the hall, he hurried over and then inside.

Multiple holes in the far wall, surrounding a high window, bore proof of their autocannon's work. Below the window was one dead body of an ICA soldier, or what was left of him.

Also out of place, several ceiling tiles were not quite set right, all above the back stall. Frank intended to try these first, but when he opened the stall, he saw what he guessed was Jamal's Sat phone on floor, near the toilet.

Snatching it up and giving it a quick look over, he could see the screen was cracked. Mouthing, "Please God," he pushed the power button, and the phone came to life. "Alright," he said to no one, "it's time to find the target room Jamal described."

Without a place to put the phone, Frank tucked it under his armpit and stuck out his rifle barrel and then he headed back out the door.

Doing a quick check for any enemy, he focused his attention on the last door on the north side of the hall.

That should be the room.

Frank rushed to this door. Fully expecting it to be locked, still he pointed his rifle forward with one hand, while putting his other on the handle and turning.

It clicked and the door opened.

The room was expansive and dark. Lights twinkled all around, providing the room's only illumination. But for the sounds of muffled gunfire outside and soft mechanical clicking inside, there were no other sounds.

When he was certain no one was there, he flicked on the light switch.

He rushed over to the back wall Jamal mentioned, but didn't immediately see anything labeled Trunk Line on it. He hoofed his way along the wall, still seeing nothing. He even eye-balled each of the multiple cabinets of computer equipment nearby. Every single one had uncountable numbers of cables and wires running through them. Nothing said, "Trunk Line."

Then he saw something.

A hatch in the floor, midway up against the wall, caught

his attention. Upon approach, he could see writing. It was the magic words: Trunk Line Access.

Time to make the call.

Frank was far from a master of communications equipment, but he assumed that like a cellphone, if he pressed the call button, he would get the last number dialed. He also assumed the last person called was Smith.

When he did this, a number flashed on the cracked screen, and it appeared to be dialing. But when he let go of the button, the number disappeared and the screen went black.

"Shit," he said under his breath, as he had a sinking feeling.

He tried again, this time holding the button down, and it rang. Letting go, thinking the connection was now made, the ringing stopped. Like before, the number disappeared from the screen, and it went blank.

The meaning of this was absolute.

Frank turned around, and with his back against the wall, he sat down beside the hatch.

Holding onto the call button, and this time not letting go, he listened. It rang once... twice... three times when the line clicked open. But with no answer.

Frank took a breath and spoke first. "I'm betting you were expecting someone else."

"Is that you, Frank?" a familiar voice asked promptly.

"How the hell are you, Smith?" Frank asked, genuinely

glad to hear his voice.

"Happy to hear you're still alive. I met your goddaughter. Amazing young woman."

Frank beamed at this, while his eyes began to get watery. He had resolved after his last capture that he'd likely not see Lexi again. It was why he wrote the note directing her to find Smith. But now, to hear Smith's words, knowing that she had successfully found him, but to know for certain that he would not see her again, brought it all home.

"When you see her, please tell her I'm so proud of her..." he started to say, but unfortunately they had so little time. "But we should get to business first. I'm speaking on Jamal's satellite phone because I'm afraid the young man didn't make it."

Frank took another breath and continued. "I have his phone because I want you to arrange the drone missile strike to target this phone. We can no longer guide them here with lasers."

Frank assumed that Smith was at the head of all of this, for the same reason why he knew Lexi needed to find him when he left this earth.

"Roger that. I've already keyed in instructions to our bird. They'll launch on my go ahead. But first, you need to put at least five hundred meters between you and that phone. More is better."

"Give the go on launch immediately. I've decided to take a front-row seat."

"Frank... Are you mortally wounded? You know there's an Army FST who can treat you at the nearby FOB?"

"Don't wait, Matt. Please tell them to launch now."

"Ah... Okay, it's keyed in. You'll have about seven minutes. Are you sure you can't get—"

"I'm sorry, but this Sat phone is barely functional. I must physically hold the call button to keep the line open. As soon as I let go, we'll be disconnected. Plus, Jamal told me that this phone is untraceable once disconnected."

A good ten seconds passed. "Copy that, Frank."

"Matt, look after Lexi for me, would you?"

"Of course, as always... You know, it's been the honor of my life to serve under you and get to know you."

"Matt, the honor is all mine."

Chapter 48

Lexi

54:21

She felt herself slip and almost fall, but she held on, with her brother above her calling out words of encouragement. Lexi looked down at the spinning fan below them and then up above at Travis coaxing her up. She wondered how her brother did this so effortlessly.

One last time, she told herself that if he could do it, so could she. But the fact was, Travis was always much better at climbing trees than she was. More importantly, he always had no fear, whereas most of her life, she was constantly afraid. But not now. Her only fear was if she failed, she wouldn't get her brother out of this bunker alive.

Lexi sucked in a couple of gulps of air and made sure she had a good hold. Using her legs, she propelled herself up the final few feet.

"I told you could do it," Travis beamed, his teeth looking extra white against the dirt and grime covering his face. "Now, can you get this vent off?"

She could see there was a latch with a lock on the other side of the steel vent that was the only thing separating them from freedom and the outside world.

Travis had explained to her that in the entire bunker complex, much of which he had explored through its HVAC duct work, there were only two other access vents they could have used. One was on the other side of the complex and therefore too far away. the other was midway, near the stairwell. But that one was way too high, as it also rose up through several hundred more feet of mountain. And at this point, they both feared they wouldn't have enough time to get there and up it.

So, they risked going up the shaft with the fan, which he said if they fell it would, "tear us up into a mixed salad of Lexi and Travis bits." He actually giggled at this, which showed his sense of humor was still there, in spite of all he had gone through.

She looked down and then back up at the lock.

"Okay, stay behind me," she announced to him.

Lexi pointed her M4 at the lock as Travis slipped behind her.

With two trigger pulls, her rifle shot out fire and a *boom-boom* that rattled her body, and she feared, busted her ear drums.

The latch clattered loose and part of it fell, banging its way down and finally thumping deeply off of something metallic below.

She pushed up on the gate, and it opened up.

Pulling herself up, she scurried out of the vent and dropped onto her back, looking up. Right then, a delightful gust of mountain air caressed her skin, carrying with it the most pleasant scents of pine sap and her eyes were rewarded with the glorious sight of billowing clouds against a deep blue sky.

"Come on out," she yelled to her brother, not hearing anything but a loud ringing in her head.

He popped up and out, like a small, blackened animal coming out of its dirty lair. His lips moved, which meant he said something, but she couldn't hear a damned thing.

He stood up straight, shoulders back, one of his arms slung around and pointed over a wall, encircling them that came up to his chin.

Lexi pushed herself up and stood up beside her brother. They were on what felt like the top of a castle tower. To their east was an open valley of green and to their west was the top of Mount Weather.

She made out from his lips, "Do..." but not the rest of what Travis said, as he urged her to look at what he was seeing in the southeast sky.

Lexi had to squint to see it.

Something was on fire, and it was shooting across the heavens...

And it was coming right toward them.

High Point Special Facility

Senator Chase

Colonel Dabber confided with Chase two pieces of news: one good and one bad. The good was that the missile was off and in only three minutes, ten seconds, the target would be destroyed. The bad: Frank had to remain at the target sight to ensure that the satellite phone he used for targeting remained on.

"Seventy seconds," stated the private.

Chase couldn't help but feel emotional for his new friend, who had done so much to protect him and his country. When they were incarcerated together, Frank shared with him multiple war stories, as well as what he knew about Farook's reign of terror."

"Forty seconds."

Chase closed his eyes and said a quick prayer for Frank. Then for all of their military currently fighting against this enemy in and around High Point Special Facility and other locations. Finally, he prayed for his country.

He opened his eyes and watched as the missile came in from the southeast and in a split second, hit the Communications Center building.

The flash of light caused all of them to shield their eyes.

Chapter 49

Chase

43:51

The Colonel announced they would be on the move, to get far away from Mount Weather, if the device did, in fact go off. They all felt certain that they were able to destroy any possibility of communications going out from HPSF, but they did not have confirmation that anyone was able to neutralize the local device. Dabber was haggling over logistics when a private interrupted him.

"Sir, we have confirmation from our drones that the MICV on sight is gone."

"What do you mean, gone? Where in the Sam Hill did it go?" Dabber demanded.

"I'm waiting for a report, sir."

"No matter, we need to evacuate this facility, A-Sap."

"Sir, I have another report. Our thermal imaging found two tangos exiting the East Portal, at least one was armed."

"Do we have assets in the area?"

"Yes, sir," Seal Team Two has just picked them up. And,

sir?"

"Yes, Private."

"One of the tangos, a woman, wants to talk to you. I have her on comms," the private said this, and turned to look at Dabber.

"Who is this? Lexi Broadmoor?"

Chase caught Dabber's attention and stated, "I can vouch for her."

"Yes, Ms. Broadmoor, continue."

Lexi

01:52

They were at a forward operating base set up about two miles from what the military called HPSF, but she knew it as Mount Weather. There they waited to see if Sal did what he said or if they would have to evacuate the rest of the east coast.

Lexi looked at the familiar faces around her, each of whom meant so much to her, while she thought about those who didn't make it.

Gladys caught a round in the shoulder and was in intensive care at the Forward Surgical Team unit nearby. Her prognosis was good, and she was reported to be telling the surgeon before going under, "You better get every bit of this damned enemy round out of me, or I will kick your butt."

Jonah, too was recovering from a gunshot wound to the arm. He reportedly never complained once.

Travis, despite all that he had suffered, including a thirty-foot fall, had only a mild concussion. "He'll be as good as new," the doctor told her. But she knew he would be even better than that.

But her godfather Frank, was said to have given his life to ensure that there was no way HPSF could communicate with any other devices. Supposedly Matt Smith had been speaking to him, but because her comms were down, she hadn't yet spoken to Smith. Everyone said that Frank was a hero. But she didn't need to be told that. She knew he was.

Lexi felt numb to the sadness, simply squeezing Travis once more, who was getting mighty tired of getting hugged by her.

Samuel gave her the look. He smiled and put an arm around her again, doing his best to comfort her. But he wasn't going to be around much either.

Moments earlier, Senator Chase was sworn in as President after Abbie Khan resigned. Just before that, he asked Samuel to join him in a new program to reinvigorate citizen militias, working directly with the US Military.

"Here it comes," someone said, among the hundred or so military and a dozen civilians.

All eyes were on a big screen, showing live footage of Area B's vents and access portals from a drone flying above.

With almost a minute to go before the device was set to go off, they saw movement.

"Sir, I'm getting confirmation," announced an Army Specialist. "The vents are closing."

They could see it themselves, especially in the vent they had come out of. It was some sort of enclosure, just below the grill she had shot out and escaped from.

In a matter of seconds, everything was sealed up and anything inside was sealed in, including reports of several thousand ICA soldiers, who had seemingly returned to die with their Mahdi.

The nightmare was finally over.

Her uncle, Abdul Farook, the leader of the terrorists who killed millions and almost succeeded in killing their country, was now entombed for good inside the bunker. Whether he was already dead or not was immaterial. The Colonel stated that once Area B was sealed off, they would never open it up again.

It should have been the ultimate triumph for Lexi. But she was numb to this, too.

When it was long past what others were calling zero hour, an announcement must have come over their communications network, because several of those in attendance were cheering and shaking each other's hands. Colonel Dabber was all smiles and took a celebratory stroll over to Lexi and Travis.

"Thanks to your heroic efforts and those of other damned fine heroes like your godfather, it looks like nothing has escaped HPSF. We are calling this crisis over."

Now everyone, except Lexi and Travis were cheering.

Chapter 50

Lexi

August 20th

"No, like this," Lexi instructed, while demonstrating how to thrust using a knife.

Travis let his arms drop and shoulders slump.

"Don't worry, you'll get the hang of it."

"It's not that. I just miss Uncle Frank."

Lexi holstered her knife and wrapped her arms around her brother. "I do too... Hey, I have an idea..."

Travis looked up at his sister, expecting to be hit with her usual sisterly advice.

"Let's go swimming!"

Travis' face lit up like a Christmas Tree. "Okay but..." he spun out of her embrace, and slowly moved away from her, "last one in is a rotten egg," he chortled, dashing toward their dock. She took off after him.

They both halted halfway there when an alarm sounded.

This was the proximity alarm that Frank had set up and Travis had improved upon in the month that they had been back. It meant that someone who didn't belong was driving up their driveway or had stepped onto their property.

They had left the gate open the last few days, because so many visitors had stopped by, it was too much of a pain to walk all the way down to the gate and let them in.

After a month of not having to worry about terrorists attacking them, they weren't too worried and left the gates opened. Yet, every evening, they set the alarms. Frank's words of "Always be ready!" were still fresh in both their minds. It was the reason why they continued to train and exercise before they had some fun.

"Are we expecting anyone this early in the morning?" Lexi asked.

Travis just shook his head, his eyes wide and full of concern.

They could both hear the vehicle driving closer now.

A horn *honked*.

"They must be friendly," she stated. "But just in case..." Lexi rushed over to the screen door and slipped in her hand to grab her AK and Travis' pistol. "Behind me," she said, jogging around the side of the house, while doing a quick check that there was a round in the chamber.

When they neared the front of the house, eyes fixed down the drive, they could see a black SUV approaching.

"I don't recognize them," said Travis, repeating Lexi's own thoughts.

Lexi and Travis stood their ground, showing the intruder they were ready to use their weapons, but not raising them in the event the approaching vehicle was friendly.

The SUV pulled up to within a few feet of them and stopped. Its window tinting and the morning's bright sunlight conspired against their ability to see who was driving the vehicle.

The driver's side door popped open, but no one stepped out. And for just a moment, Lexi imagined it was Abdul, with his twisted smile and bandaged check.

She hadn't had a nightmare starring Abdul since that day he was entombed in Mount Weather, much less given him more than a few moments of thought. That part of her life was behind her.

Or so she thought.

Reflexively, her hands went to her rifle. She was about to point the thing at the driver just to stop them from torturing her with the wait when the driver stepped out.

It was Samuel, wearing a grin longer than the State of Florida. She ran to him yelling, "Samuel!"

She hugged him, and he hugged back, and then he kissed her. Their last kiss was almost a month ago when they said goodbye and Lexi, Travis and Jonah headed back home. Other than radio conversations, every Friday—they called it their Date Night—they've had no physical contact since then.

"I missed you," he said, giving her a spin.

"Me too." She pulled away when she saw Travis was there.

"Hey Travis. How goes it?" Samuel asked, giving him a squeeze.

"Good. So, how's Virginia and the new capital?"

"Busy. It takes quite a lot setting up a new Washington, DC."

"Speaking of which..." Lexi cut in. "So, what do we owe the honor of the President's Number One coming to visit little old us?"

"Hardly. I'm a small peon at best. But I come *bearing gifts*." The last two words he said really loud.

As if on cue, the passenger door opened. Two feet and a cane poked out. Then out stepped their godfather Frank Cartwright.

"Frank," Lexi and Travis hollered in unison, both rushed past Samuel and the open doors to get to Frank.

"You're alive?" Lexi asked, not believing her own eyes.

They threw themselves at him.

"Careful with the squeezing," Frank said, in a voice more horse than she remembered.

"How?" Lexi cried. "No, where have you been?"

"Don't beat him up," Samuel said, only a few inches away. "He only just woke up from a coma a week ago. I'm sure he'll tell you the whole story, but word is he somehow fixed the radio to stay open, then escaped the Comms Center through the hatch where the trunk lines were located, and drove away in the MICV, just before the missile exploded."

"Don't forget our friend," Frank stated. He sounded like he'd swallowed broken glass.

"Of course," Samuel said. "The leader of the ICA unit our militia attacked, some guy named Faisal. He was in the MICV when Frank was trying to get distance between him and the coming explosion. Faisal attacked Frank. When the blast occurred, ole Faisal's body protected Frank enough that Frank's wounds were not too horrible."

Both Lexi and Travis still held on, fearing if they let go, Frank would disappear like he had before.

"But why did no one tell us?" Lexi looked up at Samuel, feeling a little angry at being left out in the dark all this time.

"For a couple of reasons. First, the Army didn't find Frank until a week later, when they brought a team in hazmat suits to check out the place. They found Frank, near death, and no one knew who he was until Colonel Dabber ID'd him. Then the other reason for the secrecy was that he was in a highly secure military hospital, and they didn't think he would make it until when he woke. I was just told all this yesterday, when I had planned a surprise trip here...

"Anyway, the Major will be as good as new after a few weeks of convalescing."

"What about, you know, the cancer?" Lexi asked.

"Well, turns out that the diagnosis was wrong," Frank croaked and then coughed.

"It was some benign growth in his knee," Samuel jumped in. "Part of some old war wounds. They replaced his knees and checked him all out. So, all he needs is rest."

Lexi released Frank from her hug. "Come on Travis. Let's help our godfather inside." She handed him his cane and put an arm around him to offer herself as his crutch.

"I'm good," he said. "Walk me to the back and tell me what you've been doing for the last month?" He coughed. "Slim, would you get our bags?"

"Are you staying for a while?" Lexi asked, still trying to process all this good news.

"For the night. Then I must get back in the morning." Samuel said this as he closed the doors of the truck and grabbed two duffels and two rifles out of the back. "Oh, and I forgot the other present."

Frank, with Lexi on one side and Travis on the other stopped their slow progression along the driveway.

"President Chase had me bring ten cases of Stella Artois, along with his thanks."

"I'll drink to that," Frank said.

"Me too," Lexi said.

"Me three," Travis said with a giggle.

Frank let a growing smile envelop his face. "Now that's what I call a homecoming."

The end.

Thank you for reading the *HIGHWAY Series*! There is an epilogue to this series, which didn't make it in the final edit. If you'd like to read this, give me your email and I'll send it to you.

In addition, I will also email you a free copy of my USA Today Bestselling story, *True Enemy*, which chronicles Frank's first combat mission and how he met Lexi's and Travis' father, Stanley.

Finally, I will also make available to you a downloadable map of High Point Special Facility, which includes Area B details and other important locations on Mount Weather.

If you'd like these three gifts, go to this address:

https://www.mlbanner.com/revolution-epilogue
(Give me your best email address &
I will send them to you.)

Did you like *REVOLUTION*?

In case you weren't aware, I'm an independent writer who relies on ratings and reviews to help get the word out about my books. This is why reviews are so important to me and why I truly need your help. If you liked *REVOLUTION*, please let others know, by leaving even a short review.

Thank you!

Post Review on Amazon

A Note from The Author

The Highway Series, like all my books, is based on a realistic science-based scenario and my vision for what would have transpired for my characters, with a mix of facts and fiction.

What was fiction?

Most of the towns, bases, locations are real places, but some are not. And some are a combination of real and fictional to make them fit the story. Additionally, some scenarios might not be absolutely realistic based on the timing of when the scenario takes place.

For instance, Fort Rucker is a real drone base, though its name had changed (to Fort Novosel) after the second book in the series was published. Also, at this time, it would have been hard for a group of terrorists to so easily take over the base. But in a realistic future with budget cuts and redeployment of troops, my fictional scenario created the possibility.

In another example, Longhorn Ammo Storage Depot was an amalgam of several abandoned Army bases. There is an actual Longhorn in Texas, but it had since been decommissioned and turned into a lovely public park. Additionally, as I write this, there is an abandoned Air Force base, where an entrepreneur has been trying to sell the bunkers as prepper condos. You could lease one today... If you don't mind living in the most rural part of Iowa.

These are the fun bits of writing, using reality with my own twists, to make a story hopefully more compelling for you, the reader.

Final Thoughts & Acknowledgments

Thank you once more for reading, *REVOLUTION*!

To all the men and women who have served and/or continue to serve in our U.S. Military, I offer my most heartfelt thanks. *REVOLUTION* (as well as the whole *HIGHWAY Series*) is a tribute to you and your huge sacrifices, including for many, the ultimate sacrifice, that you have made to help secure our freedoms.

But those freedoms are still in jeopardy from vanishing today.

As Ronald Reagan famously instructed us, *"Freedom is never more than one generation away from extinction. We didn't pass it to our children in the bloodstream. It must be fought for, protected, and handed on for them to do the same, or one day we will spend our sunset years telling our children and our children's children what it was once like in the United States where men were free."*

Are we that generation?

Our freedom has never been so fleeting as it is today. In this series, I portrayed a new US government formed during a terrorist takeover, which seized upon an emergency to capture power for itself by forcibly taking over our rights. Although, this particular storyline may seem unlikely to you, I would suggest that any corrupt government that wishes to remain in power, will use whatever means are necessary to retain that power, including removal of many of the rights we take for granted as Americans: right to bear arms, free speech, taxation without representation, privacy, and private property ownership, just to name a few.

Many of these rights have been marginalized incrementally, but an authoritarian power will find a means to take away all of these and more.

Never forget that one of our most important foundational documents as a country started this way in its second paragraph:

"We hold these truths to be self-evident, that all men are created equal, that they are endowed by their Creator with certain unalienable Rights, that among these are Life, Liberty and the pursuit of Happiness."

Life, Liberty and the pursuit of Happiness…

As Americans, whether serving in the military or as civilians, it is our job to protect these rights so beautifully codified in the Declaration of Independence.

Let us not be that one generation!

Michael "ML" Banner

Who is ML Banner?

Michael "ML" Banner is an award winning,
USA Today Bestselling author of Apocalyptic Thrillers

Michael writes what he loves to read: apocalyptic thrillers, which thrust regular people into extraordinary circumstances, where their actions may determine not only their own fate, but that of the world.

One of his 18 books was a USA Today Bestseller (which you can read for free), most were #1 Amazon best-sellers in one or more genres. *Highway* (the first book in this series) won the 2016 Readers Favorite Gold Medal in Thrillers and was 2016 Finalist for Kindle Book Review's Best Sci-Fi Novel. His work is traditionally published and self-published.

Often his thrillers are set in far-flung places, as Michael

uses his experiences from visiting dozens of countries—some multiple times—over the years. One of his last transatlantic cruises became the foreground of the *MADNESS Chronicles*., winner of the 2018 Readers Favorite Silver Medal in Horror.

When not traveling around the US or the world to research his next series, you'll find Michael and his wife on a beach on the Sea of Cortez (Mexico).

Want more from M.L. Banner?

Receive FREE books & *Apocalyptic Updates* - A monthly publication highlighting discounted books, cool science/discoveries, new releases, reviews, and more. Just go to:

MLBanner.com/free

Connect with M.L. Banner

Keep in contact – I would love to hear from you!

- Email: michael@mlbanner.com
- Facebook: facebook.com/authormlbanner
- Twitter: @ml_banner

Books by M.L. Banner

For a complete list of Michael's current and upcoming books: MLBanner.com/books/

HIGHWAY SERIES

True Enemy (Short)

An unlikely hero finds his true enemy.

(Link to this USA Today Bestselling short at the back of *Highway #1*)

Highway (01)

A terrorist attack forces siblings onto a highway, and an impossible journey home.

Endurance (02)

Enduring what comes next will take everything they've got, and more.

Resistance (03)

It will come down to citizen militias to resist the jihadis march.

Revolution (04)

A 2nd American revolution might be required to save the country.

ASHFALL APOCALYPSE

Ashfall Apocalypse (01)

A world-wide apocalypse has just begun.

Leticia's Soliloquy (An Ashfall Apocalypse Short)

Leticia tells her story.

(This short is exclusively available from a link at the end of book #1)

Collapse (02)

As temps plummet, a new foe seeks revenge.

Compton's Epoch (An Ashfall Apocalypse Short)

Compton reveals what makes him tick.

(This short is exclusively available from a link at the end of book #2)

Perdition (03)

Sometimes the best plan is to run. But where?

MADNESS CHRONICLES

MADNESS (01)

A parasitic infection causes mammals to attack.

PARASITIC (02)

The parasitic infection doesn't just affect animals.

SYMPTOMATIC (03)

When your loved one becomes symptomatic, what do you do?

The Final Outbreak (Books 1 - 3)

The end is coming. It's closer than you think. And it's real.

STONE AGE SERIES

Stone Age (01)

The next big solar event separates family and friends, and begins a new Stone Age.

Desolation (02)

To survive the coming desolation will require new friendships.

Max's Epoch (Stone Age Short)

Max wasn't born a prepper, he was forged into one. (This short is exclusively available on MLBanner.com)

Hell's Requiem (03)

One man struggles to survive and find his way to a scientific sanctuary.

Time Slip (Stand Alone)

The time slip was his accident; can he use it to save the one he loves?

Cicada (04)

The scientific community of Cicada may be the world's only hope, or it may lead to the end of everything.